I0661055

Nathaniel Hawthorne

The Snow-Image, and Other Twice-Told Tales

Nathaniel Hawthorne

The Snow-Image, and Other Twice-Told Tales

ISBN/EAN: 9783337088491

Printed in Europe, USA, Canada, Australia, Japan

Cover: Foto ©Andreas Hilbeck / pixelio.de

More available books at **www.hansebooks.com**

THE

AND

OTHER TWICE-TOLD TALES.

BY

NATHANIEL HAWTHORNE.

BOSTON:
JAMES R. OSGOOD AND COMPANY,
Late Ticknor & Fields, and Fields, Osgood, & Co.
1876.

PREFACE.

TO HORATIO BRIDGE, ESQ., U. S. N.

MY DEAR BRIDGE: — Some of the more crabbed of my critics, I understand, have pronounced your friend egotistical, indiscreet, and even impertinent, on account of the Prefaces and Introductions with which, on several occasions, he has seen fit to pave the reader's way into the interior edifice of a book. In the justice of this censure I do not exactly concur, for the reasons, on the one hand, that the public generally has negatived the idea of undue freedom on the author's part, by evincing, it seems to me, rather more interest in these aforesaid Introductions than in the stories which followed; and that, on the other hand, with whatever appearance of confidential intimacy, I have been especially careful to make no disclosures respecting myself which the most indifferent observer might not have been acquainted with, and which I was not perfectly willing that my worst enemy should know. I might further justify myself, on the plea that, ever since my youth, I have been addressing a very limited circle of friendly readers, without much danger of being overheard by the public at large; and that the habits thus acquired might pardonably continue, although strangers may have begun to mingle with my audience.   -

But the charge, I am bold to say, is not a reasonable one, in any view which we can fairly take of it. There is no harm, but, on the contrary, good, in arraying some of the ordinary facts of life in a slightly idealized and artistic guise. I have taken facts which relate to myself, because they chance to be nearest at hand, and likewise are my own property. And, as for egotism, a person, who has been burrowing, to his utmost ability, into the depths of our common nature, for the purposes of psychological romance, — and who pursues his researches in that dusky region, as he needs must, as well by the tact of sympathy as by the light of observation, — will smile at incurring such an imputation in virtue of a little preliminary talk about his external habits, his abode, his casual associates, and other matters entirely upon the surface. These things hide the man, instead of displaying him. You must make quite another kind of inquest, and look through the whole range of his fictitious characters, good and evil, in order to detect any of his essential traits.

Be all this as it may, there can be no question as to the propriety of my inscribing this volume of earlier and later sketches to you, and pausing here, a few moments, to speak of them, as friend speaks to friend; still being cautious, however, that the public and the critics shall overhear nothing which we care about concealing. On you, if on no other person, I am entitled to rely, to

sustain the position of my Dedicatee. If anybody is re-
sponsible for my being at this day an author, it is yourself. I know not whence your faith came; but, while
we were lads together at a country college, — gathering
blueberries, in study-hours, under those tall academic
pines; or watching the great logs, as they tumbled along
the current of the Androscoggin; or shooting pigeons
and gray squirrels in the woods; or bat-fowling in the
summer twilight; or catching trouts in that shadowy
little stream which, I suppose, is still wandering river-
ward through the forest, — though you and I will never
cast a line in it again, — two idle lads, in short (as we
need not fear to acknowledge now), doing a hundred
things that the Faculty never heard of, or else it had
been the worse for us, — still it was your prognostic
of your friend's destiny, that he was to be a writer of
fiction.

And a fiction-monger, in due season, he became. But
was there ever such a weary delay in obtaining the slightest recognition from the public, as in my case? I sat
down by the wayside of life, like a man under enchantment, and a shrubbery sprung up around me, and the
bushes grew to be saplings, and the saplings became
trees, until no exit appeared possible, through the en-
tangling depths of my obscurity. And there, perhaps, I
should be sitting at this moment, with the moss on the
imprisoning tree-trunks, and the yellow leaves of more
than a score of autumns piled above me, if it had not
been for you. For it was through your interposition
— and that, moreover, unknown to himself — that your
early friend was brought before the public, somewhat

more prominently than theretofore, in the first volume of Twice-told Tales. Not a publisher in America, I presume, would have thought well enough of my forgotten or never-noticed stories to risk the expense of print and paper; nor do I say this with any purpose of casting odium on the respectable fraternity of booksellers, for their blindness to my wonderful merit. To confess the truth, I doubted of the public recognition quite as much as they could do. So much the more generous was your confidence; and knowing, as I do, that it was founded on old friendship rather than cold criticism, I value it only the more for that.

So, now, when I turn back upon my path, lighted by a transitory gleam of public favor, to pick up a few articles which were left out of my former collections, I take pleasure in making them the memorial of our very long and unbroken connection. Some of these sketches were among the earliest that I wrote, and, after lying for years in manuscript, they at last skulked into the Annuals or Magazines, and have hidden themselves there ever since. Others were the productions of a later period; others, again, were written recently. The comparison of these various trifles — the indices of intellectual condition at far separate epochs — affects me with a singular complexity of regrets. I am disposed to quarrel with the earlier sketches, both because a mature judgment discerns so many faults, and still more because they come so nearly up to the standard of the best that I can achieve now. The ripened autumnal fruit tastes but little better than the early windfalls. It would, indeed, be mortifying to believe that the summer-time of life has passed away, without any greater progress and improvement than is indicated here. But — at least, so I would fain hope — these things are scarcely to be depended upon, as measures of the intellectual and moral man. In youth, men are apt to write more wisely than they really know or feel; and the remainder of life may be not idly spent in realizing and convincing themselves of the wisdom which they uttered long ago. The truth that was only in the fancy then may have since become a substance in the mind and heart.

I have nothing further, I think, to say : unless it be that the public need not dread my again trespassing on its kindness, with any more of these musty and mouse-nibbled leaves of old periodicals, transformed, by the magic arts of my friendly publishers, into a new book. These are the last. Or, if a few still remain, they are either such as no paternal partiality could induce the author to think worth preserving, or else they have got into some very dark and dusty hiding-place, quite out of my own remembrance and whence no researches can avail to unearth them. So there let them rest.

Very sincerely yours,

N. H.

Lenox, November 1, 1851.

1 *

CONTENTS.

THE SNOW-IMAGE:

A CHILDISH MIRACLE.

ONE afternoon of a cold winter's day, when the sun shone forth with chilly brightness, after a long storm, two children asked leave of their mother to run out and play in the new-fallen snow. The elder child was a little girl, whom, because she was of a tender and modest disposition, and was thought to be very beautiful, her parents, and other people who were familiar with her, used to call Violet. But her brother was known by the style and title of Peony, on account of the ruddiness of his broad and round little phiz, which made everybody think of sunshine and great scarlet flowers. The father of these two children, a certain Mr. Lindsey, it is important to say, was an excellent but exceedingly matter-of-fact sort of man, a dealer in hardware, and was sturdily accustomed to take what is called the common-sense view of all matters that came under his consideration. With a heart about as tender as other people's, he had a head as hard and impenetrable, and therefore, perhaps, as empty, as one of the iron pots which it was a part of his business to sell. The mother's character, on the other hand, had a strain of poetry in it, a trait of unworldly beauty, — a delicate and dewy flower,

as it were, that had survived out of her imaginative youth,
and still kept itself alive amid the dusty realities of mat-
rimony and motherhood.

So, Violet and Peony, as I began with saying, besought their mother to let them run out and play in the
new snow; for, though it had looked so dreary and dismal, drifting downward out of the gray sky, it had a very
cheerful aspect, now that the sun was shining on it.   The
children dwelt in a city, and had no wider play-place than
a little garden before the house, divided by a white fence
from the street, and with a pear-tree and two or three
plum-trees overshadowing it, and some rose-bushes just
in front of the parlor-windows.   The trees and shrubs,
however, were now leafless, and their twigs were enveloped in the light snow, which thus made a kind of wintry foliage, with here and there a pendent icicle for the
fruit.

"Yes, Violet, — yes, my little Peony," said their kind
mother; "you may go out and play in the new snow."

Accordingly, the good lady bundled up her darlings in
woollen jackets and wadded sacks, and put comforters
round their necks, and a pair of striped gaiters on each
little pair of legs, and worsted mittens on their hands,
and gave them a kiss apiece, by way of a spell to keep
away Jack Frost.   Forth sallied the two children, with a
hop-skip-and-jump, that carried them at once into the very
heart of a huge snow-drift, whence Violet emerged like a
snow-bunting, while little Peony floundered out with his
round face in full bloom.   Then what a merry time had
they!   To look at them, frolicking in the wintry garden,
you would have thought that the dark and pitiless storm
had been sent for no other purpose but to provide a new
plaything for Violet and Peony; and that they themselves
had been created, as the snow-birds were, to take delight

only in the tempest, and in the white mantle which it spread over the earth.

At last, when they had frosted one another all over with handfuls of snow, Violet, after laughing heartily at little Peony's figure, was struck with a new idea.

"You look exactly like a snow-image, Peony," said she, "if your cheeks were not so red. And that puts me in mind! Let us make an image out of snow, — an image of a little girl, — and it shall be our sister, and shall run about and play with us all winter long. Won't it be nice?"

"O, yes!" cried Peony, as plainly as he could speak, for he was but a little boy. "That will be nice! And mamma shall see it!"

"Yes," answered Violet; "mamma shall see the new little girl. But she must not make her come into the warm parlor; for, you know, our little snow-sister will not love the warmth."

And forthwith the children began this great business of making a snow-image that should run about; while their mother, who was sitting at the window and over-heard some of their talk, could not help smiling at the gravity with which they set about it. They really seemed to imagine that there would be no difficulty whatever in creating a live little girl out of the snow. And, to say the truth, if miracles are ever to be wrought, it will be by putting our hands to the work in precisely such a simple and undoubting frame of mind as that in which Violet and Peony now undertook to perform one, without so much as knowing that it was a miracle. So thought the mother; and thought, likewise, that the new snow, just fallen from heaven, would be excellent material to make new beings of, if it were not so very cold. She gazed at the children a moment longer, delighting to watch their

little figures, — the girl, tall for her age, graceful and
agile, and so delicately colored that she looked like a
cheerful thought, more than a physical reality; while
Peony expanded in breadth rather than height, and rolled
along on his short and sturdy legs as substantial as an
elephant, though not quite so big. Then the mother resumed her work. What it was I forget; but she was
either trimming a silken bonnet for Violet, or darning a
pair of stockings for little Peony's short legs. Again,
however, and again, and yet other agains, she could not
help turning her head to the window to see how the children got on with their snow-image.

Indeed, it was an exceedingly pleasant sight, those
bright little souls at their tasks! Moreover, it was really
wonderful to observe how knowingly and skilfully they
managed the matter. Violet assumed the chief direction,
and told Peony what to do, while, with her own delicate
fingers, she shaped out all the nicer parts of the snow-
figure. It seemed, in fact, not so much to be made by
the children, as to grow up under their hands, while they
were playing and prattling about it. Their mother was
quite surprised at this; and the longer she looked, the
more and more surprised she grew.

"What remarkable children mine are!" thought she,
smiling with a mother's pride; and, smiling at herself,
too, for being so proud of them. "What other children
could have made anything so like a little girl's figure
out of snow at the first trial? Well; — but now I must
finish Peony's new frock, for his grandfather is coming
to-morrow, and I want the little fellow to look handsome."

So she took up the frock, and was soon as busily at
work again with her needle as the two children with their
snow-image. But still, as the needle travelled hither and

thither through the seams of the dress, the mother made
her toil light and happy by listening to the airy voices of
Violet and Peony. They kept talking to one another all
the time, their tongues being quite as active as their feet
and hands. Except at intervals, she could not distinctly
hear what was said, but had merely a sweet impression
that they were in a most loving mood, and were enjoying
themselves highly, and that the business of making the
snow-image went prosperously on. Now and then, however, when Violet and Peony happened to raise their
voices, the words were as audible as if they had been
spoken in the very parlor, where the mother sat. O,
how delightfully those words echoed in her heart, even
though they meant nothing so very wise or wonderful,
after all!

But you must know a mother listens with her heart,
much more than with her ears; and thus she is often
delighted with the trills of celestial music, when other
people can hear nothing of the kind.

"Peony, Peony!" cried Violet to her brother, who had
gone to another part of the garden, "bring me some of
that fresh snow, Peony, from the very farthest corner,
where we have not been trampling. I want it to shape
our little snow-sister's bosom with. You know that part
must be quite pure, just as it came out of the sky!"

"Here it is, Violet!" answered Peony, in his bluff
tone, — but a very sweet tone, too, — as he came floun-
dering through the half-trodden drifts. "Here is the
snow for her little bosom. O Violet, how beau-ti-ful she
begins to look!"

"Yes," said Violet, thoughtfully and quietly; "our
snow-sister does look very lovely. I did not quite know,
Peony, that we could make such a sweet little girl as
this."

The mother, as she listened, thought how fit and delightful an incident it would be, if fairies, or, still better, if angel-children were to come from paradise, and play invisibly with her own darlings, and help them to make their snow-image, giving it the features of celestial babyhood! Violet and Peony would not be aware of their immortal playmates, — only they would see that the image grew very beautiful while they worked at it, and would think that they themselves had done it all.

"My little girl and boy deserve such playmates, if mortal children ever did!" said the mother to herself; and then she smiled again at her own motherly pride.

Nevertheless, the idea seized upon her imagination; and, ever and anon, she took a glimpse out of the window, half dreaming that she might see the golden-haired children of paradise sporting with her own golden-haired Violet and bright-cheeked Peony.

Now, for a few moments, there was a busy and earnest, but indistinct hum of the two children's voices, as Violet and Peony wrought together with one happy consent. Violet still seemed to be the guiding spirit, while Peony acted rather as a laborer, and brought her the snow from far and near. And yet the little urchin evidently had a proper understanding of the matter, too!

"Peony, Peony!" cried Violet; for her brother was again at the other side of the garden. "Bring me those light wreaths of snow that have rested on the lower branches of the pear-tree. You can clamber on the snow-drift, Peony, and reach them easily. I must have them to make some ringlets for our snow-sister's head!"

"Here they are, Violet!" answered the little boy. "Take care you do not break them. Well done! Well done! How pretty!"

"Does she not look sweetly?" said Violet, with a very satisfied tone; "and now we must have some little shining bits of ice, to make the brightness of her eyes. She is not finished yet. Mamma will see how very beautiful she is; but papa will say, 'Tush! nonsense! —come in out of the cold!'"

"Let us call mamma to look out," said Peony; and then he shouted lustily, "Mamma! mamma!! mamma!!! Look out, and see what a nice 'ittle girl we are making!"

The mother put down her work, for an instant, and looked out of the window. But it so happened that the sun — for this was one of the shortest days of the whole year — had sunken so nearly to the edge of the world, that his setting shine came obliquely into the lady's eyes. So she was dazzled, you must understand, and could not very distinctly observe what was in the garden. Still, however, through all that bright, blinding dazzle of the sun and the new snow, she beheld a small white figure in the garden, that seemed to have a wonderful deal of human likeness about it. And she saw Violet and Peony, — indeed, she looked more at them than at the image, — she saw the two children still at work; Peony bringing fresh snow, and Violet applying it to the figure as scientifically as a sculptor adds clay to his model. Indistinctly as she discerned the snow-child, the mother thought to herself that never before was there a snow-figure so cunningly made, nor ever such a dear little girl and boy to make it.

"They do everything better than other children," said she, very complacently. "No wonder they make better snow-images!"

She sat down again to her work, and made as much haste with it as possible; because twilight would soon

come, and Peony's frock was not yet finished, and grandfather was expected, by railroad, pretty early in the
morning. Faster and faster, therefore, went her flying
fingers. The children, likewise, kept busily at work in
the garden, and still the mother listened, whenever she
could catch a word. She was amused to observe how
their little imaginations had got mixed up with what
they were doing, and were carried away by it. They
seemed positively to think that the snow-child would run
about and play with them.

"What a nice playmate she will be for us, all winter
long!" said Violet. "I hope papa will not be afraid
of her giving us a cold! Sha' n't you love her dearly,
Peony ?"

"O yes!" cried Peony. "And I will hug her, and
she shall sit down close by me, and drink some of my
warm milk!"

"O no, Peony!" answered Violet, with grave wisdom.
"That will not do at all. Warm milk will not be wholesome for our little snow-sister. Little snow-people, like
her, eat nothing but icicles. No, no, Peony; we must
not give her anything warm to drink!"

There was a minute or two of silence; for Peony,
whose short legs were never weary, had gone on a pil-
grimage again to the other side of the garden. All of
a sudden, Violet cried out, loudly and joyfully, —

"Look here, Peony! Come quickly! A light has
been shining on her cheek out of that rose-colored cloud!
and the color does not go away! Is not that beautiful!"

"Yes; it is beau-ti-ful," answered Peony, pronoun-
cing the three syllables with deliberate accuracy. "O
Violet, only look at her hair! It is all like gold!"

"O, certainly," said Violet, with tranquillity, as if it

were very much a matter of course. "That color, you know, comes from the golden clouds, that we see up there in the sky. She is almost finished now. But her lips must be made very red, — redder than her cheeks. Perhaps, Peony, it will make them red, if we both kiss them!"

Accordingly, the mother heard two smart little smacks, as if both her children were kissing the snow-image on its frozen mouth. But, as this did not seem to make the lips quite red enough, Violet next proposed that the snow-child should be invited to kiss Peony's scarlet cheek.

"Come, 'ittle snow-sister, kiss me!" cried Peony.

"There! she has kissed you," added Violet, "and now her lips are very red. And she blushed a little, too!"

"O, what a cold kiss!" cried Peony.

Just then, there came a breeze of the pure west-wind, sweeping through the garden and rattling the parlor-windows. It sounded so wintry cold, that the mother was about to tap on the window-pane with her thimbled finger, to summon the two children in, when they both cried out to her with one voice. The tone was not a tone of surprise, although they were evidently a good deal excited; it appeared rather as if they were very much rejoiced at some event that had now happened, but which they had been looking for, and had reckoned upon all along.

"Mamma! mamma! We have finished our little snow-sister, and she is running about the garden with us!"

"What imaginative little beings my children are!" thought the mother, putting the last few stitches into Peony's frock. "And it is strange, too, that they make me almost as much a child as they themselves are! I can hardly help believing, now, that the snow-image has really come to life ! ”

“ Dear mamma ! ” cried Violet, “ pray look out and see what a sweet playmate we have ! ”

The mother, being thus entreated, could no longer delay to look forth from the window. The sun was now gone out of the sky, leaving, however, a rich inheritance of his brightness among those purple and golden clouds which make the sunsets of winter so magnificent. But there was not the slightest gleam or dazzle, either on the window or on the snow; so that the good lady could look all over the garden, and see everything and everybody in it. And what do you think she saw there ? Violet and Peony, of course, her own two darling children. Ah, but whom or what did she besides ? Why, if you will believe me, there was a small figure of a girl, dressed all in white, with rose-tinged cheeks and ringlets of golden hue, playing about the garden with the two children ! A stranger though she was, the child seemed to be on as familiar terms with Violet and Peony, and they with her, as if all the three had been playmates during the whole of their little lives. The mother thought to herself that it must certainly be the daughter of one of the neighbors, and that, seeing Violet and Peony in the garden, the child had run across the street to play with them. So this kind lady went to the door, intending to invite the little runaway into her comfortable parlor; for, now that the sunshine was withdrawn, the atmosphere, out of doors, was already growing very cold.

But, after opening the house-door, she stood an instant on the threshold, hesitating whether she ought to ask the child to come in, or whether she should even speak to her. Indeed, she almost doubted whether it were a real child, after all, or only a light wreath of the new-fallen snow, blown hither and thither about the garden by the intensely cold west-wind. There was certainly something very singular in the aspect of the little stranger. Among all the children of the neighborhood, the lady could remember no such face, with its pure white, and delicate rose-color, and the golden ringlets tossing about the forehead and cheeks. And as for her dress, which was entirely of white, and fluttering in the breeze, it was such as no reasonable woman would put upon a little girl, when sending her out to play, in the depth of winter. It made this kind and careful mother shiver only to look at those small feet, with nothing in the world on them, except a very thin pair of white slippers. Nevertheless, airily as she was clad, the child seemed to feel not the slightest inconvenience from the cold, but danced so lightly over the snow that the tips of her toes left hardly a print in its surface; while Violet could but just keep pace with her, and Peony's short legs compelled him to lag behind.

Once, in the course of their play, the strange child placed herself between Violet and Peony, and taking a hand of each, skipped merrily forward, and they along with her. Almost immediately, however, Peony pulled away his little fist, and began to rub it as if the fingers were tingling with cold; while Violet also released herself, though with less abruptness, gravely remarking that it was better not to take hold of hands. The white-robed damsel said not a word, but danced about, just as merrily as before. If Violet and Peony did not choose to play with her, she could make just as good a playmate of the brisk and cold west-wind, which kept blowing her all about the garden, and took such liberties with her, that they seemed to have been friends for a long time.

All this while, the mother stood on the threshold, wondering how a little girl could look so much like a flying snow-drift, or how a snow-drift could look so very like a little girl.

She called Violet, and whispered to her.

"Violet, my darling, what is this child's name?" asked she. "Does she live near us?"

"Why, dearest mamma," answered Violet, laughing to think that her mother did not comprehend so very plain an affair, "this is our little snow-sister, whom we have just been making!"

"Yes, dear mamma," cried Peony, running to his mother, and looking up simply into her face. "This is our snow-image! Is it not a nice 'ittle child?"

At this instant a flock of snow-birds came flitting through the air. As was very natural, they avoided Violet and Peony. But, — and this looked strange, — they flew at once to the white-robed child, fluttered eagerly about her head, alighted on her shoulders, and seemed to claim her as an old acquaintance. She, on her part, was evidently as glad to see these little birds, old Winter's grandchildren, as they were to see her, and welcomed them by holding out both her hands. Hereupon, they each and all tried to alight on her two palms and ten small fingers and thumbs, crowding one another off, with an immense fluttering of their tiny wings. One dear little bird nestled tenderly in her bosom; another put its bill to her lips. They were as joyous, all the while, and seemed as much in their element, as you may have seen them when sporting with a snow-storm.

Violet and Peony stood laughing at this pretty sight: for they enjoyed the merry time which their new playmate was having with these small-winged visitants, almost as much as if they themselves took part in it.

"Violet," said her mother, greatly perplexed, "tell me the truth, without any jest. Who is this little girl?"

"My darling mamma," answered Violet, looking seriously into her mother's face, and apparently surprised that she should need any further explanation, "I have told you truly who she is. It is our little snow-image, which Peony and I have been making. Peony will tell you so, as well as I."

"Yes, mamma," asseverated Peony, with much gravity in his crimson little phiz; "this is 'ittle snow-child. Is not she a nice one? But, mamma, her hand, is oh, so very cold!"

While mamma still hesitated what to think and what to do, the street-gate was thrown open, and the father of Violet and Peony appeared, wrapped in a pilot-cloth sack, with a fur cap drawn down over his ears, and the thickest of gloves upon his hands. Mr. Lindsey was a middle-aged man, with a weary and yet a happy look in his wind-flushed and frost-pinched face, as if he had been busy all the day long, and was glad to get back to his quiet home. His eyes brightened at the sight of his wife and children, although he could not help uttering a word or two of surprise, at finding the whole family in the open air, on so bleak a day, and after sunset too. He soon perceived the little white stranger, sporting to and fro in the garden, like a dancing snow-wreath, and the flock of snow-birds fluttering about her head.

"Pray, what little girl may that be?" inquired this very sensible man. "Surely her mother must be crazy, to let her go out in such bitter weather as it has been to-day, with only that flimsy white gown and those thin slippers!"

"My dear husband," said his wife, "I know no more

2

about the little thing than you do. Some neighbor's
child, I suppose. Our Violet and Peony," she added,
laughing at herself for repeating so absurd a story, "in-
sist that she is nothing but a snow-image, which they
have been busy about in the garden, almost all the afternoon."

As she said this, the mother glanced her eyes toward the spot where the children's snow-image had
been made. What was her surprise, on perceiving that
there was not the slightest trace of so much labor! — no
image at all! — no piled up heap of snow! — nothing
whatever, save the prints of little footsteps around a
vacant space!

"This is very strange!" said she.

"What is strange, dear mother?" asked Violet.
"Dear father, do not you see how it is? This is our
snow-image, which Peony and I have made, because we
wanted another playmate. Did not we, Peony?"

"Yes, papa," said crimson Peony. "This be our
'ittle snow-sister. Is she not beau-ti-ful? But she gave
me such a cold kiss!"

"Poh, nonsense, children!" cried their good, honest
father, who, as we have already intimated, had an exceedingly common-sensible way of looking at matters.
"Do not tell me of making live figures out of snow.
Come, wife; this little stranger must not stay out in the
bleak air a moment longer. We will bring her into the
parlor; and you shall give her a supper of warm bread
and milk, and make her as comfortable as you can.
Meanwhile, I will inquire among the neighbors; or, if
necessary, send the city-crier about the streets, to give
notice of a lost child."

So saying, this honest and very kind-hearted man was
going toward the little white damsel, with the best in-

tentions in the world. But Violet and Peony, each seizing their father by the hand, earnestly besought him not to make her come in.

"Dear father," cried Violet, putting herself before him, " it is true what I have been telling you ! This is our little snow-girl, and she cannot live any longer than while she breathes the cold west-wind. Do not make her come into the hot room ! "

"Yes, father," shouted Peony, stamping his little foot, so mightily was he in earnest, "this be nothing but our 'ittle snow-child ! She will not love the hot fire ! "

"Nonsense, children, nonsense, nonsense ! " cried the father, half vexed, half laughing at what he considered their foolish obstinacy. "Run into the house, this moment ! It is too late to play any longer, now. I must take care of this little girl immediately, or she will catch her death-a-cold ! "

"Husband ! dear husband ! " said his wife, in a low voice, — for she had been looking narrowly at the snow-child, and was more perplexed than ever, — "there is something very singular in all this. You will think me foolish, — but — but — may it not be that some invisible angel has been attracted by the simplicity and good faith with which our children set about their undertaking ? May he not have spent an hour of his immortality in playing with those dear little souls ? and so the result is what we call a miracle. No, no ! Do not laugh at me ; I see what a.foolish thought it is ! "

"My dear wife," replied the husband, laughing heartily, " you are as much a child as Violet and Peony."

And in one sense so she was, for all through life she had kept her heart full of childlike simplicity and faith, which was as pure and clear as crystal ; and, looking at all matters through this transparent medium, she sometimes saw truths so profound, that other people laughed at them as nonsense and absurdity.

But now kind Mr. Lindsey had entered the garden, breaking away from his two children, who still sent their shrill voices after him, beseeching him to let the snow-child stay and enjoy herself in the cold west-wind. As he approached, the snow-birds took to flight. The little white damsel, also, fled backward, shaking her head, as if to say, " Pray, do not touch me ! " and roguishly, as it appeared, leading him through the deepest of the snow. Once, the good man stumbled, and floundered down upon his face, so that, gathering himself up again, with the snow sticking to his rough pilot-cloth sack, he looked as white and wintry as a snow-image of the largest size. Some of the neighbors, meanwhile, seeing him from their windows, wondered what could possess poor Mr. Lindsey to be running about his garden in pursuit of a snow-drift, which the west-wind was driving hither and thither ! At length, after a vast deal of trouble, he chased the little stranger into a corner, where she could not possibly escape him. His wife had been looking on, and, it being nearly twilight, was wonder-struck to observe how the snow-child gleamed and sparkled, and how she seemed to shed a glow all round about her ; and when driven into the corner, she posi-tively glistened like a star ! It was a frosty kind of brightness, too, like that of an icicle in the moonlight. The wife thought it strange that good Mr. Lindsey should see nothing remarkable in the snow-child's ap-pearance.

" Come, you odd little thing ! " cried the honest man, seizing her by the hand, " I have caught you at last, and will make you comfortable in spite of yourself. We will put a nice warm pair of worsted stockings on your frozen little feet, and you shall have a good thick shawl to wrap yourself in. Your poor white nose, I am afraid, is actually frost-bitten. But we will make it all right. Come along in."

And so, with a most benevolent smile on his sagacious visage, all purple as it was with the cold, this very well-meaning gentleman took the snow-child by the hand and led her towards the house. She followed him, droopingly and reluctant; for all the glow and sparkle was gone out of her figure; and whereas just before she had resembled a bright, frosty, star-gemmed evening, with a crimson gleam on the cold horizon, she now looked as dull and languid as a thaw. As kind Mr. Lindsey led her up the steps of the door, Violet and Peony looked into his face, — their eyes full of tears, which froze before they could run down their cheeks, — and again entreated him not to bring their snow-image into the house.

"Not bring her in!" exclaimed the kind-hearted man. "Why, you are crazy, my little Violet! — quite crazy, my small Peony! She is so cold, already, that her hand has almost frozen mine, in spite of my thick gloves. Would you have her freeze to death?"

His wife, as he came up the steps, had been taking another long, earnest, almost awe-stricken gaze at the little white stranger. She hardly knew whether it was a dream or no; but she could not help fancying that she saw the delicate print of Violet's fingers on the child's neck. It looked just as if, while Violet was shaping out the image, she had given it a gentle pat with her hand, and had neglected to smooth the impression quite away.

"After all, husband," said the mother, recurring to her idea that the angels would be as much delighted to play with Violet and Peony as she herself was, — "after all, she does look strangely like a snow-image! I do believe she is made of snow!"

A puff of the west-wind blew against the snow-child, and again she sparkled like a star.

"Snow!" repeated good Mr. Lindsey, drawing the reluctant guest over his hospitable threshold. "No wonder she looks like snow. She is half frozen, poor little thing! But a good fire will put everything to rights."

Without further talk, and always with the same best intentions, this highly benevolent and common-sensible individual led the little white damsel — drooping, drooping, drooping, more and more — out of the frosty air, and into his comfortable parlor. A Heidenberg stove, filled to the brim with intensely burning anthracite, was sending a bright gleam through the isinglass of its iron door, and causing the vase of water on its top to fume and bubble with excitement. A warm, sultry smell was diffused throughout the room. A thermometer on the wall farthest from the stove stood at eighty degrees. The parlor was hung with red curtains, and covered with a red carpet, and looked just as warm as it felt. The difference betwixt the atmosphere here and the cold, wintry twilight out of doors, was like stepping at once from Nova Zembla to the hottest part of India, or from the North Pole into an oven. O, this was a fine place for the little white stranger!

The common-sensible man placed the snow-child on the hearth-rug, right in front of the hissing and fuming stove.

"Now she will be comfortable!" cried Mr. Lindsey, rubbing his hands and looking about him, with the pleasantest smile you ever saw. "Make yourself at home, my child."

Sad, sad and drooping, looked the little white maiden, as she stood on the hearth-rug, with the hot blast of the stove striking through her like a pestilence. Once, she threw a glance wistfully toward the windows, and caught a glimpse, through its red curtains, of the snow-covered roofs, and the stars glimmering frostily, and all the delicious intensity of the cold night. The bleak wind rattled the window-panes, as if it were summoning her to come forth. But there stood the snow-child, drooping, before the hot stove!

But the common-sensible man saw nothing amiss.

"Come, wife," said he, "let her have a pair of thick stockings and a woollen shawl or blanket directly; and tell Dora to give her some warm supper as soon as the milk boils. You, Violet and Peony, amuse your little friend. She is out of spirits, you see, at finding herself in a strange place. For my part, I will go around among the neighbors, and find out where she belongs."

The mother, meanwhile, had gone in search of the shawl and stockings; for her own view of the matter, however subtle and delicate, had given way, as it always did, to the stubborn materialism of her husband. Without heeding the remonstrances of his two children, who still kept murmuring that their little snow-sister did not love the warmth, good Mr. Lindsey took his departure, shutting the parlor-door carefully behind him. Turning up the collar of his sack over his ears, he emerged from the house, and had barely reached the street-gate, when he was recalled by the screams of Violet and Peony, and the rapping of a thimbled finger against the parlor window.

"Husband! husband!" cried his wife, showing her horror-stricken face through the window-panes. "There is no need of going for the child's parents!"

"We told you so, father!" screamed Violet and Peony, as he re-entered the parlor. "You would bring her in; and now our poor — dear — beau-ti-ful little snow-sister is thawed!"

And their own sweet little faces were already dissolved in tears; so that their father, seeing what strange things occasionally happen in this every-day world, felt not a little anxious lest his children might be going to thaw too! In the utmost perplexity, he demanded an explanation of his wife. She could only reply, that, being summoned to the parlor by the cries of Violet and Peony, she found no trace of the little white maiden, unless it were the remains of a heap of snow, which, while she was gazing at it, melted quite away upon the hearth-rug.

"And there you see all that is left of it!" added she, pointing to a pool of water, in front of the stove.

"Yes, father," said Violet, looking reproachfully at him, through her tears, "there is all that is left of our dear little snow-sister!"

"Naughty father!" cried Peony, stamping his foot, and — I shudder to say — shaking his little fist at the common-sensible man. "We told you how it would be! What for did you bring her in?"

And the Heidenberg stove, through the isinglass of its door, seemed to glare at good Mr. Lindsey, like a red-eyed demon, triumphing in the mischief which it had done!

This, you will observe, was one of those rare cases, which yet will occasionally happen, where common-sense finds itself at fault. The remarkable story of the snow-image, though to that sagacious class of people to whom good Mr. Lindsey belongs it may seem but a childish affair, is, nevertheless, capable of being moralized in various methods, greatly for their edification. One of its lessons, for instance, might be, that it behooves men, and especially men of benevolence, to consider well what they are about, and, before acting on their philanthropic purposes, to be quite sure that they comprehend the nature and all the relations of the business in hand. What has been established as an element of good to one being may prove absolute mischief to another; even as the warmth of the parlor was proper enough for children of flesh and blood, like Violet and Peony, — though by no means very wholesome, even for them, — but involved nothing short of annihilation to the unfortunate snow-image.

But, after all, there is no teaching anything to wise men of good Mr. Lindsey's stamp. They know everything, — oh, to be sure! — everything that has been, and everything that is, and everything that, by any future possibility, can be. And, should some phenomenon of nature or providence transcend their system, they will not recognize it, even if it come to pass under their very noses.

"Wife," said Mr. Lindsey, after a fit of silence, "see what a quantity of snow the children have brought in on their feet! It has made quite a puddle here before the stove. Pray tell Dora to bring some towels and sop it up!"

THE GREAT STONE FACE.

ONE afternoon, when the sun was going down, a mother and her little boy sat at the door of their cottage, talking about the Great Stone Face. They had but to lift their eyes, and there it was plainly to be seen, though miles away, with the sunshine brightening all its features.

And what was the Great Stone Face?

Embosomed amongst a family of lofty mountains, there was a valley so spacious that it contained many thousand inhabitants. Some of these good people dwelt in log-huts, with the black forest all around them, on the steep and difficult hillsides. Others had their homes in comfortable farm-houses, and cultivated the rich soil on the gentle slopes or level surfaces of the valley. Others, again, were congregated into populous villages, where some wild, highland rivulet, tumbling down from its birthplace in the upper mountain region, had been caught and tamed by human cunning, and compelled to turn the machinery of cotton-factories. The inhabitants of this valley, in short, were numerous, and of many modes of life. But all of them, grown people and children, had a kind of familiarity with the Great Stone Face, although some possessed the gift of distinguishing this grand natural phenomenon more perfectly than many of their neighbors.

The Great Stone Face, then, was a work of Nature in her mood of majestic playfulness, formed on the perpendicular side of a mountain by some immense rocks, which had been thrown together in such a position as, when viewed at a proper distance, precisely to resemble the features of the human countenance. It seemed as if an enormous giant, or a Titan, had sculptured his own likeness on the precipice. There was the broad arch of the forehead, a hundred feet in height; the nose, with its long bridge; and the vast lips, which, if they could have spoken, would have rolled their thunder accents from one end of the valley to the other. True it is, that if the spectator approached too near, he lost the outline of the gigantic visage, and could discern only a heap of ponderous and gigantic rocks, piled in chaotic ruin one upon another. Retracing his steps, however, the wondrous features would again be seen; and the farther he withdrew from them, the more like a human face, with all its original divinity intact, did they appear; until, as it grew dim in the distance, with the clouds and glorified vapor of the mountains clustering about it, the Great Stone Face seemed positively to be alive.

It was a happy lot for children to grow up to manhood or womanhood with the Great Stone Face before their eyes, for all the features were noble, and the expression was at once grand and sweet, as if it were the glow of a vast, warm heart, that embraced all mankind in its affections, and had room for more. It was an education only to look at it. According to the belief of many people, the valley owed much of its fertility to this benign aspect that was continually beaming over it, illuminating the clouds, and infusing its tenderness into the sunshine.

As we began with saying, a mother and her little boy

sat at their cottage-door, gazing at the Great Stone Face, and talking about it. The child's name was Ernest.

"Mother," said he, while the Titanic visage smiled on him, "I wish that it could speak, for it looks so very kindly that its voice must needs be pleasant. If I were to see a man with such a face, I should love him dearly."

"If an old prophecy should come to pass," answered his mother, "we may see a man, some time or other, with exactly such a face as that."

"What prophecy do you mean, dear mother?" eagerly inquired Ernest. "Pray tell me all about it!"

So his mother told him a story that her own mother had told to her, when she herself was younger than little Ernest; a story, not of things that were past, but of what was yet to come; a story, nevertheless, so very old, that even the Indians, who formerly inhabited this valley, had heard it from their forefathers, to whom, as they affirmed, it had been murmured by the mountain streams, and whispered by the wind among the tree-tops. The purport was, that, at some future day, a child should be born hereabouts, who was destined to become the greatest and noblest personage of his time, and whose countenance, in manhood, should bear an exact resemblance to the Great Stone Face. Not a few old-fashioned people, and young ones likewise, in the ardor of their hopes, still cherished an enduring faith in this old prophecy. But others, who had seen more of the world, had watched and waited till they were weary, and had beheld no man with such a face, nor any man that proved to be much greater or nobler than his neighbors, concluded it to be nothing but an idle tale. At all events, the great man of the prophecy had not yet appeared.

"O mother, dear mother!" cried Ernest, clapping his

hands above his head, "I do hope that I shall live to see him!"

His mother was an affectionate and thoughtful woman, and felt that it was wisest not to discourage the generous hopes of her little boy. So she only said to him, "Perhaps you may."

And Ernest never forgot the story that his mother told him. It was always in his mind, whenever he looked upon the Great Stone Face. He spent his childhood in the log-cottage where he was born, and was dutiful to his mother, and helpful to her in many things, assisting her much with his little hands, and more with his loving heart. In this manner, from a happy yet often pensive child, he grew up to be a mild, quiet, unobtrusive boy, and sun-browned with labor in the fields, but with more intelligence brightening his aspect than is seen in many lads who have been taught at famous schools. Yet Ernest had had no teacher, save only that the Great Stone Face became one to him. When the toil of the day was over, he would gaze at it for hours, until he began to imagine that those vast features recognized him, and gave him a smile of kindness and encouragement, responsive to his own look of veneration. We must not take upon us to affirm that this was a mistake, although the Face may have looked no more kindly at Ernest than at all the world besides. But the secret was, that the boy's tender and confiding simplicity discerned what other people could not see; and thus the love, which was meant for all, became his peculiar portion.

About this time, there went a rumor throughout the valley, that the great man, foretold from ages long ago, who was to bear a resemblance to the Great Stone Face, had appeared at last. It seems that, many years before, a young man had migrated from the valley and settled at

a distant seaport, where, after getting together a little
money, he had set up as a shopkeeper. His name — but
I could never learn whether it was his real one, or a
nickname that had grown out of his habits and success
in life — was Gathergold. Being shrewd and active,
and endowed by Providence with that inscrutable faculty
which develops itself in what the world calls luck, he became an exceedingly rich merchant, and owner of a whole
fleet of bulky-bottomed ships. All the countries of the
globe appeared to join hands for the mere purpose of
adding heap after heap to the mountainous accumulation
of this one man's wealth. The cold regions of the north,
almost within the gloom and shadow of the Arctic Circle,
sent him their tribute in the shape of furs; hot Africa
sifted for him the golden sands of her rivers, and gathered
up the ivory tusks of her great elephants out of the forests; the East came bringing him the rich shawls, and
spices, and teas, and the effulgence of diamonds, and the
gleaming purity of large pearls. The ocean, not to be
behindhand with the earth, yielded up her mighty whales,
that Mr. Gathergold might sell their oil, and make a
profit on it. Be the original commodity what it might,
it was gold within his grasp. It might be said of him,
as of Midas in the fable, that whatever he touched with
his finger immediately glistened, and grew yellow, and
was changed at once into sterling metal, or, which suited
him still better, into piles of coin. And, when Mr. Gathergold had become so very rich that it would have taken
him a hundred years only to count his wealth, he bethought himself of his native valley, and resolved to go
back thither, and end his days where he was born. With
this purpose in view, he sent a skilful architect to build
him such a palace as should be fit for a man of his vast
wealth to live in.

As I have said above, it had already been rumored in the valley that Mr. Gathergold had turned out to be the prophetic personage so long and vainly looked for, and that his visage was the perfect and undeniable similitude of the Great Stone Face. People were the more ready to believe that this must needs be the fact, when they beheld the splendid edifice that rose, as if by enchantment, on the site of his father's old weather-beaten farm-house. The exterior was of marble, so dazzlingly white that it seemed as though the whole structure might melt away in the sunshine, like those humbler ones which Mr. Gathergold, in his young play-days, before his fingers were gifted with the touch of transmutation, had been accustomed to build of snow. It had a richly ornamented portico, supported by tall pillars, beneath which was a lofty door, studded with silver knobs, and made of a kind of variegated wood that had been brought from beyond the sea. The windows, from the floor to the ceiling of each stately apartment, were composed, respectively, of but one enormous pane of glass, so transparently pure that it was said to be a finer medium than even the vacant atmosphere. Hardly anybody had been permitted to see the interior of this palace; but it was reported, and with good semblance of truth, to be far more gorgeous than the outside, insomuch that whatever was iron or brass in other houses was silver or gold in this; and Mr. Gathergold's bedchamber, especially, made such a glittering appearance that no ordinary man would have been able to close his eyes there. But, on the other hand, Mr. Gathergold was now so inured to wealth, that perhaps he could not have closed his eyes unless where the gleam of it was certain to find its way beneath his eyelids.

In due time, the mansion was finished; next came the

upholsterers, with magnificent furniture; then, a whole
troop of black and white servants, the harbingers of Mr.
Gathergold, who, in his own majestic person, was expected to arrive at sunset. Our friend Ernest, meanwhile, had been deeply stirred by the idea that the great
man, the noble man, the man of prophecy, after so many
ages of delay, was at length to be made manifest to his
native valley. He knew, boy as he was, that there were
a thousand ways in which Mr. Gathergold, with his vast
wealth, might transform himself into an angel of beneficence, and assume a control over human affairs as wide
and benignant as the smile of the Great Stone Face.
Full of faith and hope, Ernest doubted not that what the
people said was true, and that now he was to behold the
living likeness of those wondrous features on the mountain-side. While the boy was still gazing up the valley,
and fancying, as he always did, that the Great Stone
Face returned his gaze and looked kindly at him, the
rumbling of wheels was heard, approaching swiftly along
the winding road.

"Here he comes!" cried a group of people who were
assembled to witness the arrival. "Here comes the
great Mr. Gathergold!"

A carriage, drawn by four horses, dashed round the
turn of the road. Within it, thrust partly out of the
window, appeared the physiognomy of a little old man,
with a skin as yellow as if his own Midas-hand had
transmuted it. He had a low forehead, small, sharp
eyes, puckered about with innumerable wrinkles, and very
thin lips, which he made still thinner by pressing them
forcibly together.

"The very image of the Great Stone Face!" shouted
the people. "Sure enough, the old prophecy is true;
and here we have the great man come, at last!"

And, what greatly perplexed Ernest, they seemed actually to believe that here was the likeness which they
spoke of. By the roadside there chanced to be an old
beggar-woman and two little beggar-children, stragglers
from some far-off region, who, as the carriage rolled onward, held out their hands and lifted up their doleful
voices, most piteously beseeching charity. A yellow
claw — the very same that had clawed together so much
wealth — poked itself out of the coach-window, and
dropt some copper coins upon the ground ; so that,
though the great man's name seems to have been Gathergold, he might just as suitably have been nicknamed
Scattercopper. Still, nevertheless, with an earnest shout,
and evidently with as much good faith as ever, the people bellowed, —

"He is the very image of the Great Stone Face!"

But Ernest turned sadly from the wrinkled shrewdness of that sordid visage, and gazed up the valley,
where, amid a gathering mist, gilded by the last sunbeams, he could still distinguish those glorious features
which had impressed themselves into his soul. Their
aspect cheered him. What did the benign lips seem to
say ?

"He will come! Fear not, Ernest; the man will
come!"

The years went on, and Ernest ceased to be a boy.
He had grown to be a young man now. He attracted
little notice from the other inhabitants of the valley ; for
they saw nothing remarkable in his way of life, save
that, when the labor of the day was over, he still loved
to go apart and gaze and meditate upon the Great Stone
Face. According to their idea of the matter, it was a
folly, indeed, but pardonable, inasmuch as Ernest was
industrious, kind, and neighborly, and neglected no duty

for the sake of indulging this idle habit. They knew not that the Great Stone Face had become a teacher to him, and that the sentiment which was expressed in it would enlarge the young man's heart, and fill it with wider and deeper sympathies than other hearts. They knew not that thence would come a better wisdom than could be learned from books, and a better life than could be moulded on the defaced example of other human lives. Neither did Ernest know that the thoughts and affections which came to him so naturally, in the fields and at the fireside, and wherever he communed with himself, were of a higher tone than those which all men shared with him. A simple soul, — simple as when his mother first taught him the old prophecy, — he beheld the marvellous features beaming adown the valley, and still wondered that their human counterpart was so long in making his appearance.

By this time poor Mr. Gathergold was dead and buried; and the oddest part of the matter was, that his wealth, which was the body and spirit of his existence, had disappeared before his death, leaving nothing of him but a living skeleton, covered over with a wrinkled, yellow skin. Since the melting away of his gold, it had been very generally conceded that there was no such striking resemblance, after all, betwixt the ignoble features of the ruined merchant and that majestic face upon the mountain-side. So the people ceased to honor him during his lifetime, and quietly consigned him to forgetfulness after his decease. Once in a while, it is true, his memory was brought up in connection with the magnificent palace which he had built, and which had long ago been turned into a hotel for the accommodation of strangers, multitudes of whom came, every summer, to visit that famous natural curiosity, the Great Stone Face.

Thus, Mr. Gathergold being discredited and thrown into the shade, the man of prophecy was yet to come.

It so happened that a native-born son of the valley, many years before, had enlisted as a soldier, and, after a great deal of hard fighting, had now become an illustrious commander. Whatever he may be called in history, he was known in camps and on the battle-field under the nickname of Old Blood-and-Thunder. This war-worn veteran, being now infirm with age and wounds, and weary of the turmoil of a military life, and of the roll of the drum and the clangor of the trumpet, that had so long been ringing in his ears, had lately signified a purpose of returning to his native valley, hoping to find repose where he remembered to have left it. The inhabitants, his old neighbors and their grown-up children, were resolved to welcome the renowned warrior with a salute of cannon and a public dinner; and all the more enthusiastically, it being affirmed that now, at last, the likeness of the Great Stone Face had actually appeared. An aid-de-camp of Old Blood-and-Thunder, travelling through the valley, was said to have been struck with the resemblance. Moreover the schoolmates and early acquaintances of the general were ready to testify, on oath, that, to the best of their recollection, the aforesaid general had been exceedingly like the majestic image, even when a boy, only that the idea had never occurred to them at that period. Great, therefore, was the excitement throughout the valley; and many people, who had never once thought of glancing at the Great Stone Face for years before, now spent their time in gazing at it, for the sake of knowing exactly how General Blood-and-Thunder looked.

On the day of the great festival, Ernest, with all the

other people of the valley, left their work, and proceeded
to the spot where the sylvan banquet was prepared.
As he approached, the loud voice of the Rev. Dr.
Battleblast was heard, beseeching a blessing on the good
things set before them, and on the distinguished friend
of peace in whose honor they were assembled. The
tables were arranged in a cleared space of the woods,
shut in by the surrounding trees, except where a vista
opened eastward, and afforded a distant view of the
Great Stone Face. Over the general's chair, which
was a relic from the home of Washington, there was
an arch of verdant boughs, with the laurel profusely
intermixed, and surmounted by his country's banner,
beneath which he had won his victories. Our friend
Ernest raised himself on his tiptoes, in hopes to get a
glimpse of the celebrated guest; but there was a mighty
crowd about the tables anxious to hear the toasts and
speeches, and to catch any word that might fall from the
general in reply; and a volunteer company, doing duty
as a guard, pricked ruthlessly with their bayonets at any
particularly quiet person among the throng. So Ernest,
being of an unobtrusive character, was thrust quite into
the background, where he could see no more of Old
Blood-and-Thunder's physiognomy than if it had been
still blazing on the battle-field. To console himself, he
turned towards the Great Stone Face, which, like a
faithful and long-remembered friend, looked back and
smiled upon him through the vista of the forest. Meantime, however, he could overhear the remarks of various
individuals, who were comparing the features of the hero
with the face on the distant mountain-side.

"'T is the same face, to a hair!" cried one man,
cutting a caper for joy.

"Wonderfully like, that's a fact!" responded another.

"Like! why, I call it Old Blood-and-Thunder him-self, in a monstrous looking-glass!" cried a third. "And why not? He's the greatest man of this or any other age, beyond a doubt."

And then all three of the speakers gave a great shout, which communicated electricity to the crowd, and called forth a roar from a thousand voices, that went reverber-ating for miles among the mountains, until you might have supposed that the Great Stone Face had poured its thunder-breath into the cry. All these comments, and this vast enthusiasm, served the more to interest our friend; nor did he think of questioning that now, at length, the mountain-visage had found its human coun-terpart. It is true, Ernest had imagined that this long-looked-for personage would appear in the character of a man of peace, uttering wisdom, and doing good, and making people happy. But, taking an habitual breadth of view, with all his simplicity, he contended that Provi-dence should choose its own method of blessing man-kind, and could conceive that this great end might be effected even by a warrior and a bloody sword, should inscrutable wisdom see fit to order matters so.

"The general! the general!" was now the cry. "Hush! silence! Old Blood-and-Thunder's going to make a speech."

Even so; for, the cloth being removed, the general's health had been drunk amid shouts of applause, and he now stood upon his feet to thank the company. Ernest saw him. There he was, over the shoulders of the crowd, from the two glittering epaulets and embroidered col-lar upward, beneath the arch of green boughs with in-tertwined laurel, and the banner drooping as if to shade his brow! And there, too, visible in the same glance, through the vista of the forest, appeared the Great Stone

Face! And was there, indeed, such a resemblance as
the crowd had testified? Alas, Ernest could not recognize it! He beheld a war-worn and weather-beaten
countenance, full of energy, and expressive of an iron
will; but the gentle wisdom, the deep, broad, tender
sympathies, were altogether wanting in Old Blood-and-
Thunder's visage; and even if the G.eat Stone Face had
assumed his look of stern command, the milder traits
would still have tempered it.

"This is not the man of prophecy," sighed Ernest, to
himself, as he made his way out of the throng. "And
must the world wait longer yet?"

The mists had congregated about the distant mountain-side, and there were seen the grand and awful
features of the Great Stone Face, awful but benignant,
as if a mighty angel were sitting among the hills, and
enrobing himself in a cloud-vesture of gold and purple.
As he looked, Ernest could hardly believe but that a
smile beamed over the whole visage, with a radiance
still brightening, although without motion of the lips.
It was probably the effect of the western sunshine, melting through the thinly diffused vapors that had swept
between him and the object that he gazed at. But —
as it always did — the aspect of his marvellous friend
made Ernest as hopeful as if he had never hoped in
vain.

"Fear not, Ernest," said his heart, even as if the
Great Face were whispering him, — "fear not, Ernest;
he will come."

More years sped swiftly and tranquilly away. Ernest
still dwelt in his native valley, and was now a man of
middle age. By imperceptible degrees, he had become
known among the people. Now, as heretofore, he labored for his bread, and was the same simple-hearted

man that he had always been. But he had thought and felt so much, he had given so many of the best hours of his life to unworldly hopes for some great good to mankind, that it seemed as though he had been talking with the angels, and had imbibed a portion of their wisdom unawares. It was visible in the calm and well-considered beneficence of his daily life, the quiet stream of which had made a wide green margin all along its course. Not a day passed by, that the world was not the better because this man, humble as he was, had lived. He never stepped aside from his own path, yet would always reach a blessing to his neighbor. Almost involuntarily, too, he had become a preacher. The pure and high simplicity of his thought, which, as one of its manifestations, took shape in the good deeds that dropped silently from his hand, flowed also forth in speech. He uttered truths that wrought upon and moulded the lives of those who heard him. His auditors, it may be, never suspected that Ernest, their own neighbor and familiar friend, was more than an ordinary man; least of all did Ernest himself suspect it; but, inevitably as the murmur of a rivulet, came thoughts out of his mouth that no other human lips had spoken.

When the people's minds had had a little time to cool, they were ready enough to acknowledge their mistake in imagining a similarity between General Blood-and-Thunder's truculent physiognomy and the benign visage on the mountain-side. But now, again, there were reports and many paragraphs in the newspapers, affirming that the likeness of the Great Stone Face had appeared upon the broad shoulders of a certain eminent statesman. He, like Mr. Gathergold and Old Blood-and-Thunder, was a native of the valley, but had left it in his early days, and taken up the trades of law and politics. Instead of

the rich man's wealth and the warrior's sword, he had
but a tongue, and it was mightier than both together.
So wonderfully eloquent was he, that whatever he might
choose to say, his auditors had no choice but to believe
him ; wrong looked like right, and right like wrong ;
for when it pleased him, he could make a kind of illuminated fog with his mere breath, and obscure the natural daylight with it.   His tongue, indeed, was a magic
instrument : sometimes it rumbled like the thunder ;
sometimes it warbled like the sweetest music.   It was
the blast of war, — the song of peace ; and it seemed to
have a heart in it, when there was no such matter.   In
good truth, he was a wondrous man ; and when his
tongue had acquired him all other imaginable success,
— when it had been heard in halls of state, and in the
courts of princes and potentates, — after it had made
him known all over the world, even as a voice crying
from shore to shore, — it finally persuaded his countrymen to select him for the Presidency.   Before this time,
— indeed, as soon as he began to grow celebrated, —
his admirers had found out the resemblance between him
and the Great Stone Face ; and so much were they
struck by it, that throughout the country this distinguished gentleman was known by the name of Old
Stony Phiz.   The phrase was considered as giving a
highly favorable aspect to his political prospects ; for,
as is likewise the case with the Popedom, nobody ever
becomes President without taking a name other than his
own.

While his friends were doing their best to make him
President, Old Stony Phiz, as he was called, set out on a
visit to the valley where he was born.   Of course, he had
no other object that to shake hands with his fellow-citi-
zens, and neither thought nor cared about any effect

which his progress through the country might have upon the election. Magnificent preparations were made to receive the illustrious statesman; a cavalcade of horsemen set forth to meet him at the boundary line of the State, and all the people left their business and gathered along the wayside to see him pass. Among these was Ernest. Though more than once disappointed, as we have seen, he had such a hopeful and confiding nature, that he was always ready to believe in whatever seemed beautiful and good. He kept his heart continually open, and thus was sure to catch the blessing from on high, when it should come. So now again, as buoyantly as ever, he went forth to behold the likeness of the Great Stone Face.

The cavalcade came prancing along the road, with a great clattering of hoofs and a mighty cloud of dust, which rose up so dense and high that the visage of the mountain-side was completely hidden from Ernest's eyes. All the great men of the neighborhood were there on horseback: militia officers, in uniform; the member of Congress; the sheriff of the county; the editors of newspapers; and many a farmer, too, had mounted his patient steed, with his Sunday coat upon his back. It really was a very brilliant spectacle, especially as there were numerous banners flaunting over the cavalcade, on some of which were gorgeous portraits of the illustrious statesman and the Great Stone Face, smiling familiarly at one another, like two brothers. If the pictures were to be trusted, the mutual resemblance, it must be confessed, was marvellous. We must not forget to mention that there was a band of music, which made the echoes of the mountains ring and reverberate with the loud triumph of its strains; so that airy and soul-thrilling melodies broke out among all the heights and hollows,

3   D

as if every nook of his native valley had found a voice, to welcome the distinguished guest. But the grandest effect was when the far-off mountain precipice flung back the music; for then the Great Stone Face itself seemed to be swelling the triumphant chorus, in acknowledgment that, at length, the man of prophecy was come.

All this while the people were throwing up their hats and shouting, with enthusiasm so contagious that the heart of Ernest kindled up, and he likewise threw up his hat, and shouted, as loudly as the loudest, "Huzza for the great man! Huzza for Old Stony Phiz?" But as yet he had not seen him.

"Here he is, now!" cried those who stood near Ernest. "There! There! Look at Old Stony Phiz and then at the Old Man of the Mountain, and see if they are not as like as two twin-brothers!"

In the midst of all this gallant array, came an open barouche, drawn by four white horses; and in the barouche, with his massive head uncovered, sat the illustrious statesman, Old Stony Phiz himself.

"Confess it," said one of Ernest's neighbors to him, "the Great Stone Face has met its match at last!"

Now, it must be owned that, at his first glimpse of the countenance which was bowing and smiling from the barouche, Ernest did fancy that there was a resemblance between it and the old familiar face upon the mountain-side. The brow, with its massive depth and loftiness, and all the other features, indeed, were boldly and strongly hewn, as if in emulation of a more than heroic, of a Titanic model. But the sublimity and stateliness, the grand expression of a divine sympathy, that illuminated the mountain visage, and etherealized its ponderous granite substance into spirit, might here be sought in vain. Something had been originally left out, or had departed. And therefore the marvellously gifted states-man had always a weary gloom in the deep caverns of his eyes, as of a child that has outgrown its playthings, or a man of mighty faculties and little aims, whose life, with all its high performances, was vague and empty, because no high purpose had endowed it with reality.

Still, Ernest's neighbor was thrusting his elbow into his side, and pressing him for an answer.

"Confess! confess! Is not he the very picture of your Old Man of the Mountain?"

"No!" said Ernest, bluntly, "I see little or no like-ness."

"Then so much the worse for the Great Stone Face!" answered his neighbor; and again he set up a shout for Old Stony Phiz.

But Ernest turned away, melancholy, and almost despondent: for this was the saddest of his disappoint-ments, to behold a man who might have fulfilled the prophecy, and had not willed to do so. Meantime, the cavalcade, the banners, the music, and the barouches swept past him, with the vociferous crowd in the rear, leaving the dust to settle down, and the Great Stone Face to be revealed again, with the grandeur that it had worn for untold centuries.

"Lo, here I am, Ernest!" the benign lips seemed to say. "I have waited longer than thou, and am not yet weary. Fear not; the man will come."

The years hurried onward, treading in their haste on one another's heels. And now they began to bring white hairs, and scatter them over the head of Ernest; they made reverend wrinkles across his forehead, and furrows in his cheeks. He was an aged man. But not in vain had he grown old: more than the white hairs on his head

were the sage thoughts in his mind; his wrinkles and
furrows were inscriptions that Time had graved, and in
which he had written legends of wisdom that had been
tested by the tenor of a life. And Ernest had ceased to
be obscure. Unsought for, undesired, had come the fame
which so many seek, and made him known in the great
world, beyond the limits of the valley in which he had
dwelt so quietly. College professors, and even the active
men of cities, came from far to see and converse with
Ernest; for the report had gone abroad that this simple
husbandman had ideas unlike those of other men, not
gained from books, but of a higher tone, — a tranquil
and familiar majesty, as if he had been talking with the
angels as his daily friends. Whether it were sage,
statesman, or philanthropist, Ernest received these visit-
ors with the gentle sincerity that had characterized him
from boyhood, and spoke freely with them of whatever
came uppermost, or lay deepest in his heart or their own.
While they talked together, his face would kindle, unawares, and shine upon them, as with a mild evening
light. Pensive with the fulness of such discourse, his
guests took leave and went their way; and passing up
the valley, paused to look at the Great Stone Face, imagining that they had seen its likeness in a human countenance, but could not remember where.

While Ernest had been growing up and growing old,
a bountiful Providence had granted a new poet to this
earth. He, likewise, was a native of the valley, but had
spent the greater part of his life at a distance from that
romantic region, pouring out his sweet music amid the
bustle and din of cities. Often, however, did the mountains which had been familiar to him in his childhood
lift their snowy peaks into the clear atmosphere of his
poetry. Neither was the Great Stone Face forgotten,

for the poet had celebrated it in an ode, which was grand enough to have been uttered by its own majestic lips. This man of genius, we may say, had come down from heaven with wonderful endowments. If he sang of a mountain, the eyes of all mankind beheld a mightier grandeur reposing on its breast, or soaring to its summit, than had before been seen there. If his theme were a lovely lake, a celestial smile had now been thrown over it, to gleam forever on its surface. If it were the vast old sea, even the deep immensity of its dread bosom seemed to swell the higher, as if moved by the emotions of the song. Thus the world assumed another and a better aspect from the hour that the poet blessed it with his happy eyes. The Creator had bestowed him, as the last best touch to his own handiwork. Creation was not finished till the poet came to interpret, and so complete it.

The effect was no less high and beautiful, when his human brethren were the subject of his verse. The man or woman, sordid with the common dust of life, who crossed his daily path, and the little child who played in it, were glorified if he beheld them in his mood of poetic faith. He showed the golden links of the great chain that intertwined them with an angelic kindred; he brought out the hidden traits of a celestial birth that made them worthy of such kin. Some, indeed, there were, who thought to show the soundness of their judgment by affirming that all the beauty and dignity of the natural world existed only in the poet's fancy. Let such men speak for themselves, who undoubtedly appear to have been spawned forth by Nature with a contemptuous bitterness; she having plastered them up out of her refuse stuff, after all the swine were made. As respects all things else, the poet's ideal was the truest truth.

The songs of this poet found their way to Ernest. He read them after his customary toil, seated on the bench before his cottage-door, where for such a length of time he had filled his repose with thought, by gazing at the Great Stone Face. And now as he read stanzas that caused the soul to thrill within him, he lifted his eyes to the vast countenance beaming on him so benignantly.

"O majestic friend," he murmured, addressing the Great Stone Face, " is not this man worthy to resemble thee ? "

The Face seemed to smile, but answered not a word.

Now it happened that the poet, though he dwelt so far away, had not only heard of Ernest, but had meditated much upon his character, until he deemed nothing so desirable as to meet this man, whose untaught wisdom walked hand in hand with the noble simplicity of his life. One summer morning, therefore, he took passage by the railroad, and, in the decline of the afternoon, alighted from the cars at no great distance from Ernest's cottage. The great hotel, which had formerly been the palace of Mr. Gathergold, was close at hand, but the poet, with his carpet-bag on his arm, inquired at once where Ernest dwelt, and was resolved to be accepted as his guest.

Approaching the door, he there found the good old man, holding a volume in his hand, which alternately he read, and then, with a finger between the leaves, looked lovingly at the Great Stone Face.

"Good evening," said the poet. "Can you give a traveller a night's lodging ? "

"Willingly," answered Ernest ; and then he added, smiling, " Methinks I never saw the Great Stone Face look so hospitably at a stranger."

The poet sat down on the bench beside him, and he

and Ernest talked together. Often had the poet held intercourse with the wittiest and the wisest, but never before with a man like Ernest, whose thoughts and feelings gushed up with such a natural freedom, and who made great truths so familiar by his simple utterance of them. Angels, as had been so often said, seemed to have wrought with him at his labor in the fields; angels seemed to have sat with him by the fireside; and, dwelling with angels as friend with friends, he had imbibed the sublimity of their ideas, and imbued it with the sweet and lowly charm of household words. So thought the poet. And Ernest, on the other hand, was moved and agitated by the living images which the poet flung out of his mind, and which peopled all the air about the cottage-door with shapes of beauty, both gay and pensive. The sympathies of these two men instructed them with a profounder sense than either could have attained alone. Their minds accorded into one strain, and made delightful music which neither of them could have claimed as all his own, nor distinguished his own share from the other's. They led one another, as it were, into a high pavilion of their thoughts, so remote, and hitherto so dim, that they had never entered it before, and so beautiful that they desired to be there always.

As Ernest listened to the poet, he imagined that the Great Stone Face was bending forward to listen too. He gazed earnestly into the poet's glowing eyes.

"Who are you, my strangely gifted guest?" he said.

The poet laid his finger on the volume that Ernest had been reading.

"You have read these poems," said he. "You know me, then, — for I wrote them."

Again, and still more earnestly than before, Ernest

examined the poet's features; then turned towards the Great Stone Face; then back, with an uncertain aspect, to his guest. But his countenance fell; he shook his head, and sighed.

"Wherefore are you sad?" inquired the poet.

"Because," replied Ernest, "all through life I have awaited the fulfilment of a prophecy; and, when I read these poems, I hoped that it might be fulfilled in you."

"You hoped," answered the poet, faintly smiling, "to find in me the likeness of the Great Stone Face. And you are disappointed, as formerly with Mr. Gathergold, and Old Blood-and-Thunder, and Old Stony Phiz. Yes, Ernest, it is my doom. You must add my name to the illustrious three, and record another failure of your hopes. For — in shame and sadness do I speak it, Ernest — I am not worthy to be typified by yonder benign and majestic image."

"And why?" asked Ernest. He pointed to the volume. "Are not those thoughts divine?"

"They have a strain of the Divinity," replied the poet. "You can hear in them the far-off echo of a heavenly song. But my life, dear Ernest, has not corresponded with my thought. I have had grand dreams, but they have been only dreams, because I have lived — and that, too, by my own choice — among poor and mean realities. Sometimes even — shall I dare to say it? — I lack faith in the grandeur, the beauty, and the goodness, which my own works are said to have made more evident in nature and in human life. Why, then, pure seeker of the good and true, shouldst thou hope to find me, in yonder image of the divine?"

The poet spoke sadly, and his eyes were dim with tears. So, likewise, were those of Ernest.

At the hour of sunset, as had long been his frequent

custom, Ernest was to discourse to an assemblage of the neighboring inhabitants in the open air. He and the poet, arm in arm, still talking together as they went along, proceeded to the spot. It was a small nook among the hills, with a gray precipice behind, the stern front of which was relieved by the pleasant foliage of many creeping plants, that made a tapestry for the naked rock, by hanging their festoons from all its rugged angles. At a small elevation above the ground, set in a rich framework of verdure, there appeared a niche, spacious enough to admit a human figure, with freedom for such gestures as spontaneously accompany earnest thought and genuine emotion. Into this natural pulpit Ernest ascended, and threw a look of familiar kindness around upon his audience. They stood, or sat, or reclined upon the grass, as seemed good to each, with the departing sunshine falling obliquely over them, and mingling its subdued cheerfulness with the solemnity of a grove of ancient trees, beneath and amid the boughs of which the golden rays were constrained to pass. In another direction was seen the Great Stone Face, with the same cheer, combined with the same solemnity, in its benignant aspect.

Ernest began to speak, giving to the people of what was in his heart and mind. His words had power, because they accorded with his thoughts; and his thoughts had reality and depth, because they harmonized with the life which he had always lived. It was not mere breath that this preacher uttered; they were the words of life, because a life of good deeds and holy love was melted into them. Pearls, pure and rich, had been dissolved into this precious draught. The poet, as he listened, felt that the being and character of Ernest were a nobler strain of poetry than he had ever written. His eyes

3 *

glistening with tears, he gazed reverentially at the venerable man, and said within himself that never was there an aspect so worthy of a prophet and a sage as that mild, sweet, thoughtful countenance, with the glory of white hair diffused about it. At a distance, but distinctly to be seen, high up in the golden light of the setting sun, appeared the Great Stone Face, with hoary mists around it, like the white hairs around the brow of Ernest. Its look of grand beneficence seemed to embrace the world.

At that moment, in sympathy with a thought which he was about to utter, the face of Ernest assumed a grandeur of expression, so imbued with benevolence, that the poet, by an irresistible impulse, threw his arms aloft, and shouted, —

"Behold! Behold! Ernest is himself the likeness of the Great Stone Face!"

Then all the people looked, and saw that what the deep-sighted poet said was true. The prophecy was fulfilled. But Ernest, having finished what he had to say, took the poet's arm, and walked slowly homeward, still hoping that some wiser and better man than himself would by and by appear, bearing a resemblance to the GREAT STONE FACE.

MAIN STREET.

A RESPECTABLE-LOOKING individual makes his bow and addresses the public. In my daily walks along the principal street of my native town, it has often occurred to me, that, if its growth from infancy upward, and the vicissitude of characteristic scenes that have passed along this thoroughfare during the more than two centuries of its existence, could be presented to the eye in a shifting panorama, it would be an exceedingly effective method of illustrating the march of time. Acting on this idea, I have contrived a certain pictorial exhibition, somewhat in the nature of a puppet-show, by means of which I propose to call up the multiform and many-colored Past before the spectator, and show him the ghosts of his forefathers, amid a succession of historic incidents, with no greater trouble than the turning of a crank. Be pleased, therefore, my indulgent patrons, to walk into the show-room, and take your seats before yonder mysterious curtain. The little wheels and springs of my machinery have been well oiled; a multitude of puppets are dressed in character, representing all varieties of fashion, from the Puritan cloak and jerkin to the latest Oak Hall coat; the lamps are trimmed, and shall brighten into noontide sunshine, or fade away in moonlight, or muffle their brilliancy in a November cloud, as the nature of the scene may require; and, in short, the exhibition is just ready to commence. Unless something should go wrong, — as, for instance, the misplacing of a picture, whereby the people and events of one century might be thrust into the middle of another; or the breaking of a wire, which would bring the course of time to a sudden period, — barring, I say, the casualties to which such a complicated piece of mechanism is liable, — I flatter myself, ladies and gentlemen, that the performance will elicit your generous approbation.

Ting-a-ting-ting! goes the bell; the curtain rises; and we behold — not, indeed, the Main Street — but the track of leaf-strewn forest-land over which its dusty pavement is hereafter to extend.

You perceive, at a glance, that this is the ancient and primitive wood, — the ever-youthful and venerably old, — verdant with new twigs, yet hoary, as it were, with the snowfall of innumerable years, that have accumulated upon its intermingled branches. The white man's axe has never smitten a single tree; his footstep has never crumpled a single one of the withered leaves, which all the autumns since the flood have been harvesting beneath. Yet, see! along through the vista of impending boughs, there is already a faintly traced path, running nearly east and west, as if a prophecy or foreboding of the future street had stolen into the heart of the solemn old wood. Onward goes this hardly perceptible track, now ascending over a natural swell of land, now subsiding gently into a hollow; traversed here by a little streamlet, which glitters like a snake through the gleam of sunshine, and quickly hides itself among the underbrush, in its quest for the neighboring cove; and impeded there by the massy corpse of a giant of the forest, which had lived out its incalculable term of life, and been overthrown by mere old age, and lies buried in the new vegetation that is born of its decay. What footsteps can have worn this half-seen path? Hark! Do we not hear them now rustling softly over the leaves? We discern an Indian woman, — a majestic and queenly woman, or else her spectral image does not represent her truly, — for this is the great Squaw Sachem, whose rule, with that of her sons, extends from Mystic to Agawam. That red chief, who stalks by her side, is Wappacowet, her second husband, the priest and magician, whose incantations shall hereafter affright the pale-faced settlers with grisly phantoms, dancing and shrieking in the woods, at midnight. But greater would be the affright of the Indian necromancer, if, mirrored in the pool of water at his feet, he could catch a prophetic glimpse of the noonday marvels which the white man is destined to achieve; if he could see, as in a dream, the stone front of the stately hall, which will cast its shadow over this very spot; if he could be aware that the future edifice will contain a noble Museum, where, among countless curiosities of earth and sea, a few Indian arrow-heads shall be treasured up as memorials of a vanished race!

No such forebodings disturb the Squaw Sachem and Wappacowet. They pass on, beneath the tangled shade, holding high talk on matters of state and religion, and imagine, doubtless, that their own system of affairs will endure forever. Meanwhile, how full of its own proper life is the scene that lies around them! The gray squirrel runs up the trees, and rustles among the upper branches. Was not that the leap of a deer? And there is the whirr of a partridge! Methinks, too, I catch the cruel and stealthy eye of a wolf, as he draws back into yonder impervious density of underbrush. So, there, amid the murmur of boughs, go the Indian queen and the Indian priest; while the gloom of the broad wilderness impends over them, and its sombre mystery invests them as with something preternatural; and only momentary streaks of quivering sunlight, once in a great while, find their way down, and glimmer among the feathers in their dusky hair. Can it be that the thronged street of a city will ever pass into this twilight solitude, — over those soft heaps of the decaying tree-trunks, and through the swampy places, green with water-moss, and penetrate that hopeless entanglement of great trees, which have been uprooted and tossed together by a whirlwind? It has been a wilderness from the creation. Must it not be a wilderness forever?

Here an acidulous-looking gentleman in blue glasses, with bows of Berlin steel, who has taken a seat at the extremity of the front row, begins, at this early stage of the exhibition, to criticise.

"The whole affair is a manifest catchpenny!" observes he, scarcely under his breath. "The trees look more like weeds in a garden than a primitive forest; the Squaw Sachem and Wappacowet are stiff in their pasteboard joints; and the squirrels, the deer, and the wolf move with all the grace of a child's wooden monkey, sliding up and down a stick."

"I am obliged to you, sir, for the candor of your remarks," replies the showman, with a bow. "Perhaps they are just. Human art has its limits, and we must now and then ask a little aid from the spectator's imagination."

"You will get no such aid from mine," responds the critic. "I make it a point to see things precisely as they are. But come! go ahead! the stage is waiting!"

The showman proceeds.

Casting our eyes again over the scene, we perceive

that strangers have found their way into the solitary place. In more than one spot, among the trees, an up-heaved axe is glittering in the sunshine. Roger Conant, the first settler in Naumkeag, has built his dwelling, months ago, on the border of the forest-path; and at this moment he comes eastward through the vista of woods, with his gun over his shoulder, bringing home the choice portions of a deer. His stalwart figure, clad in a leathern jerkin and breeches of the same, strides sturdily onward, with such an air of physical force and energy that we might almost expect the very trees to stand aside, and give him room to pass. And so, in-deed, they must; for, humble as is his name in history, Roger Conant still is of that class of men who do not merely find, but make, their place in the system of human affairs; a man of thoughtful strength, he has planted the germ of a city. There stands his habi-tation, showing in its rough architecture some features of the Indian wigwam, and some of the log-cabin, and somewhat, too, of the straw-thatched cottage in Old England, where this good yeoman had his birth and breeding. The dwelling is surrounded by a cleared space of a few acres, where Indian corn grows thriv-ingly among the stumps of the trees; while the dark forest hems it in, and seems to gaze silently and solemn-ly, as if wondering at the breadth of sunshine which the white man spreads around him. An Indian, half hidden in the dusky shade, is gazing and wondering too.

Within the door of the cottage you discern the wife, with her ruddy English cheek. She is singing, doubt-less, a psalm tune, at her household work; or, perhaps she sighs at the remembrance of the cheerful gossip, and all the merry social life, of her native village beyond the vast and melancholy sea. Yet the next moment she

laughs, with sympathetic glee, at the sports of her little
tribe of children ; and soon turns round, with the home-
look in her face, as her husband's foot is heard approaching the rough-hewn threshold. How sweet must it be
for those who have an Eden in their hearts, like Roger
Conant and his wife, to find a new world to project it
into, as they have, instead of dwelling among old haunts
of men, where so many household fires have been kindled and burnt out, that the very glow of happiness has
something dreary in it ! Not that this pair are alone in
their wild Eden, for here comes Goodwife Massey, the
young spouse of Jeffrey Massey, from her home hard by,
with an infant at her breast. Dame Conant has another
of like age ; and it shall hereafter be one of the disputed
points of history which of these two babies was the first
town-born child.

But see ! Roger Conant has other neighbors within
view. Peter Palfrey likewise has built himself a house,
and so has Balch, and Norman, and Woodbury. Their
dwellings, indeed, — such is the ingenious contrivance of
this piece of pictorial mechanism, — seem to have arisen,
at various points of the scene, even while we have been
looking at it. The forest-track, trodden more and more
by the hobnailed shoes of these sturdy and ponderous
Englishmen, has now a distinctness which it never could
have acquired from the light tread of a hundred times as
many Indian moccasins. It will be a street, anon. As
we observe it now, it goes onward from one clearing to
another, here plunging into a shadowy strip of woods,
there open to the sunshine, but everywhere showing a
decided line, along which human interests have begun
to hold their career. Over yonder swampy spot, two
trees have been felled, and laid side by side to make a
causeway. In another place, the axe has cleared away a

confused intricacy of fallen trees and clustered boughs, which had been tossed together by a hurricane. So now the little children, just beginning to run alone, may trip along the path, and not often stumble over an impediment, unless they stray from it to gather wood-berries beneath the trees. And, besides the feet of grown people and children, there are the cloven hoofs of a small herd of cows, who seek their subsistence from the native grasses, and help to deepen the track of the future thoroughfare. Goats also browse along it, and nibble at the twigs that thrust themselves across the way. Not seldom, in its more secluded portions, where the black shadow of the forest strives to hide the trace of human footsteps, stalks a gaunt wolf, on the watch for a kid or a young calf; or fixes his hungry gaze on the group of children gathering berries, and can hardly forbear to rush upon them. And the Indians, coming from their distant wigwams to view the white man's settlement, marvel at the deep track which he makes, and perhaps are saddened by a flitting presentiment that this heavy tread will find its way over all the land; and that the wild woods, the wild wolf, and the wild Indian will alike be trampled beneath it. Even so shall it be. The pavements of the Main Street must be laid over the red man's grave.

Behold! here is a spectacle which should be ushered in by the peal of trumpets, if Naumkeag had ever yet heard that cheery music, and by the roar of cannon, echoing among the woods. A procession, — for, by its dignity, as marking an epoch in the history of the street, it deserves that name, — a procession advances along the pathway. The good ship Abigail has arrived from England, bringing wares and merchandise, for the comfort of the inhabitants, and traffic with the Indians; bringing

E

passengers too, and, more important than all, a governor for the new settlement. Roger Conant and Peter Palfrey, with their companions, have been to the shore to welcome him; and now, with such honor and triumph as their rude way of life permits, are escorting the seaflushed voyagers to their habitations. At the point where Endicott enters upon the scene, two venerable trees unite their branches high above his head; thus forming a triumphal arch of living verdure, beneath which he pauses, with his wife leaning on his arm, to catch the first impression of their new-found home. The old settlers gaze not less earnestly at him, than he at the hoary woods and the rough surface of the clearings. They like his bearded face, under the shadow of the broad-brimmed and steeple-crowned Puritan hat; — a visage resolute, grave, and thoughtful, yet apt to kindle with that glow of a cheerful spirit by which men of strong character are enabled to go joyfully on their proper tasks. His form, too, as you see it, in a doublet and hose of sad-colored cloth, is of a manly make, fit for toil and hardship, and fit to wield the heavy sword that hangs from his leathern belt. His aspect is a better warrant for the ruler's office than the parchment commission which he bears, however fortified it may be with the broad seal of the London council. Peter Palfrey nods to Roger Conant. "The worshipful Court of Assistants have done wisely," say they between themselves. "They have chosen for our governor a man out of a thousand." Then they toss up their hats, — they, and all the uncouth figures of their company, most of whom are clad in skins, inasmuch as their old kersey and linsey-woolsey garments have been torn and tattered by many a long month's wear, — they all toss up their hats, and salute their new governor and captain with a hearty

English shout of welcome. We seem to hear it with our own ears, so perfectly is the action represented in this life-like, this almost magic picture!

But have you observed the lady who leans upon the arm of Endicott? — a rose of beauty from an English garden, now to be transplanted to a fresher soil. It may be that, long years — centuries indeed — after this fair flower shall have decayed, other flowers of the same race will appear in the same soil, and gladden other generations with hereditary beauty. Does not the vision haunt us yet? Has not Nature kept the mould unbroken, deeming it a pity that the idea should vanish from mortal sight forever, after only once assuming earthly substance? Do we not recognize, in that fair woman's face, the model of features which still beam, at happy moments, on what was then the woodland pathway, but has long since grown into a busy street?

"This is too ridiculous! — positively insufferable!" mutters the same critic who had before expressed his disapprobation. "Here is a pasteboard figure, such as a child would cut out of a card, with a pair of very dull scissors; and the fellow modestly requests us to see in it the prototype of hereditary beauty!"

"But, sir, you have not the proper point of view," remarks the showman. "You sit altogether too near to get the best effect of my pictorial exhibition. Pray, oblige me by removing to this other bench, and I venture to assure you the proper light and shadow will transform the spectacle into quite another thing."

"Pshaw!" replies the critic; "I want no other light and shade. I have already told you that it is my business to see things just as they are."

"I would suggest to the author of this ingenious exhibition," observes a gentlemanly person, who has shown

signs of being much interested, — "I would suggest that
Anna Gower, the first wife of Governor Endicott, and who
came with him from England, left no posterity; and that,
consequently, we cannot be indebted to that honorable
lady for any specimens of feminine loveliness now extant
among us."

Having nothing to allege against this genealogical objection, the showman points again to the scene.

During this little interruption, you perceive that the
Anglo-Saxon energy — as the phrase now goes — has
been at work in the spectacle before us. So many chimneys now send up their smoke, that it begins to have the
aspect of a village street; although everything is so inar-
tificial and inceptive, that it seems as if one returning
wave of the wild nature might overwhelm it all. But the
one edifice which gives the pledge of permanence to this
bold enterprise is seen at the central point of the picture.
There stands the meeting-house, a small structure, low-
roofed, without a spire, and built of rough timber, newly
hewn, with the sap still in the logs, and here and there
a strip of bark adhering to them. A meaner temple was
never consecrated to the worship of the Deity. With
the alternative of kneeling beneath the awful vault of the
firmament, it is strange that men should creep into this
pent-up nook, and expect God's presence there. Such,
at least, one would imagine, might be the feeling of these
forest-settlers, accustomed, as they had been, to stand
under the dim arches of vast cathedrals, and to offer up
their hereditary worship in the old ivy-covered churches
of rural England, around which lay the bones of many
generations of their forefathers. How could they dispense with the carved altar-work? — how, with the pictured windows, where the light of common day was
hallowed by being transmitted through the glorified fig-

ures of saints? — how, with the lofty roof, imbued, as it must have been, with the prayers that had gone upward for centuries? — how, with the rich peal of the solemn organ, rolling along the aisles, pervading the whole church, and sweeping the soul away on a flood of audible religion? They needed nothing of all this. Their house of worship, like their ceremonial, was naked, simple, and severe. But the zeal of a recovered faith burned like a lamp within their hearts, enriching everything around them with its radiance; making of these new walls, and this narrow compass, its own cathedral; and being, in itself, that spiritual mystery and experience, of which sacred architecture, pictured windows, and the organ's grand solemnity are remote and imperfect symbols. All was well, so long as their lamps were freshly kindled at the heavenly flame. After a while, however, whether in their time or their children's, these lamps began to burn more dimly, or with a less genuine lustre; and then it might be seen how hard, cold, and confined was their system, — how like an iron cage was that which they called Liberty.

Too much of this. Look again at the picture, and observe how the aforesaid Anglo-Saxon energy is now trampling along the street, and raising a positive cloud of dust beneath its sturdy footsteps. For there the carpenters are building a new house, the frame of which was hewn and fitted in England, of English oak, and sent hither on shipboard; and here a blacksmith makes huge clang and clatter on his anvil, shaping out tools and weapons; and yonder a wheelwright, who boasts himself a London workman, regularly bred to his handicraft, is fashioning a set of wagon-wheels, the track of which shall soon be visible. The wild forest is shrinking back; the street has lost the aromatic odor of the pine-trees, and of the sweet-fern that grew beneath them. The tender and modest wild-flowers, those gentle children of savage nature that grew pale beneath the ever-brooding shade, have shrunk away and disappeared, like stars that vanish in the breadth of light. Gardens are fenced in, and display pumpkin-beds and rows of cabbages and beans; and, though the governor and the minister both view them with a disapproving eye, plants of broad-leaved tobacco, which the cultivators are enjoined to use privily, or not at all. No wolf, for a year past, has been heard to bark, or known to range among the dwellings, except that single one, whose grisly head, with a plash of blood beneath it, is now affixed to the portal of the meeting-house. The partridge has ceased to run across the too-frequented path. Of all the wild life that used to throng here, only the Indians still come into the set-tlement, bringing the skins of beaver and otter, bear and elk, which they sell to Endicott for the wares of England. And there is little John Massey, the son of Jeffrey Massey and first-born of Naumkeag, playing beside his father's threshold, a child of six or seven years old. Which is the better-grown infant, — the town or the boy?

The red men have become aware that the street is no longer free to them, save by the sufferance and permission of the settlers. Often, to impress them with an awe of English power, there is a muster and training of the town-forces, and a stately march of the mail-clad band, like this which we now see advancing up the street. There they come, fifty of them, or more; all with their iron breastplates and steel caps well burnished, and glim-mering bravely against the sun; their ponderous muskets on their shoulders, their bandaliers about their waists, their lighted matches in their hands, and the drum and fife playing cheerily before them. See! do they not step like martial men? Do they not manœuvre like soldiers who have seen stricken fields? And well they may; for this band is composed of precisely such materials as those with which Cromwell is preparing to beat down the strength of a kingdom; and his famous regiment of Ironsides might be recruited from just such men. In everything, at this period, New England was the essential spirit and flower of that which was about to become uppermost in the mother-country. Many a bold and wise man lost the fame which would have accrued to him in English history, by crossing the Atlantic with our forefathers. Many a valiant captain, who might have been foremost at Marston Moor or Naseby, exhausted his martial ardor in the command of a log-built fortress, like that which you observe on the gently rising ground at the right of the pathway, — its banner fluttering in the breeze, and the culverins and sakers showing their deadly muzzles over the rampart.

A multitude of people were now thronging to New England: some, because the ancient and ponderous framework of Church and State threatened to crumble down upon their heads; others, because they despaired of such a downfall. Among those who came to Naumkeag were men of history and legend, whose feet leave a track of brightness along any pathway which they have trodden. You shall behold their life-like images — their spectres, if you choose so to call them — passing, encountering with a familiar nod, stopping to converse together, praying, bearing weapons, laboring or resting from their labors, in the Main Street. Here, now, comes Hugh Peters, an earnest, restless man, walking swiftly, as being impelled by that fiery activity of nature which shall hereafter thrust him into the conflict of dangerous affairs, make him the chaplain and counsellor of Cromwell, and finally

bring him to a bloody end. He pauses, by the meeting-
house, to exchange a greeting with Roger Williams, whose
face indicates, methinks, a gentler spirit, kinder and more
expansive, than that of Peters; yet not less active for
what he discerns to be the will of God, or the welfare
of mankind. And look! here is a guest for Endicott,
coming forth out of the forest, through which he has
been journeying from Boston, and which, with its rude
branches, has caught hold of his attire, and has wet his
feet with its swamps and streams. Still there is something in his mild and venerable, though not aged presence — a propriety, an equilibrium, in Governor Win-
throp's nature — that causes the disarray of his costume
to be unnoticed, and gives us the same impression as if
he were clad in such grave and rich attire as we may suppose him to have worn in the Council Chamber of the
colony. Is not this characteristic wonderfully perceptible in our spectral representative of his person? But
what dignitary is this crossing from the other side to
greet the governor? A stately personage, in a dark velvet cloak, with a hoary beard, and a gold chain across his
breast; he has the authoritative port of one who has
filled the highest civic station in the first of cities. Of
all men in the world, we should least expect to meet the
Lord Mayor of London — as Sir Richard Saltonstall has
been, once and again — in a forest-bordered settlement
of the western wilderness.

Farther down the street, we see Emanuel Downing, a
grave and worthy citizen, with his son George, a strip-
ling who has a career before him; his shrewd and quick
capacity and pliant conscience shall not only exalt him
high, but secure him from a downfall. Here is another
figure, on whose characteristic make and expressive action I will stake the credit of my pictorial puppet-show.

Have you not already detected a quaint, sly humor in
that face, — an eccentricity in the manner, — a certain
indescribable waywardness, — all the marks, in short, of
an original man, unmistakably impressed, yet kept down
by a sense of clerical restraint? That is Nathaniel Ward,
the minister of Ipswich, but better remembered as the
simple cobbler of Agawam. He hammered his sole so
faithfully, and stitched his upper-leather so well, that the
shoe is hardly yet worn out, though thrown aside for
some two centuries past. And next, among these Puritans
and Roundheads, we observe the very model of a Cavalier, with the curling lovelock, the fantastically trimmed
beard, the embroidery, the ornamented rapier, the gilded
dagger, and all other foppishnesses that distinguished the
wild gallants who rode headlong to their overthrow in
the cause of King Charles. This is Morton of Merry
Mount, who has come hither to hold a council with Endicott, but will shortly be his prisoner. Yonder pale,
decaying figure of a white-robed woman, who glides
slowly along the street, is the Lady Arabella, looking
for her own grave in the virgin soil. That other female
form, who seems to be talking — we might almost say
preaching or expounding — in the centre of a group of
profoundly attentive auditors, is Ann Hutchinson. And
here comes Vane —

"But, my dear sir," interrupts the same gentleman
who before questioned the showman's genealogical accuracy, "allow me to observe that these historical person-
ages could not possibly have met together in the Main
Street. They might, and probably did, all visit our old
town, at one time or another, but not simultaneously;
and you have fallen into anachronisms that I positively
shudder to think of!"

"The fellow," adds the scarcely civil critic, "has

4

learned a bead-roll of historic names, whom he lugs into his pictorial puppet-show, as he calls it, helter-skelter, without caring whether they were contemporaries or not, — and sets them all by the ears together. But was there ever such a fund of impudence? To hear his running commentary, you would suppose that these miserable slips of painted pasteboard, with hardly the remotest outlines of the human figure, had all the character and expression of Michael Angelo's pictures. Well! go on, sir!"

"Sir, you break the illusion of the scene," mildly remonstrates the showman.

"Illusion! What illusion?" rejoins the critic, with a contemptuous snort. "On the word of a gentleman, I see nothing illusive in the wretchedly bedaubed sheet of canvas that forms your background, or in these pasteboard slips that hitch and jerk along the front. The only illusion, permit me to say, is in the puppet-showman's tongue, — and that but a wretched one, into the bargain!"

"We public men," replies the showman, meekly, "must lay our account, sometimes, to meet an uncandid severity of criticism. But — merely for your own pleasure, sir — let me entreat you to take another point of view. Sit farther back, by that young lady, in whose face I have watched the reflection of every changing scene; only oblige me by sitting there; and, take my word for it, the slips of pasteboard shall assume spiritual life, and the bedaubed canvas become an airy and changeable reflex of what it purports to represent."

"I know better," retorts the critic, settling himself in his seat, with sullen but self-complacent immovableness. "And, as for my own pleasure, I shall best consult it by remaining precisely where I am."

The showman bows, and waves his hand; and, at the signal, as if time and vicissitude had been awaiting his permission to move onward, the mimic street becomes alive again.

Years have rolled over our scene, and converted the forest-track into a dusty thoroughfare, which, being intersected with lanes and cross-paths, may fairly be designated as the Main Street. On the ground-sites of many of the log-built sheds, into which the first settlers crept for shelter, houses of quaint architecture have now risen. These later edifices are built, as you see, in one generally accordant style, though with such subordinate variety as keeps the beholder's curiosity excited, and causes each structure, like its owner's character, to produce its own peculiar impression. Most of them have one huge chimney in the centre, with flues so vast that it must have been easy for the witches to fly out of them, as they were wont to do, when bound on an aerial visit to the Black Man in the forest. Around this great chimney the wooden house clusters itself, in a whole community of gable-ends, each ascending into its own separate peak; the second story, with its lattice-windows, projecting over the first; and the door, which is perhaps arched, provided on the outside with an iron hammer, wherewith the visitor's hand may give a thundering rat-a-tat. The timber framework of these houses, as compared with those of recent date, is like the skeleton of an old giant, beside the frail bones of a modern man of fashion. Many of them, by the vast strength and soundness of their oaken substance, have been preserved through a length of time which would have tried the stability of brick and stone; so that, in all the progressive decay and continual reconstruction of the street, down to our own days, we shall still behold these old edifices occupying their long-accustomed sites. For instance, on the upper corner of that green lane which shall hereafter be North Street, we see the Curwen House, newly built, with the carpenters still at work on the roof nailing down the last sheaf of shingles. On the lower corner stands another dwelling, — destined, at some period of its existence, to be the abode of an unsuccessful alchemist, — which shall likewise survive to our own generation, and perhaps long outlive it. Thus, through the medium of these patriarchal edifices, we have now established a sort of kindred and hereditary acquaintance with the Main Street.

Great as is the transformation produced by a short term of years, each single day creeps through the Puritan settlement sluggishly enough. It shall pass before your eyes, condensed into the space of a few moments. The gray light of early morning is slowly diffusing itself over the scene; and the bellman, whose office it is to cry the hour at the street-corners, rings the last peal upon his hand bell, and goes wearily homewards, with the owls, the bats, and other creatures of the night. Lattices are thrust back on their hinges, as if the town were opening its eyes, in the summer morning. Forth stumbles the still drowsy cowherd, with his horn; putting which to his lips, it emits a bellowing bray, impossible to be represented in the picture, but which reaches the pricked-up ears of every cow in the settlement, and tells her that the dewy pasture-hour is come. House after house awakes, and sends the smoke up curling from its chimney, like frosty breath from living nostrils; and as those white wreaths of smoke, though impregnated with earthy admixtures, climb skyward, so, from each dwelling, does the morning worship — its spiritual essence, bearing up its human imperfection — find its way to the heavenly Father's throne.

The breakfast-hour being passed, the inhabitants do not, as usual, go to their fields or workshops, but remain within doors; or perhaps walk the street, with a grave sobriety, yet a disengaged and unburdened aspect, that belongs neither to a holiday nor a Sabbath. And, indeed, this passing day is neither, nor is it a common week-day, although partaking of all the three. It is the Thursday Lecture; an institution which New England has long ago relinquished, and almost forgotten, yet which it would have been better to retain, as bearing relations to both the spiritual and ordinary life, and bringing each acquainted with the other. The tokens of its observance, however, which here meet our eyes, are of rather a questionable cast. It is, in one sense, a day of public shame; the day on which transgressors, who have made themselves liable to the minor severities of the Puritan law, receive their reward of ignominy. At this very moment, the constable has bound an idle fellow to the whipping-post, and is giving him his deserts with a cat-o'-nine-tails. Ever since sunrise, Daniel Fairfield has been standing on the steps of the meeting-house, with a halter about his neck, which he is condemned to wear visibly throughout his lifetime; Dorothy Talby is chained to a post at the corner of Prison Lane, with the hot sun blazing on her matronly face, and all for no other offence than lifting her hand against her husband; while, through the bars of that great wooden cage, in the centre of the scene, we discern either a human being or a wild beast, or both in one, whom this public infamy causes to roar, and gnash his teeth, and shake the strong oaken bars, as if he would break forth, and tear in pieces the little children who have been peeping at him. Such are the profitable sights that serve the good people to while away the earlier part of lecture-day. Betimes in the forenoon, a traveller — the first traveller that has come hitherward this morning — rides slowly into the street on his patient steed. He seems a clergyman ; and, as he draws near, we recognize the minister of Lynn, who was pre-engaged to lecture here, and has been revolving his discourse, as he rode through the hoary wilderness. Behold, now, the whole town thronging into the meeting-house, mostly with such sombre visages that the sunshine becomes little better than a shadow when it falls upon them. There go the Thirteen Men, grim rulers of a grim community! There goes John Massey, the first town-born child, now a youth of twenty, whose eye wanders with peculiar interest towards that buxom damsel who comes up the steps at the same instant. There hobbles Goody Foster, a sour and bitter old beldam, looking as if she went to curse, and not to pray, and whom many of her neighbors suspect of taking an occasional airing on a broomstick. There, too, slinking shamefacedly in, you observe that same poor do-nothing and good-for-nothing whom we saw castigated just now at the whipping-post. Last of all, there goes the tithing-man, lugging in a couple of small boys, whom he has caught at play beneath God's blessed sunshine, in a back lane. What native of Naumkeag, whose recollections go back more than thirty years, does not still shudder at that dark ogre of his infancy, who perhaps had long ceased to have an actual existence, but still lived in his childish belief, in a horrible idea, and in the nurse's threat, as the Tidy Man!

It will be hardly worth our while to wait two, or it may be three, turnings of the hour-glass, for the conclusion of the lecture. Therefore, by my control over light and darkness, I cause the dusk, and then the starless night, to brood over the street; and summon forth again the bellman, with his lantern casting a gleam about his

footsteps, to pace wearily from corner to corner, and
shout drowsily the hour to drowsy or dreaming ears.
Happy are we, if for nothing else, yet because we did
not live in those days. In truth, when the first novelty
and stir of spirit had subsided, — when the new settlement, between the forest-border and the sea, had become
actually a little town, — its daily life must have trudged
onward with hardly anything to diversify and enliven it,
while also its rigidity could not fail to cause miserable
distortions of the moral nature. Such a life was sinister
to the intellect, and sinister to the heart; especially when
one generation had bequeathed its religious gloom, and
the counterfeit of its religious ardor, to the next; for
these characteristics, as was inevitable, assumed the form
both of hypocrisy and exaggeration, by being inherited
from the example and precept of other human beings,
and not from an original and spiritual source. The sons
and grandchildren of the first settlers were a race of
lower and narrower souls than their progenitors had been.
The latter were stern, severe, intolerant, but not super-
stitious, not even fanatical; and endowed, if any men of
that age were, with a far-seeing worldly sagacity. But
it was impossible for the succeeding race to grow up, in
heaven's freedom, beneath the discipline which their
gloomy energy of character had established; nor, it may
be, have we even yet thrown off all the unfavorable influ-
ences which, among many good ones, were bequeathed to
us by our Puritan forefathers. Let us thank God for
having given us such ancestors; and let each successive
generation thank him, not less fervently, for being one
step further from them in the march of ages.

"What is all this?" cries the critic. "A sermon?
If so, it is not in the bill."

"Very true," replies the showman; "and I ask par-
don of the audience."

Look now at the street, and observe a strange people
entering it. Their garments are torn and disordered,
their faces haggard, their figures emaciated; for they
have made their way hither through pathless deserts,
suffering hunger and hardship, with no other shelter
than a hollow tree, the lair of a wild beast, or an Indian
wigwam.   Nor, in the most inhospitable and dangerous
of such lodging-places, was there half the peril that awaits
them in this thoroughfare of Christian men, with those
secure dwellings and warm hearths on either side of it, and
yonder meeting-house as the central object of the scene.
These wanderers have received from Heaven a gift that,
in all epochs of the world, has brought with it the penal-
ties of mortal suffering and persecution, scorn, enmity,
and death itself; — a gift that, thus terrible to its pos-
sessors, has ever been most hateful to all other men,
since its very existence seems to threaten the overthrow
of whatever else the toilsome ages have built up; — the
gift of a new idea.   You can discern it in them, illuminating their faces — their whole persons, indeed, however earthly and cloddish — with a light that inevitably
shines through, and makes the startled community aware
that these men are not as they themselves are, — not
brethren nor neighbors of their thought.   Forthwith, it
is as if an earthquake rumbled through the town, making
its vibrations felt at every hearthstone, and especially
causing the spire of the meeting-house to totter.   The
Quakers have come.   We are in peril!   See! they trample upon our wise and well-established laws in the person
of our chief magistrate; for Governor Endicott is passing, now an aged man, and dignified with long habits of
authority, — and not one of the irreverent vagabonds
has moved his hat.   Did you note the ominous frown of
the white-bearded Puritan governor, as he turned himself

about, and, in his anger, half uplifted the staff that has become a needful support to his old age? Here comes old Mr. Norris, our venerable minister. Will they doff their hats, and pay reverence to him? No: their hats stick fast to their ungracious heads, as if they grew there; and—impious varlets that they are, and worse than the heathen Indians!—they eye our reverend pastor with a peculiar scorn, distrust, unbelief, and utter denial of his sanctified pretensions, of which he himself immediately becomes conscious; the more bitterly conscious, as he never knew nor dreamed of the like before.

But look yonder! Can we believe our eyes? A Quaker woman, clad in sackcloth, and with ashes on her head, has mounted the steps of the meeting-house. She addresses the people in a wild, shrill voice,—wild and shrill it must be to suit such a figure,—which makes them tremble and turn pale, although they crowd open-mouthed to hear her. She is bold against established authority; she denounces the priest and his steeple-house. Many of her hearers are appalled; some weep; and others listen with a rapt attention, as if a living truth had now, for the first time, forced its way through the crust of habit, reached their hearts, and awakened them to life. This matter must be looked to; else we have brought our faith across the seas with us in vain; and it had been better that the old forest were still standing here, waving its tangled boughs and murmuring to the sky out of its desolate recesses, instead of this goodly street, if such blasphemies be spoken in it.

So thought the old Puritans. What was their mode of action may be partly judged from the spectacles which now pass before your eyes. Joshua Buffum is standing in the pillory. Cassandra Southwick is led to prison. And there a woman,—it is Ann Coleman,—

naked from the waist upward, and bound to the tail of
a cart, is dragged through the Main Street at the pace
of a brisk walk, while the constable follows with a whip
of knotted cords. A strong-armed fellow is that constable; and each time that he flourishes his lash in the
air, you see a frown wrinkling and twisting his brow,
and, at the same instant, a smile upon his lips. He
loves his business, faithful officer that he is, and puts
his soul into every stroke, zealous to fulfil the injunc-
tion of Major Hawthorne's warrant, in the spirit and to
the letter. There came down a stroke that has drawn
blood! Ten such stripes are to be given in Salem, ten
in Boston, and ten in Dedham; and, with those thirty
stripes of blood upon her, she is to be driven into the
forest. The crimson trail goes wavering along the Main
Street; but Heaven grant that, as the rain of·so many
years has wept upon it, time after time, and washed it
all away, so there may have been a dew of mercy, to
cleanse this cruel blood-stain out of the record of the
persecutor's life!

Pass on, thou spectral constable, and betake thee to
thine own place of torment. Meanwhile, by the silent
operation of the mechanism behind the scenes, a considerable space of time would seem to have lapsed over
the street. The older dwellings now begin to look
weather-beaten, through the effect of the many eastern
storms that have moistened their unpainted shingles and
clapboards, for not less than forty years. Such is the
age we would assign to the town, judging by the aspect
of John Massey, the first town-born child, whom his
neighbors now call Goodman Massey, and whom we see
yonder, a grave, almost autumnal-looking man, with
children of his own about him. To the patriarchs of
the settlement, no doubt, the Main Street is still but an

affair of yesterday, hardly more antique, even if destined
to be more permanent, than a path shovelled through the
snow. But to the middle-aged and elderly men who
came hither in childhood or early youth, it presents the
aspect of a long and well-established work, on which
they have expended the strength and ardor of their life.
And the younger people, native to the street, whose
earliest recollections are of creeping over the paternal
threshold, and rolling on the grassy margin of the track,
look at it as one of the perdurable things of our mortal
state, — as old as the hills of the great pasture, or the
headland at the harbor's mouth. Their fathers and
grandsires tell them how, within a few years past, the
forest stood here, with but a lonely track beneath its
tangled shade. Vain legend! They cannot make it
true and real to their conceptions. With them, moreover, the Main Street is a street indeed, worthy to hold
its way with the thronged and stately avenues of cities
beyond the sea. The old Puritans tell them of the
crowds that hurry along Cheapside and Fleet Street and
the Strand, and of the rush of tumultuous life at Temple
Bar. They describe London Bridge, itself a street, with
a row of houses on each side. They speak of the vast
structure of the Tower, and the solemn grandeur of
Westminster Abbey. The children listen, and still inquire if the streets of London are longer and broader
than the one before their father's door; if the Tower is
bigger than the jail in Prison Lane; if the old Abbey
will hold a larger congregation than our meeting-house.
Nothing impresses them, except their own experience.

It seems all a fable, too, that wolves have ever
prowled here; and not less so, that the Squaw Sachem,
and the Sagamore her son, once ruled over this region,
and treated as sovereign potentates with the English

settlers, then so few and storm-beaten, now so powerful. There stand some school-boys, you observe, in a little group around a drunken Indian, himself a prince of the Squaw Sachem's lineage. He brought hither some beaver-skins for sale, and has already swallowed the larger portion of their price, in deadly draughts of fire-water. Is there not a touch of pathos in that picture? and does it not go far towards telling the whole story of the vast growth and prosperity of one race, and the fated decay of another? — the children of the stranger making game of the great Squaw Sachem's grandson!

But the whole race of red men have not vanished with that wild princess and her posterity. This march of soldiers along the street betokens the breaking out of King Philip's war; and these young men, the flower of Essex, are on their way to defend the villages on the Connecticut; where, at Bloody Brook, a terrible blow shall be smitten, and hardly one of that gallant band be left alive. And there, at that stately mansion, with its three peaks in front, and its two little peaked towers, one on either side of the door, we see brave Captain Gardner issuing forth, clad in his embroidered buff-coat, and his plumed cap upon his head. His trusty sword, in its steel scabbard, strikes clanking on the doorstep. See how the people throng to their doors and windows, as the cavalier rides past, reining his mettled steed so gallantly, and looking so like the very soul and emblem of martial achievement, — destined, too, to meet a warrior's fate, at the desperate assault on the fortress of the Narragansetts!

"The mettled steed looks like a pig," interrupts the critic, "and Captain Gardner himself like the Devil, though a very tame one, and on a most diminutive scale."

"Sir, sir!" cries the persecuted showman, losing all patience, — for, indeed, he had particularly prided himself on these figures of Captain Gardner and his horse, — "I see that there is no hope of pleasing you. Pray, sir, do me the favor to take back your money, and withdraw!"

"Not I!" answers the unconscionable critic. "I am just beginning to get interested in the matter. Come! turn your crank, and grind out a few more of these fooleries!"

The showman rubs his brow impulsively, whisks the little rod with which he points out the notabilities of the scene, but, finally, with the inevitable acquiescence of all public servants, resumes his composure and goes on.

Pass onward, onward, Time! Build up new houses here, and tear down thy works of yesterday, that have already the rusty moss upon them! Summon forth the minister to the abode of the young maiden, and bid him unite her to the joyful bridegroom! Let the youthful parents carry their first-born to the meeting-house, to receive the baptismal rite! Knock at the door, whence the sable line of the funeral is next to issue! Provide other successive generations of men, to trade, talk, quarrel, or walk in friendly intercourse along the street, as their fathers did before them! Do all thy daily and accustomed business, Father Time, in this thoroughfare, which thy footsteps, for so many years, have now made dusty! But here, at last, thou leadest along a procession which, once witnessed, shall appear no more, and be remembered only as a hideous dream of thine, or a frenzy of thy old brain.

"Turn your crank, I say," bellows the remorseless critic, "and grind it out, whatever it be, without further preface!"

The showman deems it best to comply.

Then, here comes the worshipful Captain Curwen, sheriff of Essex, on horseback, at the head of an armed guard, escorting a company of condemned prisoners from the jail to their place of execution on Gallows Hill. The witches! There is no mistaking them! The witches! As they approach up Prison Lane, and turn into the Main Street, let us watch their faces, as if we made a part of the pale crowd that presses so eagerly about them, yet shrinks back with such shuddering dread, leaving an open passage betwixt a dense throng on either side. Listen to what the people say.

There is old George Jacobs, known hereabouts, these sixty years, as a man whom we thought upright in all his way of life, quiet, blameless, a good husband before his pious wife was summoned from the evil to come, and a good father to the children whom she left him. Ah! but when that blessed woman went to heaven, George Jacobs's heart was empty, his hearth lonely, his life broken up; his children were married, and betook themselves to habitations of their own; and Satan, in his wanderings up and down, beheld this forlorn old man, to whom life was a sameness and a weariness, and found the way to tempt him. So the miserable sinner was prevailed with to mount into the air, and career among the clouds; and he is proved to have been present at a witch-meeting as far off as Falmouth, on the very same night that his next neighbors saw him, with his rheumatic stoop, going in at his own door. There is John Willard, too; an honest man we thought him, and so shrewd and active in his business, so practical, so intent on every-day affairs, so constant at his little place of trade, where he bartered English goods for Indian corn and all kinds of country produce! How could such a man find time, or what could put it into his mind, to leave his proper calling, and become a wizard? It is a mystery, unless the Black Man tempted him with great heaps of gold. See that aged couple,—a sad sight, truly,—John Proctor, and his wife Elizabeth. If there were two old people in all the county of Essex who seemed to have led a true Christian life, and to be treading hopefully the little remnant of their earthly path, it was this very pair. Yet have we heard it sworn, to the satisfaction of the worshipful Chief-Justice Sewell, and all the court and jury, that Proctor and his wife have shown their withered faces at children's bed-sides, mocking, making mouths, and affrighting the poor little innocents in the night-time. They, or their spec-tral appearances, have stuck pins into the afflicted ones, and thrown them into deadly fainting-fits with a touch, or but a look. And, while we supposed the old man to be reading the Bible to his old wife,—she meanwhile knit-ting in the chimney-corner,—the pair of hoary reprobates have whisked up the chimney, both on one broomstick, and flown away to a witch-communion, far into the depths of the chill, dark forest. How foolish! Were it only for fear of rheumatic pains in their old bones, they had better have stayed at home. But away they went; and the laughter of their decayed, cackling voices has been heard at midnight, aloft in the air. Now, in the sunny noontide, as they go tottering to the gallows, it is the Devil's turn to laugh.

Behind these two,—who help another along, and seem to be comforting and encouraging each other, in a manner truly pitiful, if it were not a sin to pity the old witch and wizard,—behind them comes a woman, with a dark proud face that has been beautiful, and a figure that is still majestic. Do you know her? It is Martha Carrier, whom the Devil found in a humble cottage, and looked into her discontented heart, and saw pride there, and tempted her with his promise that she should be Queen of Hell. And now, with that lofty demeanor, she is passing to her kingdom, and, by her unquenchable pride, transforms this escort of shame into a triumphal procession, that shall attend her to the gates of her infernal palace, and seat her upon the fiery throne. Within this hour, she shall assume her royal dignity.

Last of the miserable train comes a man clad in black, of small stature and a dark complexion, with a clerical band about his neck. Many a time, in the years gone by, that face has been uplifted heavenward from the pulpit of the East Meeting-House, when the Rev. Mr. Burroughs seemed to worship God. What! — he? The holy man! — the learned! — the wise! How has the Devil tempted him? His fellow-criminals, for the most part, are obtuse, uncultivated creatures, some of them scarcely half-witted by nature, and others greatly decayed in their intellects through age. They were an easy prey for the destroyer. Not so with this George Burroughs, as we judge by the inward light which glows through his dark countenance, and, we might almost say, glorifies his figure, in spite of the soil and haggardness of long imprisonment, — in spite of the heavy shadow that must fall on him, while death is walking by his side. What bribe could Satan offer, rich enough to tempt and overcome this man? Alas! it may have been in the very strength of his high and searching intellect, that the Tempter found the weakness which betrayed him. He yearned for knowledge; he went groping onward into a world of mystery; at first, as the witnesses have sworn, he summoned up the ghosts of his two dead wives, and talked with them of matters beyond the grave; and, when their responses failed to satisfy the

intense and sinful craving of his spirit, he called on
Satan, and was heard. Yet — to look at him — who,
that had not known the proof, could believe him guilty?
Who would not say, while we see him offering comfort
to the weak and aged partners of his horrible crime, —
while we hear his ejaculations of prayer, that seem to
bubble up out of the depths of his heart, and fly heavenward, unawares, — while we behold a radiance brightening on his features as from the other world, which is but
a few steps off, — who would not say, that, over the
dusty track of the Main Street, a Christian saint is now
going to a martyr's death? May not the Arch-Fiend
have been too subtle for the court and jury, and betrayed
them — laughing in his sleeve, the while — into the
awful error of pouring out sanctified blood as an acceptable sacrifice upon God's altar? Ah! no; for listen to
wise Cotton Mather, who, as he sits there on his horse,
speaks comfortably to the perplexed multitude, and tells
them that all has been religiously and justly done, and
that Satan's power shall this day receive its death-blow
in New England.

Heaven grant it be so! — the great scholar must be
right; so lead the poor creatures to their death! Do
you see that group of children and half-grown girls, and,
among them, an old, hag-like Indian woman, Tituba by
name? Those are the Afflicted Ones. Behold, at this
very instant, a proof of Satan's power and malice!
Mercy Parris, the minister's daughter, has been smitten
by a flash of Martha Carrier's eye, and falls down in
the street, writhing with horrible spasms and foaming at
the mouth, like the possessed one spoken of in Scripture.
Hurry on the accursed witches to the gallows, ere they
do more mischief! — ere they fling out their withered
arms, and scatter pestilence by handfuls among the

crowd!—ere, as their parting legacy, they cast a blight over the land, so that henceforth it may bear no fruit nor blade of grass, and be fit for nothing but a sepulchre for their unhallowed carcasses! So, on they go; and old George Jacobs has stumbled, by reason of his infirmity; but Goodman Proctor and his wife lean on one another, and walk at a reasonably steady pace, considering their age. Mr. Burroughs seems to administer counsel to Martha Carrier, whose face and mien, methinks, are milder and humbler than they were. Among the multitude, meanwhile, there is horror, fear, and distrust; and friend looks askance at friend, and the husband at his wife, and the wife at him, and even the mother at her little child; as if, in every creature that God has made, they suspected a witch, or dreaded an accuser. Never, never again, whether in this or any other shape, may Universal Madness riot in the Main Street!

I perceive in your eyes, my indulgent spectators, the criticism which you are too kind to utter. These scenes, you think, are all too sombre. So, indeed, they are; but the blame must rest on the sombre spirit of our forefathers, who wove their web of life with hardly a single thread of rose-color or gold, and not on me, who have a tropic-love of sunshine, and would gladly gild all the world with it, if I knew where to find so much. That you may believe me, I will exhibit one of the only class of scenes, so far as my investigation has taught me, in which our ancestors were wont to steep their tough old hearts in wine and strong drink, and indulge an outbreak of grisly jollity.

Here it comes, out of the same house whence we saw brave Captain Gardner go forth to the wars. What! A coffin, borne on men's shoulders, and six aged gentlemen as pall-bearers, and a long train of mourners, with black gloves and black hat-bands, and everything black, save a white handkerchief in each mourner's hand, to wipe away his tears withal. Now, my kind patrons, you are angry with me. You were bidden to a bridal-dance, and find yourselves walking in a funeral proces-sion. Even so; but look back through all the social customs of New England, in the first century of her existence, and read all her traits of character; and if you find one occasion, other than a funeral feast, where jollity was sanctioned by universal practice, I will set fire to my puppet-show without another word. These are the obsequies of old Governor Bradstreet, the patri-arch and survivor of the first settlers, who, having inter-married with the Widow Gardner, is now resting from his labors, at the great age of ninety-four. The white-bearded corpse, which was his spirit's earthly garniture, now lies beneath yonder coffin-lid. Many a cask of ale and cider is on tap, and many a draught of spiced wine and aqua-vitæ has been quaffed. Else why should the bearers stagger, as they tremulously uphold the coffin? — and the aged pall-bearers, too, as they strive to walk solemnly beside it? — and wherefore do the mourners tread on one another's heels? — and why, if we may ask without offence, should the nose of the Rev. Mr. Noyes, through which he has just been delivering the funeral discourse, glow like a ruddy coal of fire? Well, well, old friends! Pass on, with your burden of mortality, and lay it in the tomb with jolly hearts. People should be permitted to enjoy themselves in their own fashion; every man to his taste; but New England must have been a dismal abode for the man of pleasure, when the only boon-companion was Death!

Under cover of a mist that has settled over the scene, a few years flit by, and escape our notice. As the atmos-

phere becomes transparent, we perceive a decrepit grand-
sire, hobbling along the street. Do you recognize him?
We saw him, first, as the baby in Goodwife Massey's
arms, when the primeval trees were flinging their shadow
over Roger Conant's cabin; we have seen him, as the
boy, the youth, the man, bearing his humble part in
all the successive scenes, and forming the index-figure
whereby to note the age of his coeval town. And here
he is, old Goodman Massey, taking his last walk, — often
pausing, — often leaning over his staff, — and calling to
mind whose dwelling stood at such and such a spot, and
whose field or garden occupied the site of those more
recent houses. He can render a reason for all the bends
and deviations of the thoroughfare, which, in its flexible
and plastic infancy, was made to swerve aside from a
straight line, in order to visit every settler's door. The
Main Street is still youthful; the coeval man is in his
latest age. Soon he will be gone, a patriarch of four-
score, yet shall retain a sort of infantine life in our local
history, as the first town-born child.

Behold here a change, wrought in the twinkling of an
eye, like an incident in a tale of magic, even while your
observation has been fixed upon the scene. The Main
Street has vanished out of sight. In its stead appears a
wintry waste of snow, with the sun just peeping over it,
cold and bright, and tingeing the white expanse with the
faintest and most ethereal rose-color. This is the Great
Snow of 1717, famous for the mountain-drifts in which
it buried the whole country. It would seem as if the
street, the growth of which we have noted so attentively,
following it from its first phase, as an Indian track, until
it reached the dignity of sidewalks, were all at once
obliterated, and resolved into a drearier pathlessness
than when the forest covered it. The gigantic swells

and billows of the snow have swept over each man's metes and bounds, and annihilated all the visible distinctions of human property. So that now the traces of former times and hitherto accomplished deeds being done away, mankind should be at liberty to enter on new paths, and guide themselves by other laws than heretofore; if, indeed, the race be not extinct, and it be worth our while to go on with the march of life, over the cold and desolate expanse that lies before us. It may be, however, that matters are not so desperate as they appear. That vast icicle, glittering so cheerlessly in the sunshine, must be the spire of the meeting-house, incrusted with frozen sleet. Those great heaps, too, which we mistook for drifts, are houses, buried up to their eaves, and with their peaked roofs rounded by the depth of snow upon them. There, now, comes a gush of smoke from what I judge to be the chimney of the Ship Tavern; — and another — another — and another — from the chimneys of other dwellings, where fireside comfort, domestic peace, the sports of children, and the quietude of age are living yet, in spite of the frozen crust above them.

But it is time to change the scene. Its dreary monotony shall not test your fortitude like one of our actual New England winters, which leaves so large a blank — so melancholy a death-spot — in lives so brief that they ought to be all summer-time. Here, at least, I may claim to be ruler of the seasons. One turn of the crank shall melt away the snow from the Main Street, and show the trees in their full foliage, the rose-bushes in bloom, and a border of green grass along the sidewalk. There! But what! How! The scene will not move. A wire is broken. The street continues buried beneath the snow, and the fate of Herculaneum and Pompeii has its parallel in this catastrophe.

Alas! my kind and gentle audience, you know not the extent of your misfortune. The scenes to come were far better than the past. The street itself would have been more worthy of pictorial exhibition; the deeds of its inhabitants not less so. And how would your interest have deepened, as, passing out of the cold shadow of antiquity, in my long and weary course, I should arrive within the limits of man's memory, and, leading you at last into the sunshine of the present, should give a reflex of the very life that is flitting past us! Your own beauty, my fair townswomen, would have beamed upon you, out of my scene. Not a gentleman that walks the street but should have beheld his own face and figure, his gait, the peculiar swing of his arm, and the coat that he put on yesterday. Then, too, — and it is what I chiefly regret, — I had expended a vast deal of light and brilliancy on a representation of the street in its whole length, from Buffum's Corner downward, on the night of the grand illumination for General Taylor's triumph. Lastly, I should have given the crank one other turn, and have brought out the future, showing you who shall walk the Main Street to-morrow, and, perchance, whose funeral shall pass through it!

But these, like most other human purposes, lie unac-complished; and I have only further to say, that any lady or gentlemen who may feel dissatisfied with the evening's entertainment shall receive back the admission fee at the door.

"Then give me mine," cries the critic, stretching out his palm. "I said that your exhibition would prove a humbug, and so it has turned out. So, hand over my quarter!"

ETHAN BRAND:

A CHAPTER FROM AN ABORTIVE ROMANCE.

BARTRAM the lime-burner, a rough, heavy-looking man, begrimed with charcoal, sat watching his kiln, at nightfall, while his little son played at building houses with the scattered fragments of marble, when, on the hillside below them, they heard a roar of laughter, not mirthful, but slow, and even solemn, like a wind shaking the boughs of the forest.

"Father, what is that?" asked the little boy, leaving his play, and pressing betwixt his father's knees.

"O, some drunken man, I suppose," answered the lime-burner; "some merry fellow from the bar-room in the village, who dared not laugh loud enough within doors lest he should blow the roof of the house off. So here he is, shaking his jolly sides at the foot of Graylock."

"But, father," said the child, more sensitive than the obtuse, middle-aged clown, "he does not laugh like a man that is glad. So the noise frightens me!"

"Don't be a fool, child!" cried his father, gruffly. "You will never make a man, I do believe; there is too much of your mother in you. I have known the rustling of a leaf startle you. Hark! Here comes the merry fellow now. You shall see that there is no harm in him."

Bartram and his little son, while they were talking thus, sat watching the same lime-kiln that had been the scene of Ethan Brand's solitary and meditative life, before he began his search for the Unpardonable Sin. Many years, as we have seen, had now elapsed, since that portentous night when the IDEA was first developed. The kiln, however, on the mountain-side, stood unimpaired, and was in nothing changed since he had thrown his dark thoughts into the intense glow of its furnace, and melted them, as it were, into the one thought that took possession of his life. It was a rude, round, tower-like structure, about twenty feet high, heavily built of rough stones, and with a hillock of earth heaped about the larger part of its circumference ; so that the blocks and fragments of marble might be drawn by cart-loads, and thrown in at the top. There was an opening at the bottom of the tower, like an oven-mouth, but large enough to admit a man in a stooping posture, and provided with a massive iron door. With the smoke and jets of flame issuing from the chinks and crevices of this door, which seemed to give admittance into the hillside, it resembled nothing so much as the private entrance to the infernal regions, which the shepherds of the Delectable Mountains were accustomed to show to pilgrims.

There are many such lime-kilns in that tract of country, for the purpose of burning the white marble which composes a large part of the substance of the hills. Some of them, built years ago, and long deserted, with weeds growing in the vacant round of the interior, which is open to the sky, and grass and wild-flowers rooting themselves into the chinks of the stones, look already like relics of antiquity, and may yet be overspread with the lichens of centuries to come. Others, where the lime-burner still feeds his daily and night-long fire, afford points of interest to the wanderer among the hills, who seats himself on a log of wood or a fragment of marble, to hold a chat with the solitary man. It is a lonesome, and, when the character is inclined to thought, may be an intensely thoughtful occupation; as it proved in the case of Ethan Brand, who had mused to such strange purpose, in days gone by, while the fire in this very kiln was burning.

The man who now watched the fire was of a different order, and troubled himself with no thoughts save the very few that were requisite to his business. At frequent intervals, he flung back the clashing weight of the iron door, and, turning his face from the insufferable glare, thrust in huge logs of oak, or stirred the immense brands with a long pole. Within the furnace were seen the curling and riotous flames, and the burning marble, almost molten with the intensity of heat; while without, the reflection of the fire quivered on the dark intricacy of the surrounding forest, and showed in the foreground a bright and ruddy little picture of the hut, the spring beside its door, the athletic and coal-begrimed figure of the lime-burner, and the half-frightened child, shrinking into the protection of his father's shadow. And when again the iron door was closed, then reappeared the tender light of the half-full moon, which vainly strove to trace out the indistinct shapes of the neighboring mountains; and, in the upper sky, there was a flitting congregation of clouds, still faintly tinged with the rosy sunset, though thus far down into the valley the sunshine had vanished long and long ago.

The little boy now crept still closer to his father, as footsteps were heard ascending the hillside, and a human form thrust aside the bushes that clustered beneath the trees.

"Halloo! who is it?" cried the lime-burner, vexed at his son's timidity, yet half infected by it. "Come forward, and show yourself, like a man, or I'll fling this chunk of marble at your head!"

"You offer me a rough welcome," said a gloomy voice, as the unknown man drew nigh. "Yet I neither claim nor desire a kinder one, even at my own fireside."

To obtain a distincter view, Bartram threw open the iron door of the kiln, whence immediately issued a gush of fierce light, that smote full upon the stranger's face and figure. To a careless eye there appeared nothing very remarkable in his aspect, which was that of a man in a coarse, brown, country-made suit of clothes, tall and thin, with the staff and heavy shoes of a wayfarer. As he advanced, he fixed his eyes — which were very bright — intently upon the brightness of the furnace, as if he beheld, or expected to behold, some object worthy of note within it.

"Good evening, stranger," said the lime-burner; "whence come you, so late in the day?"

"I come from my search," answered the wayfarer; "for, at last, it is finished."

"Drunk! — or crazy!" muttered Bartram to himself. "I shall have trouble with the fellow. The sooner I drive him away, the better."

The little boy, all in a tremble, whispered to his father, and begged him to shut the door of the kiln, so that there might not be so much light; for that there was something in the man's face which he was afraid to look at, yet could not look away from. And, indeed, even the lime-burner's dull and torpid sense began to be impressed by an indescribable something in that thin, rugged, thoughtful visage, with the grizzled hair hanging wildly about it, and those deeply sunken eyes, which gleamed like fires within the entrance of a mysterious cavern. But, as he closed the door, the stranger turned towards him, and spoke in a quiet, familiar way, that made Bartram feel as if he were a sane and sensible man, after all.

"Your task draws to an end, I see," said he. "This marble has already been burning three days. A few hours more will convert the stone to lime."

"Why, who are you?" exclaimed the lime-burner. "You seem as well acquainted with my business as I am myself."

"And well I may be," said the stranger; "for I followed the same craft many a long year, and here, too, on this very spot. But you are a new-comer in these parts. Did you never hear of Ethan Brand?"

"The man that went in search of the Unpardonable Sin?" asked Bartram, with a laugh.

"The same," answered the stranger. "He has found what he sought, and therefore he comes back again."

"What! then you are Ethan Brand himself?" cried the lime-burner, in amazement. "I am a new-comer here, as you say, and they call it eighteen years since you left the foot of Graylock. But, I can tell you, the good folks still talk about Ethan Brand, in the village yonder, and what a strange errand took him away from his lime-kiln. Well, and so you have found the Unpardonable Sin?"

"Even so!" said the stranger, calmly.

"If the question is a fair one," proceeded Bartram, "where might it be?"

Ethan Brand laid his finger on his own heart.

"Here!" replied he.

And then, without mirth in his countenance, but as if moved by an involuntary recognition of the infinite absurdity of seeking throughout the world for what was the closest of all things to himself, and looking into every heart, save his own, for what was hidden in no other breast, he broke into a laugh of scorn. It was the same slow, heavy laugh, that had almost appalled the lime-burner when it heralded the wayfarer's approach.

The solitary mountain-side was made dismal by it. Laughter, when out of place, mistimed, or bursting forth from a disordered state of feeling, may be the most terrible modulation of the human voice. The laughter of one asleep, even if it be a little child, — the madman's laugh, — the wild, screaming laugh of a born idiot, — are sounds that we sometimes tremble to hear, and would always willingly forget. Poets have imagined no utterance of fiends or hobgoblins so fearfully appropriate as a laugh. And even the obtuse lime-burner felt his nerves shaken, as this strange man looked inward at his own heart, and burst into laughter that rolled away into the night, and was indistinctly reverberated among the hills.

"Joe," said he to his little son, "scamper down to the tavern in the village, and tell the jolly fellows there that Ethan Brand has come back, and that he has found the Unpardonable Sin!"

The boy darted away on his errand, to which Ethan Brand made no objection, nor seemed hardly to notice it. He sat on a log of wood, looking steadfastly at the iron door of the kiln. When the child was out of sight, and his swift and light footsteps ceased to be heard treading first on the fallen leaves and then on the rocky mountain-path, the lime-burner began to regret his departure. He felt that the little fellow's presence had been a barrier between his guest and himself, and that he must now deal, heart to heart, with a man who, on his own confession, had committed the one only crime for which

Heaven could afford no mercy. That crime, in its indistinct blackness, seemed to overshadow him. The lime-burner's own sins rose up within him, and made his memory riotous with a throng of evil shapes that asserted their kindred with the Master Sin, whatever it might be, which it was within the scope of man's corrupted nature to conceive and cherish. They were all of one family; they went to and fro between his breast and Ethan Brand's, and carried dark greetings from one to the other.

Then Bartram remembered the stories which had grown traditionary in reference to this strange man, who had come upon him like a shadow of the night, and was making himself at home in his old place, after so long absence that the dead people, dead and buried for years, would have had more right to be at home, in any familiar spot, than he. Ethan Brand, it was said, had conversed with Satan himself in the lurid blaze of this very kiln. The legend had been matter of mirth heretofore, but looked grisly now. According to this tale, before Ethan Brand departed on his search, he had been accustomed to evoke a fiend from the hot furnace of the lime-kiln, night after night, in order to confer with him about the Unpardonable Sin; the man and the fiend each laboring to frame the image of some mode of guilt which could neither be atoned for nor forgiven. And, with the first gleam of light upon the mountain-top, the fiend crept in at the iron door, there to abide the intensest element of fire, until again summoned forth to share in the dreadful task of extending man's possible guilt beyond the scope of Heaven's else infinite mercy.

While the lime-burner was struggling with the horror of these thoughts, Ethan Brand rose from the log, and flung open the door of the kiln. The action was in such accordance with the idea in Bartram's mind, that he almost expected to see the Evil One issue forth, red-hot from the raging furnace.

"Hold! hold!" cried he, with a tremulous attempt to laugh; for he was ashamed of his fears, although they overmastered him. "Don't, for mercy's sake, bring out your Devil now!"

"Man!" sternly replied Ethan Brand, "what need have I of the Devil? I have left him behind me, on my track. It is with such half-way sinners as you that he busies himself. Fear not, because I open the door. I do but act by old custom, and am going to trim your fire, like a lime-burner, as I was once."

He stirred the vast coals, thrust in more wood, and bent forward to gaze into the hollow prison-house of the fire, regardless of the fierce glow that reddened upon his face. The lime-burner sat watching him, and half suspected his strange guest of a purpose, if not to evoke a fiend, at least to plunge bodily into the flames, and thus vanish from the sight of man. Ethan Brand, however, drew quietly back, and closed the door of the kiln.

"I have looked," said he, "into many a human heart that was seven times hotter with sinful passions than yonder furnace is with fire. But I found not there what I sought. No, not the Unpardonable Sin!"

"What is the Unpardonable Sin?" asked the lime-burner; and then he shrank farther from his companion, trembling lest his question should be answered.

"It is a sin that grew within my own breast," replied Ethan Brand, standing erect, with a pride that distinguishes all enthusiasts of his stamp. "A sin that grew nowhere else! The sin of an intellect that triumphed over the sense of brotherhood with man and reverence for God, and sacrificed everything to its own mighty claims! The only sin that deserves a recompense of immortal agony! Freely, were it to do again, would I incur the guilt. Unshrinkingly I accept the retribution!"

"The man's head is turned," muttered the lime-burner to himself. "He may be a sinner, like the rest of us, — nothing more likely, — but, I'll be sworn, he is a madman too."

Nevertheless, he felt uncomfortable at his situation, alone with Ethan Brand on the wild mountain-side, and was right glad to hear the rough murmur of tongues, and the footsteps of what seemed a pretty numerous party, stumbling over the stones and rustling through the underbrush. Soon appeared the whole lazy regiment that was wont to infest the village tavern, comprehending three or four individuals who had drunk flip beside the bar-room fire through all the winters, and smoked their pipes beneath the stoop through all the summers, since Ethan Brand's departure. Laughing boisterously, and mingling all their voices together in unceremonious talk, they now burst into the moonshine and narrow streaks of firelight that illuminated the open space before the lime-kiln. Bartram set the door ajar again, flooding the spot with light, that the whole company might get a fair view of Ethan Brand, and he of them.

There, among other old acquaintances, was a once ubiquitous man, now almost extinct, but whom we were formerly sure to encounter at the hotel of every thriving village throughout the country. It was the stage-agent. The present specimen of the genus was a wilted and smoke-dried man, wrinkled and red-nosed, in a smartly cut, brown, bobtailed coat, with brass buttons, who, for a length of time unknown, had kept his desk and corner

in the bar-room, and was still puffing what seemed to be
the same cigar that he had lighted twenty years before.
He had great fame as a dry joker, though, perhaps, less
on account of any intrinsic humor than from a certain
flavor of brandy-toddy and tobacco-smoke, which impregnated all his ideas and expressions, as well as his
person. Another well-remembered though strangely altered face was that of Lawyer Giles, as people still called
him in courtesy; an elderly ragamuffin, in his soiled shirt-
sleeves and tow-cloth trousers. This poor fellow had
been an attorney, in what he called his better days, a
sharp practitioner, and in great vogue among the village
litigants; but flip, and sling, and toddy, and cocktails,
imbibed at all hours, morning, noon, and night, had
caused him to slide from intellectual to various kinds and
degrees of bodily labor, till, at last, to adopt his own
phrase, he slid into a soap-vat. In other words, Giles
was now a soap-boiler, in a small way. He had come to
be but the fragment of a human being, a part of one foot
having been chopped off by an axe, and an entire hand
torn away by the devilish grip of a steam-engine. Yet,
though the corporeal hand was gone, a spiritual member
remained; for, stretching forth the stump, Giles steadfastly averred that he felt an invisible thumb and fingers
with as vivid a sensation as before the real ones were am-
putated. A maimed and miserable wretch he was; but
one, nevertheless, whom the world could not trample on,
and had no right to scorn, either in this or any previous
stage of his misfortunes, since he had still kept up the
courage and spirit of a man, asked nothing in charity,
and with his one hand — and that the left one — fought
a stern battle against want and hostile circumstances.

Among the throng, too, came another personage, who,
with certain points of similarity to Lawyer Giles, had

many more of difference. It was the village doctor; a man of some fifty years, whom, at an earlier period of his life, we introduced as paying a professional visit to Ethan Brand during the latter's supposed insanity. He was now a purple-visaged, rude, and brutal, yet half-gentlemanly figure, with something wild, ruined, and desperate in his talk, and in all the details of his gesture and manners. Brandy possessed this man like an evil spirit, and made him as surly and savage as a wild beast, and as miserable as a lost soul; but there was supposed to be in him such wonderful skill, such native gifts of healing, beyond any which medical science could impart, that society caught hold of him, and would not let him sink out of its reach. So, swaying to and fro upon his horse, and grumbling thick accents at the bedside, he visited all the sick-chambers for miles about among the mountain towns, and sometimes raised a dying man, as it were, by miracle, or quite as often, no doubt, sent his patient to a grave that was dug many a year too soon. The doctor had an everlasting pipe in his mouth, and, as somebody said, in allusion to his habit of swearing, it was always alight with hell-fire.

These three worthies pressed forward, and greeted Ethan Brand each after his own fashion, earnestly inviting him to partake of the contents of a certain black bottle, in which, as they averred, he would find something far better worth seeking for than the Unpardonable Sin. No mind, which has wrought itself by intense and solitary meditation into a high state of enthusiasm, can endure the kind of contact with low and vulgar modes of thought and feeling to which Ethan Brand was now subjected. It made him doubt — and, strange to say, it was a painful doubt — whether he had indeed found the Unpardonable Sin, and found it within him-

5 *

self. The whole question on which he had exhausted
life, and more than life, looked like a delusion.

"Leave me," he said bitterly, "ye brute beasts, that
have made yourselves so, shrivelling up your souls with
fiery liquors! I have done with you. Years and years
ago, I groped into your hearts, and found nothing there
for my purpose. Get ye gone!"

"Why, you uncivil scoundrel," cried the fierce doctor,
"is that the way you respond to the kindness of your
best friends? Then let me tell you the truth. You
have no more found the Unpardonable Sin than yonder
boy Joe has. You are but a crazy fellow, — I told you
so twenty years ago, — neither better nor worse than a
crazy fellow, and the fit companion of old Humphrey,
here!"

He pointed to an old man, shabbily dressed, with long
white hair, thin visage, and unsteady eyes. For some
years past this aged person had been wandering about
among the hills, inquiring of all travellers whom he met
for his daughter. The girl, it seemed, had gone off with
a company of circus-performers; and occasionally tidings of her came to the village, and fine stories were
told of her glittering appearance as she rode on horseback in the ring, or performed marvellous feats on the
tight-rope.

The white-haired father now approached Ethan Brand,
and gazed unsteadily into his face.

"They tell me you have been all over the earth," said
he, wringing his hands with earnestness. "You must
have seen my daughter, for she makes a grand figure in
the world, and everybody goes to see her. Did she send
any word to her old father, or say when she was coming
back?"

Ethan Brand's eye quailed beneath the old man's.

That daughter, from whom he so earnestly desired a word of greeting, was the Esther of our tale, the very girl whom, with such cold and remorseless purpose, Ethan Brand had made the subject of a psychological experiment, and wasted, absorbed, and perhaps annihilated her soul, in the process.

"Yes," murmured he, turning away from the hoary wanderer; "it is no delusion. There is an Unpardonable Sin!"

While these things were passing, a merry scene was going forward in the area of cheerful light, beside the spring and before the door of the hut. A number of the youth of the village, young men and girls, had hurried up the hillside, impelled by curiosity to see Ethan Brand, the hero of so many a legend familiar to their childhood. Finding nothing, however, very remarkable in his aspect, — nothing but a sunburnt wayfarer, in plain garb and dusty shoes, who sat looking into the fire, as if he fancied pictures among the coals, — these young people speedily grew tired of observing him. As it happened, there was other amusement at hand. An old German Jew, travelling with a diorama on his back, was passing down the mountain-road towards the village just as the party turned aside from it, and, in hopes of eking out the profits of the day, the showman had kept them company to the lime-kiln.

"Come, old Dutchman," cried one of the young men, "let us see your pictures, if you can swear they are worth looking at!"

"O yes, Captain," answered the Jew, — whether as a matter of courtesy or craft, he styled everybody Captain, — "I shall show you, indeed, some very superb pictures!"

So, placing his box in a proper position, he invited the

young men and girls to look through the glass orifices
of the machine, and proceeded to exhibit a series of the
most outrageous scratchings and daubings, as specimens
of the fine arts, that ever an itinerant showman had the
face to impose upon his circle of spectators. The pictures were worn out, moreover, tattered, full of cracks and
wrinkles, dingy with tobacco-smoke, and otherwise in a
most pitiable condition. Some purported to be cities,
public edifices, and ruined castles in •Europe; others
represented Napoleon's battles and Nelson's sea-fights;
and in the midst of these would be seen a gigantic,
brown, hairy hand, — which might have been mistaken
for the Hand of Destiny, though, in truth, it was only
the showman's, — pointing its forefinger to various scenes
of the conflict, while its owner gave historical illustra-
tions. When, with much merriment at its abominable
deficiency of merit, the exhibition was concluded, the
German bade little Joe put his head into the box.
Viewed through the magnifying-glasses, the boy's round,
rosy visage assumed the strangest imaginable aspect of
an immense Titanic child, the mouth grinning broadly,
and the eyes and every other feature overflowing with
fun at the joke. Suddenly, however, that merry face
turned pale, and its expression changed to horror, for
this easily impressed and excitable child had become
sensible that the eye of Ethan Brand was fixed upon
him through the glass.

"You make the little man to be afraid, Captain," said
the German Jew, turning up the dark and strong outline of his visage, from his stooping posture. "But
look again, and, by chance, I shall cause you to see
somewhat that is very fine, upon my word!"

Ethan Brand gazed into the box for an instant, and
then starting back, looked fixedly at the German. What

had he seen? Nothing, apparently; for a curious youth, who had peeped in almost at the same moment, beheld only a vacant space of canvas.

"I remember you now," muttered Ethan Brand to the showman.

"Ah, Captain," whispered the Jew of Nuremburg, with a dark smile, "I find it to be a heavy matter in my show-box, — this Unpardonable Sin! By my faith, Captain, it has wearied my shoulders, this long day, to carry it over the mountain."

"Peace," answered Ethan Brand, sternly, "or get thee into the furnace yonder!"

The Jew's exhibition had scarcely concluded, when a great, elderly dog — who seemed to be his own master, as no person in the company laid claim to him — saw fit to render himself the object of public notice. Hitherto, he had shown himself a very quiet, well-disposed old dog, going round from one to another, and, by way of being sociable, offering his rough head to be patted by any kindly hand that would take so much trouble. But now, all of a sudden, this grave and venerable quadruped, of his own mere motion, and without the slightest suggestion from anybody else, began to run round after his tail, which, to heighten the absurdity of the proceeding, was a great deal shorter than it should have been. Never was seen such headlong eagerness in pursuit of an object that could not possibly be attained; never was heard such a tremendous outbreak of growling, snarling, barking, and snapping, — as if one end of the ridiculous brute's body were at deadly and most unforgivable enmity with the other. Faster and faster, round about went the cur; and faster and still faster fled the unapproachable brevity of his tail; and louder and fiercer grew his yells of rage and animosity; until, utterly exhausted, and as far from the goal as ever, the foolish old dog ceased his performance as suddenly as he had begun it. The next moment he was as mild, quiet, sensible, and respectable in his deportment, as when he first scraped acquaintance with the company.

As may be supposed, the exhibition was greeted with universal laughter, clapping of hands, and shouts of encore, to which the canine performer responded by wagging all that there was to wag of his tail, but appeared totally unable to repeat his very successful effort to amuse the spectators.

Meanwhile, Ethan Brand had resumed his seat upon the log, and moved, it might be, by a perception of some remote analogy between his own case and that of this self-pursuing cur, he broke into the awful laugh, which, more than any other token, expressed the condition of his inward being. From that moment, the merriment of the party was at an end; they stood aghast, dreading lest the inauspicious sound should be reverberated around the horizon, and that mountain would thunder it to mountain, and so the horror be prolonged upon their ears. Then, whispering one to another that it was late, — that the moon was almost down, — that the August night was growing chill, — they hurried homewards, leaving the lime-burner and little Joe to deal as they might with their unwelcome guest. Save for these three human beings, the open space on the hillside was a solitude, set in a vast gloom of forest. Beyond that darksome verge, the firelight glimmered on the stately trunks and almost black foliage of pines, intermixed with the lighter verdure of sapling oaks, maples, and poplars, while here and there lay the gigantic corpses of dead trees, decaying on the leaf-strewn soil. And it seemed to little Joe — a timorous and imaginative child — that the silent forest was holding its breath, until some fearful thing should happen.

Ethan Brand thrust more wood into the fire, and closed the door of the kiln; then looking over his shoulder at the lime-burner and his son, he bade, rather than advised, them to retire to rest.

"For myself, I cannot sleep," said he. "I have matters that it concerns me to meditate upon. I will watch the fire, as I used to do in the old time."

"And call the Devil out of the furnace to keep you company, I suppose," muttered Bartram, who had been making intimate acquaintance with the black bottle above mentioned. "But watch, if you like, and call as many devils as you like! For my part, I shall be all the better for a snooze. Come, Joe!"

As the boy followed his father into the hut, he looked back at the wayfarer, and the tears came into his eyes, for his tender spirit had an intuition of the bleak and terrible loneliness in which this man had enveloped himself.

When they had gone, Ethan Brand sat listening to the crackling of the kindled wood, and looking at the little spirts of fire that issued through the chinks of the door. These trifles, however, once so familiar, had but the slightest hold of his attention, while deep within his mind he was reviewing the gradual but marvellous change that had been wrought upon him by the search to which he had devoted himself. He remembered how the night dew had fallen upon him, — how the dark forest had whispered to him, — how the stars had gleamed upon him, — a simple and loving man, watching his fire in the years gone by, and ever musing as it burned. He remembered with what tenderness, with what love and sympathy for mankind, and what pity for human guilt

and woe, he had first begun to contemplate those ideas
which afterwards became the inspiration of his life; with
what reverence he had then looked into the heart of
man, viewing it as a temple originally divine, and, however desecrated, still to be held sacred by a brother;
with what awful fear he had deprecated the success of
his pursuit, and prayed that the Unpardonable Sin might
never be revealed to him.   Then ensued that vast intellectual development, which, in its progress, disturbed the
counterpoise between his mind and heart.   The Idea
that possessed his life had operated as a means of education; it had gone on cultivating his powers to the
highest point of which they were susceptible; it had
raised him from the level of an unlettered laborer to
stand on a star-lit eminence, whither the philosophers
of the earth, laden with the lore of universities, might
vainly strive to clamber after him.   So much for the
intellect!   But where was the heart?   That, indeed, had
withered, — had contracted, — had hardened, — had perished!   It had ceased to partake of the universal throb.
He had lost his hold of the magnetic chain of humanity.
He was no longer a brother-man, opening the chambers
or the dungeons of our common nature by the key of
holy sympathy, which gave him a right to share in all
its secrets; he was now a cold observer, looking on mankind as the subject of his experiment, and, at length,
converting man and woman to be his puppets, and pulling the wires that moved them to such degrees of crime
as were demanded for his study.

   Thus Ethan Brand became a fiend.   He began to be
so from the moment that his moral nature had ceased to
keep the pace of improvement with his intellect.   And
now, as his highest effort and inevitable development, —
as the bright and gorgeous flower, and rich, delicious

fruit of his life's labor, — he had produced the Unpardonable Sin!

"What more have I to seek? what more to achieve?" said Ethan Brand to himself. "My task is done, and well done!"

Starting from the log with a certain alacrity in his gait and ascending the hillock of earth that was raised against the stone circumference of the lime-kiln, he thus reached the top of the structure. It was a space of perhaps ten feet across, from edge to edge, presenting a view of the upper surface of the immense mass of broken marble with which the kiln was heaped. All these innumerable blocks and fragments of marble were red-hot and vividly on fire, sending up great spouts of blue flame, which quivered aloft and danced madly, as within a magic circle, and sank and rose again, with continual and multitudinous activity. As the lonely man bent forward over this terrible body of fire,.the blasting heat smote up against his person with a breath that, it might be supposed, would have scorched and shrivelled him up in a moment.

Ethan Brand stood erect, and raised his arms on high. The blue flames played upon his face, and imparted the wild and ghastly light which alone could have suited its expression; it was that of a fiend on the verge of plunging into his gulf of intensest torment.

"O Mother Earth," cried he, "who art no more my Mother, and into whose bosom this frame shall never be resolved! O mankind, whose brotherhood I have cast off, and trampled thy great heart beneath my feet! O stars of heaven, that shone on me of old, as if to light me onward and upward! — farewell all, and forever. Come, deadly element of Fire, — henceforth my familiar friend! Embrace me, as I do thee!"

That night the sound of a fearful peal of laughter rolled heavily through the sleep of the lime-burner and his little son; dim shapes of horror and anguish haunted their dreams, and seemed still present in the rude hovel, when they opened their eyes to the daylight.

"Up, boy, up!" cried the lime-burner, staring about him. "Thank Heaven, the night is gone, at last; and rather than pass such another, I would watch my lime-kiln, wide awake, for a twelvemonth. This Ethan Brand, with his humbug of an Unpardonable Sin, has done me no such mighty favor, in taking my place!"

He issued from the hut, followed by little Joe, who kept fast hold of his father's hand. The early sunshine was already pouring its gold upon the mountain-tops; and though the valleys were still in shadow, they smiled cheerfully in the promise of the bright day that was hastening onward. The village, completely shut in by hills, which swelled away gently about it, looked as if it had rested peacefully in the hollow of the great hand of Providence. Every dwelling was distinctly visible; the little spires of the two churches pointed upwards, and caught a fore-glimmering of brightness from the sun-gilt skies upon their gilded weathercocks. The tavern was astir, and the figure of the old, smoke-dried stage-agent, cigar in mouth, was seen beneath the stoop. Old Graylock was glorified with a golden cloud upon his head. Scattered likewise over the breasts of the surrounding mountains, there were heaps of hoary mist, in fantastic shapes, some of them far down into the valley, others high up towards the summits, and still others, of the same family of mist or cloud, hovering in the gold radiance of the upper atmosphere. Stepping from one to another of the clouds that rested on the hills, and thence to the loftier brotherhood that sailed in air, it seemed almost as if a mortal man might thus ascend into the heavenly regions. Earth was so mingled with sky that it was a day-dream to look at it.

To supply that charm of the familiar and homely, which Nature so readily adopts into a scene like this, the stage-coach was rattling down the mountain-road, and the driver sounded his horn, while echo caught up the notes, and intertwined them into a rich and varied and elaborate harmony, of which the original performer could lay claim to little share. The great hills played a concert among themselves, each contributing a strain of airy sweetness.

Little Joe's face brightened at once.

"Dear father," cried he, skipping cheerily to and fro, "that strange man is gone, and the sky and the mountains all seem glad of it!"

"Yes," growled the lime-burner, with an oath, "but he has let the fire go down, and no thanks to him if five hundred bushels of lime are not spoiled. If I catch the fellow hereabouts again, I shall feel like tossing him into the furnace!"

With his long pole in his hand, he ascended to the top of the kiln. After a moment's pause, he called to his son.

"Come up here, Joe!" said he.

So little Joe ran up the hillock, and stood by his father's side. The marble was all burnt into perfect, snow-white lime. But on its surface, in the midst of the circle, — snow-white too, and thoroughly converted into lime, — lay a human skeleton, in the attitude of a person who, after long toil, lies down to long repose. Within the ribs — strange to say — was the shape of a human heart.

"Was the fellow's heart made of marble?" cried Bartram, in some perplexity at this phenomenon. "At any rate, it is burnt into what looks like special good lime; and, taking all the bones together, my kiln is half a bushel the richer for him."

So saying, the rude lime-burner lifted his pole, and, letting it fall upon the skeleton, the relics of Ethan Brand were crumbled into fragments.

A BELL'S BIOGRAPHY.

HEARKEN to our neighbor with the iron tongue. While I sit musing over my sheet of foolscap, he emphatically tells the hour, in tones loud enough for all the town to hear, though doubtless intended only as a gentle hint to myself, that I may begin his biography before the evening shall be further wasted. Unquestionably, a personage in such an elevated position, and making so great a noise in the world, has a fair claim to the services of a biographer. He is the representative and most illustrious member of that innumerable class, whose characteristic feature is the tongue, and whose sole business, to clamor for the public good. If any of his noisy brethren, in our tongue-governed democracy, be envious of the superiority which I have assigned him, they have my free consent to hang themselves as high as he. And, for his history, let not the reader apprehend an empty repetition of ding-dong-bell. He has been the passive hero of wonderful vicissitudes, with which I have chanced to become acquainted, possibly from his own mouth; while the careless multitude supposed him to be talking merely of the time of day, or calling them to dinner or to church, or bidding drowsy people go bedward, or the dead to their graves. Many a revolution has it been his fate to go through, and invariably with a prodigious uproar. And whether or no he have told me his reminiscences, this at least is true, that the more I study his deep-toned language, the more sense, and sentiment, and soul, do I discover in it.

This bell — for we may as well drop our quaint personification — is of antique French manufacture, and the symbol of the cross betokens that it was meant to be suspended in the belfry of a Romish place of worship. The old people hereabout have a tradition, that a considerable part of the metal was supplied by a brass cannon, captured in one of the victories of Louis the Fourteenth over the Spaniards, and that a Bourbon princess threw her golden crucifix into the molten mass. It is said, likewise, that a bishop baptized and blessed the bell, and prayed that a heavenly influence might mingle with its tones. When all due ceremonies had been performed, the Grand Monarque bestowed the gift — than which none could resound his beneficence more loudly — on the Jesuits, who were then converting the American Indians to the spiritual dominion of the Pope. So the bell, — our self-same bell, whose familiar voice we may hear at all hours, in the streets, — this very bell sent forth its first-born accents from the tower of a log-built chapel, westward of Lake Champlain, and near the mighty stream of the St. Lawrence. It was called Our Lady's Chapel of the Forest. The peal went forth as if to redeem and consecrate the heathen wilderness. The wolf growled at the sound, as he prowled stealthily through the underbrush; the grim bear turned his back, and stalked sullenly away; the startled doe leaped up, and led her fawn into a deeper solitude. The red men wondered what awful voice was speaking amid the wind that roared through the tree-tops; and, following reverentially its summons, the dark-robed fathers blessed them, as they drew near the cross-crowned chapel. In a little time, there was a crucifix on every dusky bosom. The Indians knelt beneath the lowly roof, worshipping in the same forms that were observed under the vast dome of St. Peter's, when the Pope performed high mass in the presence of kneeling princes. All the religious festivals, that awoke the chiming bells of lofty cathedrals, called forth a peal from Our Lady's Chapel of the Forest. Loudly rang the bell of the wilderness while the streets of Paris echoed with rejoicings for the birthday of the Bourbon, or whenever France had triumphed on some European battle-field. And the solemn woods were saddened with a melancholy knell, as often as the thick-strewn leaves were swept away from the virgin soil, for the burial of an Indian chief.

Meantime, the bells of a hostile people and a hostile faith were ringing on Sabbaths and lecture-days, at Boston and other Puritan towns. Their echoes died away hundreds of miles southeastward of Our Lady's Chapel. But scouts had threaded the pathless desert that lay between, and, from behind the huge tree-trunks, perceived the Indians assembling at the summons of the bell. Some bore flaxen-haired scalps at their girdles, as if to lay those bloody trophies on Our Lady's altar. It was reported, and believed, all through New England, that the Pope of Rome, and the King of France, had established this little chapel in the forest, for the purpose of stirring up the red men to a crusade against the English settlers. The latter took energetic measures to secure their religion and their lives. On the eve of an especial fast of the Romish Church, while the bell tolled dismally, and the priests were chanting a doleful stave, a band of New England rangers rushed from the surrounding woods. Fierce shouts, and the report of musketry, pealed suddenly within the chapel. The ministering priests threw themselves before the altar, and were slain even on its steps. If, as antique traditions tell us, no grass will grow where the blood of martyrs has been shed, there should be a barren spot, to this very day, on the site of that desecrated altar.

While the blood was still plashing from step to step, the leader of the rangers seized a torch, and applied it to the drapery of the shrine. The flame and smoke arose, as from a burnt-sacrifice, at once illuminating and obscuring the whole interior of the chapel, — now hiding the dead priests in a sable shroud, now revealing them and their slayers in one terrific glare. Some already wished that the altar-smoke could cover the deed from the sight of Heaven. But one of the rangers — a man of sanctified aspect, though his hands were bloody — approached the captain.

"Sir," said he, "our village meeting-house lacks a bell, and hitherto we have been fain to summon the good people to worship by beat of drum. Give me, I pray you, the bell of this popish chapel, for the sake of the godly Mr. Rogers, who doubtless hath remembered us in the prayers of the congregation, ever since we began our march. Who can tell what share of this night's good success we owe to that holy man's wrestling with the Lord?"

"Nay, then," answered the captain, "if good Mr. Rogers hath holpen our enterprise, it is right that he should share the spoil. Take the bell and welcome, Deacon Lawson, if you will be at the trouble of carrying it home. Hitherto it hath spoken nothing but papistry, and that too in the French or Indian gibberish; but I warrant me, if Mr. Rogers consecrate it anew, it will talk like a good English and Protestant bell."

So Deacon Lawson and half a score of his townsmen took down the bell, suspended it on a pole, and bore it away on their sturdy shoulders, meaning to carry it to the shore of Lake Champlain, and thence homeward by water. Far through the woods gleamed the flames of Our Lady's Chapel, flinging fantastic shadows from the clustered foliage, and glancing on brooks that had never caught the sunlight. As the rangers traversed the mid-night forest, staggering under their heavy burden, the tongue of the bell gave many a tremendous stroke, — clang, clang, clang! — a most doleful sound, as if it were tolling for the slaughter of the priests and the ruin of the chapel. Little dreamed Deacon Lawson and his townsmen that it was their own funeral knell. A war-party of Indians had heard the report of musketry, and seen the blaze of the chapel, and now were on the track of the rangers, summoned to vengeance by the bell's dismal murmurs. In the midst of a deep swamp, they made a sudden onset on the retreating foe. Good Dea-con Lawson battled stoutly, but had his skull cloven by a tomahawk, and sank into the depths of the morass, with the ponderous bell above him. And, for many a year thereafter, our hero's voice was heard no more on earth, neither at the hour of worship, nor at festivals nor funerals.

And is he still buried in that unknown grave? Scarcely so, dear reader. Hark! How plainly we hear him at this moment, the spokesman of Time, proclaim-ing that it is nine o'clock at night! We may therefore safely conclude that some happy chance has restored him to upper air.

But there lay the bell, for many silent years; and the wonder is, that he did not lie silent there a century, or perhaps a dozen centuries, till the world should have for-

6

gotten not only his voice, but the voices of the whole brotherhood of bells. How would the first accent of his iron tongue have startled his resurrectionists! But he was not fated to be a subject of discussion among the antiquaries of far posterity. Near the close of the Old French War, a party of New England axe-men, who preceded the march of Colonel Bradstreet toward Lake Ontario, were building a bridge of logs through a swamp. Plunging down a stake, one of these pioneers felt it graze against some hard, smooth substance. He called his comrades, and, by their united efforts, the top of the bell was raised to the surface, a rope made fast to it, and thence passed over the horizontal limb of a tree. Heave-oh! up they hoisted their prize, dripping with moisture, and festooned with verdant water-moss. As the base of the bell emerged from the swamp, the pioneers perceived that a skeleton was clinging with its bony fingers to the clapper, but immediately relaxing its nerveless grasp, sank back into the stagnant water. The bell then gave forth a sullen clang. No wonder that he was in haste to speak, after holding his tongue for such a length of time! The pioneers shoved the bell to and fro, thus ringing a loud and heavy peal, which echoed widely through the forest, and reached the ears of Colonel Bradstreet, and his three thousand men. The soldiers paused on their march; a feeling of religion, mingled with home-tenderness, overpowered their rude hearts; each seemed to hear the clangor of the old church-bell, which had been familiar to him from infancy, and had tolled at the funerals of all his forefathers. By what magic had that holy sound strayed over the wide-murmuring ocean, and become audible amid the clash of arms, the loud crashing of the artillery over the rough wilderness-path, and the melancholy roar of the wind among the boughs?

The New-Englanders hid their prize in a shadowy nook, betwixt a large gray stone and the earthy roots of an overthrown tree ; and when the campaign was ended, they conveyed our friend to Boston, and put him up at auction on the sidewalk of King Street. He was suspended, for the nonce, by a block and tackle, and being swung backward and forward, gave such loud and clear testimony to his own merits, that the auctioneer had no need to say a word. The highest bidder was a rich old representative from our town, who piously bestowed the bell on the meeting-house where he had been a worshipper for half a century. The good man had his reward. By a strange coincidence, the very first duty of the sexton, after the bell had been hoisted into the belfry, was to toll the funeral knell of the donor. Soon, however, those doleful echoes were drowned by a triumphant peal for the surrender of Quebec.

Ever since that period, our hero has occupied the same elevated station, and has put in his word on all matters of public importance, civil, military, or religious. On the day when Independence was first proclaimed in the street beneath, he uttered a peal which many deemed ominous and fearful, rather than triumphant. But he has told the same story these sixty years, and none mistake his meaning now. When Washington, in the fulness of his glory, rode through our flower-strewn streets, this was the tongue that bade the Father of his Country welcome! Again the same voice was heard, when La Fayette came to gather in his half-century's harvest of gratitude. Meantime, vast changes have been going on below. His voice, which once floated over a little provincial seaport, is now reverberated between brick edifices, and strikes the ear amid the buzz and tumult of a city. On the Sabbaths of olden time, the summons of the bell was obeyed by a picturesque and varied throng; stately gentlemen in purple velvet coats, embroidered waistcoats, white wigs, and gold-laced hats, stepping with grave courtesy beside ladies in flowered satin gowns, and hoop-petticoats of majestic circumference; while behind followed a liveried slave or bondsman, bearing the psalm-book, and a stove for his mistress's feet.   The commonalty, clad in homely garb, gave precedence to their betters at the door of the meeting-house, as if admitting that there were distinctions between them, even in the sight of God.   Yet, as their coffins were borne one after another through the street, the bell has tolled a requiem for all alike.   What mattered it, whether or no there were a silver scutcheon on the coffin-lid?   "Open thy bosom, Mother Earth!"   Thus spake the bell.   "Another of thy children is coming to his long rest.   Take him to thy bosom, and let him slumber in peace."   Thus spake the bell, and Mother Earth received her child.   With the self-same tones will the present generation be ushered to the embraces of their mother; and Mother Earth will still receive her children.   Is not thy tongue a-weary, mournful talker of two centuries?   O funeral bell! wilt thou never be shattered with thine own melancholy strokes?   Yea, and a trumpet-call shall arouse the sleepers, whom thy heavy clang could awake no more!

Again — again thy voice, reminding me that I am wasting the "midnight oil."   In my lonely fantasy, I can scarce believe that other mortals have caught the sound, or that it vibrates elsewhere than in my secret soul.   But to many hast thou spoken.   Anxious men have heard thee on their sleepless pillows, and bethought themselves anew of to-morrow's care.   In a brief interval of wakefulness, the sons of toil have heard thee, and say, "Is so much of our quiet slumber spent? — is the morning so near at hand?" Crime has heard thee, and mutters, "Now is the very hour!" Despair answers thee, "Thus much of this weary life is gone!" The young mother, on her bed of pain and ecstasy, has counted thy echoing strokes, and dates from them her first-born's share of life and immortality. The bridegroom and the bride have listened, and feel that their night of rapture flits like a dream away. Thine accents have fallen faintly on the ear of the dying man, and warned him that, ere thou speakest again, his spirit shall have passed whither no voice of time can ever reach. Alas for the departing traveller, if thy voice — the voice of fleeting time — have taught him no lessons for Eternity!

SYLPH ETHEREGE.

ON a bright summer evening, two persons stood among the shrubbery of a garden, stealthily watching a young girl, who sat in the window-seat of a neighboring mansion. One of these unseen observers, a gentleman, was youthful, and had an air of high breeding and refinement, and a face marked with intellect, though otherwise of unprepossessing aspect. His features wore even an ominous, though somewhat mirthful expression, while he pointed his long forefinger at the girl, and seemed to regard her as a creature completely within the scope of his influence.

"The charm works!" said he, in a low, but emphatic whisper.

"Do you know, Edward Hamilton, — since so you choose to be named, — do you know." said the lady beside him, "that I have almost a mind to break the spell at once? What if the lesson should prove too severe! True, if my ward could be thus laughed out of her fantastic nonsense, she might be the better for it through life. But then, she is such a delicate creature! And, besides, are you not ruining your own chance, by putting forward this shadow of a rival?"

"But will he not vanish into thin air, at my bidding?" rejoined Edward Hamilton. "Let the charm work!"

The girl's slender and sylph-like figure, tinged with radiance from the sunset clouds, and overhung with the rich drapery of the silken curtains, and set within the deep frame of the window, was a perfect picture; or, rather, it was like the original loveliness in a painter's fancy, from which the most finished picture is but an imperfect copy. Though her occupation excited so much interest in the two spectators, she was merely gazing at a miniature which she held in her hand, encased in white satin and red morocco; nor did there appear to be any other cause for the smile of mockery and malice with which Hamilton regarded her.

"The charm works!" muttered he, again. "Our pretty Sylvia's scorn will have a dear retribution!"

At this moment the girl raised her eyes, and, instead of a life-like semblance of the miniature, beheld the ill-omened shape of Edward Hamilton, who now stepped forth from his concealment in the shrubbery.

Sylvia Etherege was an orphan girl, who had spent her life, till within a few months past, under the guardianship, and in the secluded dwelling, of an old bachelor uncle. While yet in her cradle, she had been the destined bride of a cousin, who was no less passive in the betrothal than herself. Their future union had been projected, as the means of uniting two rich estates, and was rendered highly expedient, if not indispensable, by the testamentary dispositions of the parents on both sides. Edgar Vaughan, the promised bridegroom, had been bred from infancy in Europe, and had never seen the beautiful girl whose heart he was to claim as his inheritance. But already, for several years, a correspondence had been kept up between the cousins, and had produced an intellectual intimacy, though it could but imperfectly acquaint them with each other's character.

Sylvia was shy, sensitive, and fanciful; and her guardian's secluded habits had shut her out from even so much of the world as is generally open to maidens of her age. She had been left to seek associates and friends for herself in the haunts of imagination, and to converse with them, sometimes in the language of dead poets, oftener in the poetry of her own mind. The companion whom she chiefly summoned up was the cousin with whose idea her earliest thoughts had been connected. She made a vision of Edgar Vaughan, and tinted it with stronger hues than a mere fancy-picture, yet graced it with so many bright and delicate perfections, that her cousin could nowhere have encountered so dangerous a rival. To this shadow she cherished a romantic fidelity. With its airy presence sitting by her side, or gliding along her favorite paths, the loneliness of her young life was blissful; her heart was satisfied with love, while yet its virgin purity was untainted by the earthliness that the touch of a real lover would have left there. Edgar Vaughan seemed to be conscious of her character; for, in his letters, he gave her a name that was happily appropriate to the sensitiveness of her disposition, the delicate peculiarity of her manners, and the ethereal beauty both of her mind and person. Instead of Sylvia, he called her Sylph, — with the prerogative of a cousin and a lover, — his dear Sylph Etherege.

When Sylvia was seventeen, her guardian died, and she passed under the care of Mrs. Grosvenor, a lady of wealth and fashion, and Sylvia's nearest relative, though a distant one. While an inmate of Mrs. Grosvenor's family, she still preserved somewhat of her life-long habits of seclusion, and shrank from a too familiar intercourse with those around her. Still, too, she was faithful to her cousin, or to the shadow which bore his name.

The time now drew near when Edgar Vaughan, whose education had been completed by an extensive range of travel, was to revisit the soil of his nativity. Edward Hamilton, a young gentleman, who had been Vaughan's companion, both in his studies and rambles, had already recrossed the Atlantic, bringing letters to Mrs. Grosvenor and Sylvia Etherege. These credentials insured him an earnest welcome, which, however, on Sylvia's part, was not followed by personal partiality, or even the regard that seemed due to her cousin's most intimate friend. As she herself could have assigned no cause for her repugnance, it might be termed instinctive. Hamilton's person, it is true, was the reverse of attractive, especially when beheld for the first time. Yet, in the eyes of the most fastidious judges, the defect of natural grace was compensated by the polish of his manners, and by the intellect which so often gleamed through his dark features. Mrs. Grosvenor, with whom he immediately became a prodigious favorite, exerted herself to overcome Sylvia's dislike. But, in this matter, her ward could neither be reasoned with nor persuaded. The presence of Edward Hamilton was sure to render her cold, shy, and distant, abstracting all the vivacity from her deportment, as if a cloud had come betwixt her and the sunshine.

The simplicity of Sylvia's demeanor rendered it easy for so keen an observer as Hamilton to detect her feelings. Whenever any slight circumstance made him sensible of them, a smile might be seen to flit over the young man's sallow visage. None, that had once beheld this smile, were in any danger of forgetting it; whenever they recalled to memory the features of Edward Hamilton, they were always duskily illuminated by this expression of mockery and malice.

In a few weeks after Hamilton's arrival, he presented to Sylvia Etherege a miniature of her cousin, which, as he informed her, would have been delivered sooner, but was detained with a portion of his baggage. This was the miniature in the contemplation of which we beheld Sylvia so absorbed, at the commencement of our story. Such, in truth, was too often the habit of the shy and musing girl. The beauty of the pictured countenance was almost too perfect to represent a human creature, that had been born of a fallen and world-worn race, and had lived to manhood amid ordinary troubles and enjoyments, and must become wrinkled with age and care. It seemed too bright for a thing formed of dust, and doomed to crumble into dust again. Sylvia feared that such a being would be too refined and delicate to love a simple girl like her. Yet, even while her spirit drooped with that apprehension, the picture was but the masculine counterpart of Sylph Etherege's sylph-like beauty. There was that resemblance between her own face and the miniature which is said often to exist between lovers whom Heaven has destined for each other, and which, in this instance, might be owing to the kindred blood of the two parties. Sylvia felt, indeed, that there was something familiar in the countenance, so like a friend did the eyes smile upon her, and seem to imply a knowledge of her thoughts. She could account for this impression only by supposing that, in some of her day-dreams, imagination had conjured up the true similitude of her distant and unseen lover.

But now could Sylvia give a brighter semblance of reality to those day-dreams. Clasping the miniature to her heart, she could summon forth, from that haunted cell of pure and blissful fantasies, the life-like shadow, to roam with her in the moonlight garden. Even at

•

noontide it sat with her in the arbor, when the sunshine threw its broken flakes of gold into the clustering shade. The effect upon her mind was hardly less powerful than if she had actually listened to, and reciprocated, the vows of Edgar Vaughan; for, though the illusion never quite deceived her, yet the remembrance was as distinct as of a remembered interview. Those heavenly eyes gazed forever into her soul, which drank at them as at a fountain, and was disquieted if reality threw a momentary cloud between. She heard the melody of a voice breathing sentiments with which her own chimed in like music. O happy, yet hapless girl! Thus to create the being whom she loves, to endow him with all the attributes that were most fascinating to her heart, and then to flit with the airy creature into the realm of fantasy and moonlight, where dwelt his dreamy kindred! For her lover wiled Sylvia away from earth, which seemed strange, and dull, and darksome, and lured her to a country where her spirit roamed in peaceful rapture, deeming that it had found its home. Many, in their youth, have visited that land of dreams, and wandered so long in its enchanted groves, that, when banished thence, they feel like exiles everywhere.

The dark-browed Edward Hamilton, like the villain of a tale, would often glide through the romance wherein poor Sylvia walked. Sometimes, at the most blissful moment of her ecstasy, when the features of the miniature were pictured brightest in the air, they would suddenly change, and darken, and be transformed into his visage. And always, when such change occurred, the intrusive visage wore that peculiar smile with which Hamilton had glanced at Sylvia.

Before the close of summer, it was told Sylvia Etherege that Vaughan had arrived from France, and

that she would meet him — would meet, for the first
time, the loved of years — that very evening. We will
not tell how often and how earnestly she gazed upon the
miniature, thus endeavoring to prepare herself for the
approaching interview, lest the throbbing of her timorous heart should stifle the words of welcome. While
the twilight grew deeper and duskier, she sat with Mrs.
Grosvenor in an inner apartment, lighted only by the
softened gleam from an alabaster lamp, which was burning at a distance on the centre-table of the drawing-
room. Never before had Sylph Etherege looked so
sylph-like. She had communed with a creature of imagination, till her own loveliness seemed but the creation of a delicate and dreamy fancy. Every vibration
of her spirit was visible in her frame, as she listened to
the rattling of wheels and the tramp upon the pavement,
and deemed that even the breeze bore the sound of her
lover's footsteps, as if he trode upon the viewless air.
Mrs. Grosvenor, too, while she watched the tremulous
flow of Sylvia's feelings, was deeply moved; she looked
uneasily at the agitated girl, and was about to speak,
when the opening of the street-door arrested the words
upon her lips.

Footsteps ascended the staircase, with a confident and
familiar tread, and some one entered the drawing-room.
From the sofa where they sat, in the inner apartment,
Mrs. Grosvenor and Sylvia could not discern the visitor.

"Sylph!" cried a voice. "Dearest Sylph! Where
are you, sweet Sylph Etherege? Here is your Edgar
Vaughan!"

But instead of answering, or rising to meet her lover,
— who had greeted her by the sweet and fanciful name,
which, appropriate as it was to her character, was known
only to him, — Sylvia grasped Mrs. Grosvenor's arm,

while her whole frame shook with the throbbing of her heart.

"Who is it?" gasped she. "Who calls me Sylph?"

Before Mrs. Grosvenor could reply, the stranger entered the room, bearing the lamp in his hand. Approaching the sofa, he displayed to Sylvia the features of Edward Hamilton, illuminated by that evil smile, from which his face derived so marked an individuality.

"Is not the miniature an admirable likeness?" inquired he.

Sylvia shuddered, but had not power to turn away her white face from his gaze. The miniature, which she had been holding in her hand, fell down upon the floor, where Hamilton, or Vaughan, set his foot upon it, and crushed the ivory counterfeit to fragments.

"There, my sweet Sylph," he exclaimed. "It was I that created your phantom-lover, and now I annihilate him! Your dream is rudely broken. Awake, Sylph Etherege, awake to truth! I am the only Edgar Vaughan!"

"We have gone too far, Edgar Vaughan," said Mrs. Grosvenor, catching Sylvia in her arms. The revengeful freak, which Vaughan's wounded vanity had suggested, had been countenanced by this lady, in the hope of curing Sylvia of her romantic notions, and reconciling her to the truths and realities of life. "Look at the poor child!" she continued. "I protest I tremble for the consequences!"

"Indeed, madam!" replied Vaughan, sneeringly, as he threw the light of the lamp on Sylvia's closed eyes and marble features. "Well, my conscience is clear. I did but look into this delicate creature's heart : and with the pure fantasies that I found there, I made what seemed a man, — and the delusive shadow has wiled her away to Shadow-land, and vanished there! It is no new tale. Many a sweet maid has shared the lot of poor Sylph Etherege!"

"And now, Edgar Vaughan," said Mrs. Grosvenor, as Sylvia's heart began faintly to throb again, "now try, in good earnest, to win back her love from the phantom which you conjured up. If you succeed, she will be the better, her whole life long, for the lesson we have given her."

Whether the result of the lesson corresponded with Mrs. Grosvenor's hopes, may be gathered from the closing scene of our story. It had been made known to the fashionable world that Edgar Vaughan had returned from France, and, under the assumed name of Edward Hamilton, had won the affections of the lovely girl to whom he had been affianced in his boyhood. The nuptials were to take place at an early date. One evening, before the day of anticipated bliss arrived, Edgar Vaughan entered Mrs. Grosvenor's drawing-room, where he found that lady and Sylph Etherege.

"Only that Sylvia makes no complaint," remarked Mrs. Grosvenor, "I should apprehend that the town air is ill-suited to her constitution. She was always, indeed, a delicate creature; but now she is a mere gossamer. Do but look at her! Did you ever imagine anything so fragile?"

Vaughan was already attentively observing his mistress, who sat in a shadowy and moonlighted recess of the room, with her dreamy eyes fixed steadfastly upon his own. The bough of a tree was waving before the window, and sometimes enveloped her in the gloom of its shadow, into which she seemed to vanish.

"Yes," he said, to Mrs. Grosvenor. "I can scarcely deem her 'of the earth, earthy.' No wonder that I call her Sylph! Methinks she will fade into the moonlight, which falls upon her through the window. Or, in the open air, she might flit away upon the breeze, like a wreath of mist!"

Sylvia's eyes grew yet brighter. She waved her hand to Edgar Vaughan, with a gesture of ethereal triumph.

"Farewell!" she said. "I will neither fade into the moonlight, nor flit away upon the breeze. Yet you cannot keep me here!"

There was something in Sylvia's look and tones that startled Mrs. Grosvenor with a terrible apprehension. But, as she was rushing towards the girl, Vaughan held her back.

"Stay!" cried he, with a strange smile of mockery and anguish. "Can our sweet Sylph be going to heaven, to seek the original of the miniature?"

THE CANTERBURY PILGRIMS.

THE summer moon, which shines in so many a tale, was beaming over a broad extent of uneven country. Some of its brightest rays were flung into a spring of water, where no traveller, toiling, as the writer has, up the hilly road beside which it gushes, ever failed to quench his thirst. The work of neat hands and considerate art was visible about this blessed fountain. An open cistern, hewn and hollowed out of solid stone, was placed above the waters, which filled it to the brim, but, by some invisible outlet, were conveyed away without dripping down its sides. Though the basin had not room for another drop, and the continual gush of water made a tremor on the surface, there was a secret charm that forbade it to overflow. I remember, that when I had slaked my summer thirst, and sat panting by the cistern, it was my fanciful theory, that Nature could not afford to lavish so pure a liquid, as she does the waters of all meaner fountains.

While the moon was hanging almost perpendicularly over this spot, two figures appeared on the summit of the hill, and came with noiseless footsteps down towards the spring. They were then in the first freshness of youth; nor is there a wrinkle now on either of their brows, and yet they wore a strange, old-fashioned garb. One, a young man with ruddy cheeks, walked beneath the canopy of a broad-brimmed gray hat; he seemed to have inherited his great-grandsire's square-skirted coat, and a waistcoat that extended its immense flaps to his knees; his brown locks, also, hung down behind, in a mode unknown to our times. By his side was a sweet young damsel, her fair features sheltered by a prim little bonnet, within which appeared the vestal muslin of a cap; her close, long-waisted gown, and indeed her whole attire, might have been worn by some rustic beauty who had faded half a century before. But that there was something too warm and life-like in them, I would here have compared this couple to the ghosts of two young lovers, who had died long since in the glow of passion, and now were straying out of their graves, to renew the old vows, and shadow forth the unforgotten kiss of their earthly lips, beside the moonlit spring.

"Thee and I will rest here a moment, Miriam," said the young man, as they drew near the stone cistern, "for there is no fear that the elders know what we have done; and this may be the last time we shall ever taste this water."

Thus speaking, with a little sadness in his face, which was also visible in that of his companion, he made her sit down on a stone, and was about to place himself very close to her side; she, however, repelled him, though not unkindly.

"Nay, Josiah," said she, giving him a timid push with her maiden hand, "thee must sit farther off, on that other stone, with the spring between us. What would the sisters say, if thee were to sit so close to me?"

"But we are of the world's people now, Miriam," answered Josiah.

The girl persisted in her prudery, nor did the youth,

in fact, seem altogether free from a similar sort of shyness; so they sat apart from each other, gazing up the hill, where the moonlight discovered the tops of a group of buildings. While their attention was thus occupied, a party of travellers, who had come wearily up the long ascent, made a halt to refresh themselves at the spring. There were three men, a woman, and a little girl and boy. Their attire was mean, covered with the dust of the summer's day, and damp with the night-dew; they all looked woebegone, as if the cares and sorrows of the world had made their steps heavier as they climbed the hill; even the two little children appeared older in evil days than the young man and maiden who had first approached the spring.

"Good evening to you, young folks," was the salutation of the travellers; and "Good evening, friends," replied the youth and damsel.

"Is that white building the Shaker meeting-house?" asked one of the strangers. "And are those the red roofs of the Shaker village?"

"Friend, it is the Shaker village," answered Josiah, after some hesitation.

The travellers, who, from the first, had looked suspiciously at the garb of these young people, now taxed them with an intention which all the circumstances, indeed, rendered too obvious to be mistaken.

"It is true, friends," replied the young man, summoning up his courage. "Miriam and I have a gift to love each other, and we are going among the world's people, to live after their fashion. And ye know that we do not transgress the law of the land; and neither ye, nor the elders themselves, have a right to hinder us.

"Yet you think it expedient to depart without leave-taking," remarked one of the travellers.

"Yea, ye-a," said Josiah, reluctantly, "because father Job is a very awful man to speak with; and being aged himself, he has but little charity for what he calls the iniquities of the flesh."

"Well," said the stranger, "we will neither use force to bring you back to the village, nor will we betray you to the elders. But sit you here awhile, and when you have heard what we shall tell you of the world which we have left, and into which you are going, perhaps you will turn back with us of your own accord. What say you?" added he, turning to his companions. "We have travelled thus far without becoming known to each other. Shall we tell our stories, here by this pleasant spring, for our own pastime, and the benefit of these misguided young lovers?"

In accordance with this proposal, the whole party stationed themselves round the stone cistern; the two children, being very weary, fell asleep upon the damp earth, and the pretty Shaker girl, whose feelings were those of a nun or a Turkish lady, crept as close as possible to the female traveller, and as far as she well could from the unknown men. The same person who had hitherto been the chief spokesman now stood up, waving his hat in his hand, and suffered the moonlight to fall full upon his front.

"In me," said he, with a certain majesty of utterance, — "in me, you behold a poet."

Though a lithographic print of this gentleman is extant, it may be well to notice that he was now nearly forty, a thin and stooping figure, in a black coat, out at elbows; notwithstanding the ill condition of his attire, there were about him several tokens of a peculiar sort of foppery, unworthy of a mature man, particularly in the arrangement of his hair, which was so disposed as to give

all possible loftiness and breadth to his forehead. However, he had an intelligent eye, and, on the whole, a
marked countenance.

"A poet!" repeated the young Shaker, a little puzzled
how to understand such a designation, seldom heard in
the utilitarian community where he had spent his life.
"O, ay, Miriam, he means a varse-maker, thee must
know."

This remark jarred upon the susceptible nerves of the
poet; nor could he help wondering what strange fatality
had put into this young man's mouth an epithet, which
ill-natured people had affirmed to be more proper to his
merit than the one assumed by himself.

"True, I am a verse-maker," he resumed, "but my
verse is no more than the material body into which I
breathe the celestial soul of thought. Alas! how many
a pang has it cost me, this same insensibility to the
ethereal essence of poetry, with which you have here
tortured me again, at the moment when I am to relinquish my profession forever! O Fate! why hast thou
warred with Nature, turning all her higher and more
perfect gifts to the ruin of me, their possessor? What
is the voice of song, when the world lacks the ear of
taste? How can I rejoice in my strength and delicacy
of feeling, when they have but made great sorrows out
of little ones? Have I dreaded scorn like death, and
yearned for fame as others pant for vital air, only to
find myself in a middle state between obscurity and
infamy? But I have my revenge! I could have given
existence to a thousand bright creations. I crush them
into my heart, and there let them putrefy! I shake off
the dust of my feet against my countrymen! But posterity, tracing my footsteps up this weary hill, will cry
shame upon the unworthy age that drove one of the

fathers of American song to end his days in a Shaker village!"

During this harangue, the speaker gesticulated with great energy; and, as poetry is the natural language of passion, there appeared reason to apprehend his final explosion into an ode extempore. The reader must understand that, for all these bitter words, he was a kind, gentle, harmless, poor fellow enough, whom Nature, tossing her ingredients together without looking at her recipe, had sent into the world with too much of one sort of brain, and hardly any of another.

"Friend," said the young Shaker, in some perplexity, "thee seemest to have met with great troubles; and, doubtless, I should pity them, if — if I could but under-stand what they were."

"Happy in your ignorance!" replied the poet, with an air of sublime superiority. "To your coarser mind, perhaps, I may seem to speak of more important griefs, when I add, what I had wellnigh forgotten, that I am out at elbows, and almost starved to death. At any rate, you have the advice and example of one individual to warn you back; for I am come hither, a disappointed man, flinging aside the fragments of my hopes, and seek-ing shelter in the calm retreat which you are so anxious to leave."

"I thank thee, friend," rejoined the youth, "but I do not mean to be a poet, nor, Heaven be praised! do I think Miriam ever made a varse in her life. So we need not fear thy disappointments. But, Miriam," he added, with real concern, "thee knowest that the elders admit nobody that has not a gift to be useful. Now, what under the sun can they do with this poor varse-maker?"

"Nay, Josiah, do not thee discourage the poor man," said the girl, in all simplicity and kindness. "Our hymns are very rough, and perhaps they may trust him to smooth them."

Without noticing this hint of professional employment, the poet turned away, and gave himself up to a sort of vague revery, which he called thought. Sometimes he watched the moon, pouring a silvery liquid on the clouds, through which it slowly melted till they became all bright; then he saw the same sweet radiance dancing on the leafy trees which rustled as if to shake it off, or sleeping on the high tops of hills, or hovering down in distant valleys, like the material of unshaped dreams; lastly, he looked into the spring, and there the light was mingling with the water. In its crystal bosom, too, beholding all heaven reflected there, he found an emblem of a pure and tranquil breast. He listened to that most ethereal of all sounds, the song of crickets, coming in full choir upon the wind, and fancied that, if moonlight could be heard, it would sound just like that. Finally, he took a draught at the Shaker spring, and, as if it were the true Castalia, was forthwith moved to compose a lyric, a Farewell to his Harp, which he swore should be its closing strain, the last verse that an ungrateful world should have from him. This effusion, with two or three other little pieces, subsequently written, he took the first opportunity to send, by one of the Shaker brethren, to Concord, where they were published in the New Hampshire Patriot.

Meantime, another of the Canterbury pilgrims, one so different from the poet that the delicate fancy of the latter could hardly have conceived of him, began to relate his sad experience. He was a small man, of quick and unquiet gestures, about fifty years old, with a narrow forehead, all wrinkled and drawn together. He held in his hand a pencil, and a card of some commission-mer-

chant in foreign parts, on the back of which, for there
was light enough to read or write by, he seemed ready
to figure out a calculation.

"Young man," said he, abruptly, "what quantity of
land do the Shakers own here, in Canterbury?"

"That is more than I can tell thee, friend," answered
Josiah, "but it is a very rich establishment, and for a
long way by the roadside thee may guess the land to be
ours, by the neatness of the fences."

"And what may be the value of the whole," continued
the stranger, "with all the buildings and improvements,
pretty nearly, in round numbers?"

"O, a monstrous sum,—more than I can reckon,"
replied the young Shaker.

"Well, sir," said the pilgrim, "there was a day, and
not very long ago, neither, when I stood at my counting-
room window, and watched the signal flags of three of
my own ships entering the harbor, from the East Indies,
from Liverpool, and from up the Straits, and I would
not have given the invoice of the least of them for the
title-deeds of this whole Shaker settlement. You stare.
Perhaps, now, you won't believe that I could have put
more value on a little piece of paper, no bigger than the
palm of your hand, than all these solid acres of grain,
grass, and pasture-land would sell for?"

"I won't dispute it, friend," answered Josiah, "but I
know I had rather have fifty acres of this good land than
a whole sheet of thy paper."

"You may say so now," said the ruined merchant,
bitterly, "for my name would not be worth the paper I
should write it on. Of course, you must have heard of
my failure?"

And the stranger mentioned his name, which, however
mighty it might have been in the commercial world, the

young Shaker had never heard of among the Canterbury hills.

"Not heard of my failure!" exclaimed the merchant, considerably piqued. "Why, it was spoken of on 'Change in London, and from Boston to New Orleans men trembled in their shoes. At all events, I did fail, and you see me here on my road to the Shaker village, where, doubtless (for the Shakers are a shrewd sect), they will have a due respect for my experience, and give me the management of the trading part of the concern, in which case I think I can pledge myself to double their capital in four or five years. Turn back with me, young man; for though you will never meet with my good luck, you can hardly escape my bad."

"I will not turn back for this," replied Josiah, calmly, "any more than for the advice of the varse-maker, between whom and thee, friend, I see a sort of likeness, though I can't justly say where it lies. But Miriam and I can earn our daily bread among the world's people, as well as in the Shaker village. And do we want anything more, Miriam?"

"Nothing more, Josiah," said the girl, quietly.

"Yea, Miriam, and daily bread for some other little mouths, if God send them," observed the simple Shaker lad.

Miriam did not reply, but looked down into the spring, where she encountered the image of her own pretty face, blushing within the prim little bonnet. The third pilgrim now took up the conversation. He was a sunburnt countryman, of tall frame and bony strength, on whose rude and manly face there appeared a darker, more sullen and obstinate despondency, than on those of either the poet or the merchant.

"Well, now, youngster," he began, "these folks have

had their say, so I'll take my turn. My story will cut
but a poor figure by the side of theirs; for I never supposed that I could have a right to meat and drink, and
great praise besides, only for tagging rhymes together,
as it seems this man does; nor ever tried to get the substance of hundreds into my own hands, like the trader
there. When I was about of your years, I married me
a wife, — just such a neat and pretty young woman as
Miriam, if that's her name, — and all I asked of Providence was an ordinary blessing on the sweat of my brow,
so that we might be decent and comfortable, and have
daily bread for ourselves, and for some other little mouths
that we soon had to feed. We had no very great prospects before us; but I never wanted to be idle; and I
thought it a matter of course that the Lord would help
me, because I was willing to help myself."

"And did n't he help thee, friend?" demanded Josiah,
with some eagerness.

"No," said the yeoman, sullenly; "for then you would
not have seen me here. I have labored hard for years;
and my means have been growing narrower, and my living poorer, and my heart colder and heavier, all the time;
till at last I could bear it no longer. I set myself down
to calculate whether I had best go on the Oregon expedi-
tion, or come here to the Shaker village; but I had not
hope enough left in me to begin the world over again;
and, to make my story short, here I am. And now,
youngster, take my advice, and turn back; or else, some
few years hence, you'll have to climb this hill, with as
heavy a heart as mine."

This simple story had a strong effect on the young
fugitives. The misfortunes of the poet and merchant
had won little sympathy from their plain good sense and
unworldly feelings, qualities which made them such un-

prejudiced and inflexible judges, that few men would have chosen to take the opinion of this youth and maiden as to the wisdom or folly of their pursuits. But here was one whose simple wishes had resembled their own, and who, after efforts which almost gave him a right to claim success from fate, had failed in accomplishing them.

"But thy wife, friend?" exclaimed the young man. "What became of the pretty girl, like Miriam? O, I am afraid she is dead!"

"Yea, poor man, she must be dead, — she and the children, too," sobbed Miriam.

The female pilgrim had been leaning over the spring, wherein latterly a tear or two might have been seen to fall, and form its little circle on the surface of the water. She now looked up, disclosing features still comely, but which had acquired an expression of fretfulness, in the same long course of evil fortune that had thrown a sullen gloom over the temper of the unprosperous yeoman.

"I am his wife," said she, a shade of irritability just perceptible in the sadness of her tone. "These poor little things, asleep on the ground, are two of our children. We had two more, but God has provided better for them than we could, by taking them to himself."

"And what would thee advise Josiah and me to do?" asked Miriam, this being the first question which she had put to either of the strangers.

"'T is a thing almost against nature for a woman to try to part true lovers," answered the yeoman's wife, after a pause; "but I'll speak as truly to you as if these were my dying words. Though my husband told you some of our troubles, he did n't mention the greatest, and that which makes all the rest so hard to bear. If you and your sweetheart marry, you'll be kind and pleasant to each other for a year or two, and while that's the case, you never will repent; but, by and by, he'll grow gloomy, rough, and hard to please, and you'll be peevish, and full of little angry fits, and apt to be complaining by the fireside, when he comes to rest himself from his troubles out of doors; so your love will wear away by little and little, and leave you miserable at last. It has been so with us; and yet my husband and I were true lovers once, if ever two young folks were."

As she ceased, the yeoman and his wife exchanged a glance, in which there was more and warmer affection than they had supposed to have escaped the frost of a wintry fate, in either of their breasts. At that moment, when they stood on the utmost verge of married life, one word fitly spoken, or perhaps one peculiar look, had they had mutual confidence enough to reciprocate it, might have renewed all their old feelings, and sent them back, resolved to sustain each other amid the struggles of the world. But the crisis passed, and never came again. Just then, also, the children, roused by their mother's voice, looked up, and added their wailing accents to the testimony borne by all the Canterbury pilgrims against the world from which they fled.

"We are tired and hungry!" cried they. "Is it far to the Shaker village?"

The Shaker youth and maiden looked mournfully into each other's. eyes. They had but stepped across the threshold of their homes, when lo! the dark array of cares and sorrows that rose up to warn them back. The varied narratives of the strangers had arranged themselves into a parable; they seemed not merely instances of woful fate that had befallen others, but shadowy omens of disappointed hope and unavailing toil, domestic grief and estranged affection, that would cloud the onward path of these poor fugitives. But after one instant's hesitation, they opened their arms, and sealed their resolve with as pure and fond an embrace as ever youthful love had hallowed.

"We will not go back," said they. "The world never can be dark to us, for we will always love one another."

Then the Canterbury pilgrims went up the hill, while the poet chanted a drear and desperate stanza of the Farewell to his Harp, fitting music for that melancholy band. They sought a home where all former ties of nature or society would be sundered, and all old distinctions levelled, and a cold and passionless security be substituted for mortal hope and fear, as in that other refuge of the world's weary outcasts, the grave. The lovers drank at the Shaker spring, and then, with chastened hopes, but more confiding affections, went on to mingle in an untried life.

OLD NEWS.

1.

ERE is a volume of what were once newspapers, each on a small half-sheet, yellow and time-stained, of a coarse fabric, and imprinted with a rude old type. Their aspect conveys a singular impression of antiquity, in a species of literature which we are accustomed to consider as connected only with the present moment. Ephemeral as they were intended and supposed to be, they have long outlived the printer and his whole subscription-list, and have proved more durable, as to their physical existence, than most of the timber, bricks, and stone of the town where they were issued. These are but the least of their triumphs. The government, the interests, the opinions, in short, all the moral circumstances that were contemporary with their publication, have passed away, and left no better record of what they were than may be found in these frail leaves. Happy are the editors of newspapers! Their productions excel all others in immediate popularity, and are certain to acquire another sort of value with the lapse of time. They scatter their leaves to the wind, as the sibyl did, and posterity collects them, to be treasured up among the best materials of its wisdom. With hasty pens they write for immortality.

It is pleasant to take one of these little dingy half-
sheets between the thumb and finger, and picture forth
the personage who, above ninety years ago, held it, wet
from the press, and steaming, before the fire. Many of
the numbers bear the name of an old colonial dignitary.
There he sits, a major, a member of the council, and a
weighty merchant, in his high-backed arm-chair, wearing
a solemn wig and grave attire, such as befits his imposing
gravity of mien, and displaying but little finery, except a
huge pair of silver shoe-buckles, curiously carved. Observe the awful reverence of his visage, as he reads his
Majesty's most gracious speech; and the deliberate wisdom with which he ponders over some paragraph of provincial politics, and the keener intelligence with which he
glances at the ship-news and commercial advertisements.
Observe, and smile! He may have been a wise man in
his day; but, to us, the wisdom of the politician appears
like folly, because we can compare its prognostics with
actual results; and the old merchant seems to have
busied himself about vanities, because we know that the
expected ships have been lost at sea, or mouldered at the
wharves; that his imported broadcloths were long ago
worn to tatters, and his cargoes of wine quaffed to the
lees; and that the most precious leaves of his ledger have
become waste-paper. Yet, his avocations were not so vain
as our philosophic moralizing. In this world we are the
things of a moment, and are made to pursue momentary
things, with here and there a thought that stretches mist-
ily towards eternity, and perhaps may endure as long.
All philosophy that would abstract mankind from the
present is no more than words.

The first pages of most of these old papers are as so-
porific as a bed of poppies. Here we have an erudite
clergyman, or perhaps a Cambridge professor, occupying

several successive weeks with a criticism on Tate and Brady, as compared with the New England version of the Psalms. Of course, the preference is given to the native article. Here are doctors disagreeing about the treatment of a putrid fever then prevalent, and blackguarding each other with a characteristic virulence that renders the controversy not altogether unreadable. Here are President Wigglesworth and the Rev. Dr. Colman, endeavoring to raise a fund for the support of missionaries among the Indians of Massachusetts Bay. Easy would be the duties of such a mission now! Here — for there is nothing new under the sun — are frequent complaints of the disordered state of the currency, and the project of a bank with a capital of five hundred thousand pounds, secured on lands. Here are literary essays, from the Gentleman's Magazine; and squibs against the Pretender, from the London newspapers. And here, occasionally, are specimens of New England humor, laboriously light and lamentably mirthful, as if some very sober person, in his zeal to be merry, were dancing a jig to the tune of a funeral-psalm. All this is wearisome, and we must turn the leaf.

There is a good deal of amusement, and some profit, in the perusal of those little items which characterize the manners and circumstances of the country. New England was then in a state incomparably more picturesque than at present, or than it has been within the memory of man; there being, as yet, only a narrow strip of civilization along the edge of a vast forest, peopled with enough of its original race to contrast the savage life with the old customs of another world. The white population, also, was diversified by the influx of all sorts of expatriated vagabonds, and by the continual importation of bond-servants from Ireland and elsewhere, so that there was a wild and unsettled multitude, forming a strong minority to the sober descendants of the Puritans. Then, there were the slaves, contributing their dark shade to the picture of society. The consequence of all this was a great variety and singularity of action and incident, many instances of which might be selected from these columns, where they are told with a simplicity and quaintness of style that bring the striking points into very strong relief. It is natural to suppose, too, that these circumstances affected the body of the people, and made their course of life generally less regular than that of their descendants. There is no evidence that the moral standard was higher then than now; or, indeed, that morality was so well defined as it has since become. There seem to have been quite as many frauds and robberies, in proportion to the number of honest deeds; there were murders, in hot-blood and in malice; and bloody quarrels over liquor. Some of our fathers also appear to have been yoked to unfaithful wives, if we may trust the frequent notices of elopements from bed and board. The pillory, the whipping-post, the prison, and the gallows, each had their use in those old times; and, in short, as often as our imagination lives in the past, we find it a ruder and rougher age than our own, with hardly any perceptible advantages, and much that gave life a gloomier tinge.

In vain we endeavor to throw a sunny and joyous air over our picture of this period; nothing passes before our fancy but a crowd of sad-visaged people, moving duskily through a dull gray atmosphere. It is certain that winter rushed upon them with fiercer storms than now, blocking up the narrow forest-paths, and overwhelming the roads along the sea-coast with mountain snow-drifts; so that weeks elapsed before the newspaper could

announce how many travellers had perished, or what
wrecks had strewn the shore. The cold was more
piercing then, and lingered further into the spring, making the chimney-corner a comfortable seat till long past
May-day. By the number of such accidents on record,
we might suppose that the thunder-stone, as they termed
it, fell oftener and deadlier on steeples, dwellings, and
unsheltered wretches. In fine, our fathers bore the brunt
of more raging and pitiless elements than we. There
were forebodings, also, of a more fearful tempest than
those of the elements. At two or three dates, we have
stories of drums, trumpets, and all sorts of martial music,
passing athwart the midnight sky, accompanied with the
roar of cannon and rattle of musketry, prophetic echoes
of the sounds that were soon to shake the land. Besides
these airy prognostics, there were rumors of French fleets
on the coast, and of the march of French and Indians
through the wilderness, along the borders of the settlements. The country was saddened, moreover, with
grievous sickness. The small-pox raged in many of the
towns, and seems, though so familiar a scourge, to have
been regarded with as much affright as that which drove
the throng from Wall Street and Broadway at the approach of a new pestilence. There were autumnal fevers
too, and a contagious and destructive throat-distemper, —
diseases unwritten in medical books. The dark super-
stition of former days had not yet been so far dispelled
as not to heighten the gloom of the present times. There
is an advertisement, indeed, by a committee of the Legis-
lature, calling for information as to the circumstances of
sufferers in the "late calamity of 1692," with a view to
reparation for their losses and misfortunes. But the
tenderness with which, after above forty years, it was
thought expedient to allude to the witchcraft delusion,

7 *

indicates a good deal of lingering error, as well as the advance of more enlightened opinions. The rigid hand of Puritanism might yet be felt upon the reins of government, while some of the ordinances intimate a disorderly spirit on the part of the people. The Suffolk justices, after a preamble that great disturbances have been committed by persons entering town and leaving it in coaches, chaises, calashes, and other wheel-carriages, on the evening before the Sabbath, give notice that a watch will hereafter be set at the "fortification-gate," to prevent these outrages. It is amusing to see Boston assuming the aspect of a walled city, guarded, probably, by a detachment of church-members, with a deacon at their head. Governor Belcher makes proclamation against certain "loose and dissolute people" who have been wont to stop passengers in the streets, on the Fifth of November, "otherwise called Pope's Day," and levy contributions for the building of bonfires. In this instance, the populace are more puritanic than the magistrate.

The elaborate solemnities of funerals were in accordance with the sombre character of the times. In cases of ordinary death, the printer seldom fails to notice that the corpse was "very decently interred." But when some mightier mortal has yielded to his fate, the decease of the "worshipful" such-a-one is announced, with all his titles of deacon, justice, counsellor, and colonel; then follows an heraldic sketch of his honorable ancestors, and lastly an account of the black pomp of his funeral, and the liberal expenditure of scarfs, gloves, and mourning-rings. The burial train glides slowly before us, as we have seen it represented in the woodcuts of that day, the coffin, and the bearers, and the lamentable friends, trailing their long black garments, while grim Death, a most misshapen skeleton, with all kinds of doleful emblems, stalks hideously in front. There was a coach-maker at this period, one John Lucas, who seems to have gained the chief of his living by letting out a sable coach to funerals.

It would not be fair, however, to leave quite so dismal an impression on the reader's mind; nor should it be forgotten that happiness may walk soberly in dark attire, as well as dance lightsomely in a gala-dress. And this reminds us that there is an incidental notice of the "dancing-school near the Orange-Tree," whence we may infer that the saltatory art was occasionally practised, though perhaps chastened into a characteristic gravity of movement. This pastime was probably confined to the aristocratic circle, of which the royal governor was the centre. But we are scandalized at the attempt of Jona-than Furness to introduce a more reprehensible amuse-ment: he challenges the whole country to match his black gelding in a race for a hundred pounds, to be decided on Metonomy Common or Chelsea Beach. Noth-ing as to the manners of the times can be inferred from this freak of an individual. There were no daily and continual opportunities of being merry; but sometimes the people rejoiced, in their own peculiar fashion, oftener with a calm, religious smile than with a broad laugh, as when they feasted, like one great family, at Thanksgiving time, or indulged a livelier mirth throughout the pleasant days of Election-week. This latter was the true holiday season of New England. Military musters were too seriously important in that warlike time to be classed among amusements; but they stirred up and enlivened the public mind, and were occasions of solemn festival to the governor and great men of the province, at the expense of the field-officers. The Revolution blotted a feast-day out of our calendar; for the anniversary of the king's birth appears to have been celebrated with most imposing pomp, by salutes from Castle William, a military parade, a grand dinner at the town-house, and a brilliant illumination in the evening. There was nothing forced nor feigned in these testimonials of loyalty to George the Second. So long as they dreaded the re-establishment of a popish dynasty, the people were fervent for the house of Hanover: and, besides, the immediate magistracy of the country was a barrier between the monarch and the occasional discontents of the colonies; the waves of faction sometimes reached the governor's chair, but never swelled against the throne. Thus, until oppression was felt to proceed from the king's own hand, New England rejoiced with her whole heart on his Majesty's birthday.

But the slaves, we suspect, were the merriest part of the population, since it was their gift to be merry in the worst of circumstances; and they endured, comparatively, few hardships, under the domestic sway of our fathers. There seems to have been a great trade in these human commodities. No advertisements are more frequent than those of "a negro fellow, fit for almost any household work"; "a negro woman, honest, healthy, and capable"; "a negro wench of many desirable qualities"; "a negro man, very fit for a taylor." We know not in what this natural fitness for a tailor consisted, unless it were some peculiarity of conformation that enabled him to sit cross-legged. When the slaves of a family were inconveniently prolific, — it being not quite orthodox to drown the superfluous offspring, like a litter of kittens, — notice was promulgated of "a negro child to be given away." Sometimes the slaves assumed the property of their own persons, and made their escape; among many such instances, the governor raises a hue-

and-cry after his negro Juba. But, without venturing a
word in extenuation of the general system, we confess
our opinion that Cæsar, Pompey, Scipio, and all such
great Roman namesakes, would have been better advised
had they stayed at home, foddering the cattle, cleaning
dishes, — in fine, performing their moderate share of the
labors of life, without being harassed by its cares. The
sable inmates of the mansion were not excluded from the
domestic affections: in families of middling rank, they
had their places at the board ; and when the circle closed
round the evening hearth, its blaze glowed on their dark
shining faces, intermixed familiarly with their master's
children. It must have contributed to reconcile them to
their lot, that they saw white men and women imported
from Europe as they had been from Africa, and sold,
though only for a term of years, yet as actual slaves to
the highest bidder. Slave labor being but a small part
of the industry of the country, it did not change the
character of the people ; the latter, on the contrary,
modified and softened the institution, making it a patriarchal, and almost a beautiful, peculiarity of the times.

Ah! We had forgotten the good old merchant, over
whose shoulder we were peeping, while he read the
newspaper. Let us now suppose him putting on his
three-cornered gold-laced hat, grasping his cane, with a
head inlaid of ebony and mother-of-pearl, and setting
forth, through the crooked streets of Boston, on various
errands, suggested by the advertisements of the day.
Thus he communes with himself: I must be mindful,
says he, to call at Captain Scut's, in Creek Lane, and
examine his rich velvet, whether it be fit for my apparel
on Election-day, — that I may wear a stately aspect in
presence of the governor and my brethren of the council.
I will look in, also, at the shop of Michael Cario, the

jeweller: he has silver buckles of a new fashion; and
mine have lasted me some half-score years. My fair
daughter Miriam shall have an apron of gold brocade,
and a velvet mask, — though it would be a pity the
wench should hide her comely visage; and also a French
cap, from Robert Jenkins's, on the north side of the
town-house. He hath beads, too, and ear-rings, and
necklaces, of all sorts; these are but vanities, nevertheless, they would please the silly maiden well. My dame
desireth another female in the kitchen; wherefore, I
must inspect the lot of Irish lasses, for sale by Samuel
Waldo, aboard the schooner Endeavor; as also the likely
negro wench, at Captain Bulfinch's. It were not amiss
that I took my daughter Miriam to see the royal wax-
work, near the town-dock, that she may learn to honor
our most gracious King and Queen, and their royal
progeny, even in their waxen images; not that I would
approve of image-worship. The camel, too, that strange
beast from Africa, with two great humps, to be seen near
the Common; methinks I would fain go thither, and see
how the old patriarchs were wont to ride. I will tarry
awhile in Queen Street, at the bookstore of my good
friends Kneeland & Green, and purchase Dr. Colman's
new sermon, and the volume of discourses by Mr. Henry
Flynt; and look over the controversy on baptism, between the Rev. Peter Clarke and an unknown adversary;
and see whether this George Whitefield be as great in
print as he is famed to be in the pulpit. By that time,
the auction will have commenced at the Royal Exchange,
in King Street. Moreover, I must look to the disposal
of my last cargo of West India rum and muscovado
sugar; and also the lot of choice Cheshire cheese, lest
it grow mouldy. It were well that I ordered a cask of
good English beer, at the lower end of Milk Street.

Then am I to speak with certain dealers about the lot of
stout old Vidonia, rich Canary, and Oporto wines, which
I have now lying in the cellar of the Old South meeting-
house.   But, a pipe or two of the rich Canary shall be
reserved, that it may grow mellow in mine own wine-
cellar, and gladden my heart when it begins to droop
with old age.

Provident old gentleman!   But, was he mindful of
his sepulchre?   Did he bethink him to call at the work-
shop of Timothy Sheaffe, in Cold Lane, and select such
a gravestone as would best please him?   There wrought
the man whose handiwork, or that of his fellow-crafts-
men, was ultimately in demand by all the busy multitude who have left a record of their earthly toil in these
old time-stained papers.   And now, as we turn over the
volume, we seem to be wandering among the mossy
stones of a burial-ground.

II. THE OLD FRENCH WAR.

At a period about twenty years subsequent to that
of our former sketch, we again attempt a delineation of
some of the characteristics of life and manners in New
England.   Our text-book, as before, is a file of antique
newspapers.   The volume which serves us for a writing-
desk is a folio of larger dimensions than the one before
described; and the papers are generally printed on a
whole sheet, sometimes with a supplemental leaf of news
and advertisements.   They have a venerable appearance,
being overspread with a duskiness of more than seventy
years, and discolored, here and there, with the deeper

stains of some liquid, as if the contents of a wineglass
had long since been splashed upon the page. Still, the
old book conveys an impression that, when the separate
numbers were flying about town, in the first day or two
of their respective existences, they might have been fit
reading for very stylish people. Such newspapers could
have been issued nowhere but in a metropolis the centre,
not only of public and private affairs, but of fashion and
gayety. Without any discredit to the colonial press,
these might have been, and probably were, spread out on
the tables of the British coffee-house, in King Street, for
the perusal of the throng of officers who then drank their
wine at that celebrated establishment. To interest these
military gentlemen, there were bulletins of the war
between Prussia and Austria; between England and
France, on the old battle-plains of Flanders ; and between
the same antagonists, in the newer fields of the East
Indies, — and in our own trackless woods, where white
men never trod until they came to fight there. Or,
the travelled American, the petit-maître of the colonies,
— the ape of London foppery, as the newspaper was the
semblance of the London journals, — he, with his gray
powdered periwig, his embroidered coat, lace ruffles,
and glossy silk stockings, golden-clocked, — his buckles
of glittering paste, at knee-band and shoe-strap, — his
scented handkerchief, and chapeau beneath his arm, —
even such a dainty figure need not have disdained to
glance at these old yellow pages, while they were the
mirror of passing times. For his amusement, there were
essays of wit and humor, the light literature of the day,
which, for breadth and license, might have proceeded
from the pen of Fielding or Smollet; while, in other
columns, he would delight his imagination with the
enumerated items of all sorts of finery, and with the

rival advertisements of half a dozen peruke-makers. In short, newer manners and customs had almost entirely superseded those of the Puritans, even in their own city of refuge.

It was natural that, with the lapse of time and increase of wealth and population, the peculiarities of the early settlers should have waxed fainter and fainter through the generations of their descendants, who also had been alloyed by a continual accession of emigrants from many countries and of all characters. It tended to assimilate the colonial manners to those of the mother-country, that the commercial intercourse was great, and that the merchants often went thither in their own ships. Indeed, almost every man of adequate fortune felt a yearning desire, and even judged it a filial duty, at least once in his life, to visit the home of his ancestors. They still called it their own home, as if New England were to them, what many of the old Puritans had considered it, not a permanent abiding-place, but merely a lodge in the wilderness, until the trouble of the times should be passed. The example of the royal governors must have had much influence on the manners of the colonists; for these rulers assumed a degree of state and splendor which had never been practised by their predecessors, who differed in nothing from republican chief-magistrates, under the old charter. The officers of the crown, the public characters in the interest of the administration, and the gentlemen of wealth and good descent, generally noted for their loyalty, would constitute a dignified circle, with the governor in the centre, bearing a very passable resemblance to a court. Their ideas, their habits, their code of courtesy, and their dress would have all the fresh glitter of fashions immediately derived from the fountain-head, in England. To prevent their modes of

K

life from becoming the standard with all who had the
ability to imitate them, there was no longer an undue
severity of religion, nor as yet any disaffection to British supremacy, nor democratic prejudices against pomp.
Thus, while the colonies were attaining that strength
which was soon to render them an independent republic,
it might have been supposed that the wealthier classes
were growing into an aristocracy, and ripening for hereditary rank, while the poor were to be stationary in their
abasement, and the country, perhaps, to be a sister mon-
archy with England. Such, doubtless, were the plausi-
ble conjectures deduced from the superficial phenomena
of our connection with a monarchical government, until
the prospective nobility were levelled with the mob, by
the mere gathering of winds that preceded the storm
of the Revolution. The portents of that storm were not
yet visible in the air. A true picture of society, therefore, would have the rich effect produced by distinctions
of rank that seemed permanent, and by appropriate habits
of splendor on the part of the gentry.

The people at large had been somewhat changed in
character, since the period of our last sketch, by their
great exploit, the conquest of Louisburg. After that
event, the New-Englanders never settled into precisely
the same quiet race which all the world had imagined
them to be. They had done a deed of history, and were
anxious to add new ones to the record. They had
proved themselves powerful enough to influence the
result of a war, and were thenceforth called upon, and
willingly consented, to join their strength against the
enemies of England; on those fields, at least, where victory would redound to their peculiar advantage. And
now, in the heat of the Old French War, they might
well be termed a martial people. Every man was a sol-

dier, or the father or brother of a soldier; and the whole land literally echoed with the roll of the drum, either beating up for recruits.among the towns and villages, or striking the march towards the frontiers. Besides the provincial troops, there were twenty-three British regiments in the northern colonies. The country has never known a period of such excitement and warlike life, except during the Revolution, — perhaps scarcely then; for that was a lingering war, and this a stirring and eventful one.

One would think that no very wonderful talent was requisite for an historical novel, when the rough and hurried paragraphs of these newspapers can recall the past so magically. We seem to be waiting in the street for the arrival of the post-rider — who is seldom more than twelve hours beyond his time — with letters, by way of Albany, from the various departments of the army. Or, we may fancy ourselves in the circle of listeners, all with necks stretched out towards an old gentleman in the centre, who deliberately puts on his spectacles, unfolds the wet newspaper, and gives us the details of the broken and contradictory reports, which have been flying from mouth to mouth, ever since the courier alighted at Secretary Oliver's office. Sometimes we have an account of the Indian skirmishes near Lake George, and how a ranging party of provincials were so closely pursued, that they threw away their arms, and eke their shoes, stockings, and breeches, barely reaching the camp in their shirts, which also were terribly tattered by the bushes. Then, there is a journal of the siege of Fort Niagara, so minute that it almost numbers the cannon-shot and bombs, and describes the effect of the latter missiles on the French commandant's stone mansion, within the fortress. In the letters of the provincial officers, it is amusing to observe

how some of them endeavor to catch the careless and
jovial turn of old campaigners. One gentleman tells us
that he holds a brimming glass in his hand, intending to
drink the health of his correspondent, unless a cannon-
ball should dash the liquor from his lips; in the midst of
his letter he hears the bells of the French churches ringing, in Quebec, and recollects that it is Sunday; where-
upon, like a good Protestant, he resolves to disturb the
Catholic worship by a few thirty-two pound shot. While
this wicked man of war was thus making a jest of religion, his pious mother had probably put up a note, that
very Sabbath-day, desiring the "prayers of the congregation for a son gone a soldiering." We trust, however,
that there were some stout old worthies who were not
ashamed to do as their fathers did, but went to prayer,
with their soldiers, before leading them to battle; and
doubtless fought none the worse for that. If we had
enlisted in the Old French War, it should have been
under such a captain; for we love to see a man keep
the characteristics of his country.*

These letters, and other intelligence from the army,
are pleasant and lively reading, and stir up the mind
like the music of a drum and fife. It is less agreeable
to meet with accounts of women slain and scalped, and

* The contemptuous jealousy of the British army, from the
general downwards, was very galling to the provincial troops.
In one of the newspapers, there is an admirable letter of a New
England man, copied from the London Chronicle, defending
the provincials with an ability worthy of Franklin, and somewhat in his style. The letter is remarkable, also, because it takes
up the cause of the whole range of colonies, as if the writer
looked upon them all as constituting one country, and that his
own. Colonial patriotism had not hitherto been so broad a
sentiment.

infants dashed against trees, by the Indians on the frontiers. It is a striking circumstance, that innumerable
bears, driven from the woods, by the uproar of contend-
ing armies in their accustomed haunts, broke into the
settlements, and committed great ravages among children, as well as sheep and swine. Some of them prowled
where bears had never been for a century, penetrating
within a mile or two of Boston; a fact that gives a strong
and gloomy impression of something very terrific going
on in the forest, since these savage beasts fled townward
to avoid it. But it is impossible to moralize about such
trifles, when every newspaper contains tales of military
enterprise, and often a huzza for victory; as, for instance, the taking of Ticonderoga, long a place of awe
to the provincials, and one of the bloodiest spots in the
present war. Nor is it unpleasant, among whole pages
of exultation, to find a note of sorrow for the fall of some
brave officer; it comes wailing in, like a funeral strain
amidst a peal of triumph, itself triumphant too. Such
was the lamentation over Wolfe. Somewhere, in this
volume of newspapers, though we cannot now lay our
finger upon the passage, we recollect a report that General Wolfe was slain, not by the enemy, but by a shot
from his own soldiers.

In the advertising columns, also, we are continually
reminded that the country was in a state of war. Governor Pownall makes proclamation for the enlisting of
soldiers, and directs the militia colonels to attend to the
discipline of their regiments, and the selectmen of every
town to replenish their stocks of ammunition. The magazine, by the way, was generally kept in the upper loft of
the village meeting-house. The provincial captains are
drumming up for soldiers, in every newspaper. Sir
Jeffrey Amherst advertises for batteaux-men, to be em-

ployed on the lakes; and gives notice to the officers of
seven British regiments, dispersed on the recruiting service, to rendezvous in Boston. Captain Hallowell, of
the province ship-of-war King George, invites able-bodied
seamen to serve his Majesty, for fifteen pounds, old tenor,
per month. By the rewards offered, there would appear
to have been frequent desertions from the New England
forces: we applaud their wisdom, if not their valor or
integrity. Cannon of all calibres, gunpowder and balls,
firelocks, pistols, swords, and hangers, were common
articles of merchandise. Daniel Jones, at the sign of
the hat and helmet, offers to supply officers with scarlet
broadcloth, gold-lace for hats and waistcoats, cockades,
and other military foppery, allowing credit until the pay-
rolls shall be made up. This advertisement gives us
quite a gorgeous idea of a provincial captain in full
dress.

At the commencement of the campaign of 1759, the
British general informs the farmers of New England
that a regular market will be established at Lake George,
whither they are invited to bring provisions and refresh-
ments of all sorts, for the use of the army. ' Hence, we
may form a singular picture of petty traffic, far away
from any permanent settlements, among the hills which
border that romantic lake, with the solemn woods overshadowing the scene. Carcasses of bullocks and fat
porkers are placed upright against the huge trunks of
the trees; fowls hang from the lower branches, bobbing
against the heads of those beneath; butter-firkins, great
cheeses, and brown loaves of household bread, baked in
distant ovens, are collected under temporary shelters or
pine-boughs, with gingerbread, and pumpkin-pies, perhaps, and other toothsome dainties. Barrels of cider
and spruce-beer are running freely into the wooden can-

teens of the soldiers. Imagine such a scene, beneath the dark forest canopy, with here and there a few straggling sunbeams, to dissipate the gloom. See the shrewd yeomen, haggling with their scarlet-coated customers, abating somewhat in their prices, but still dealing at monstrous profit; and then complete the picture with circumstances that bespeak war and danger. A cannon shall be seen to belch its smoke from among the trees, against some distant canoes on the lake; the traffickers shall pause, and seem to hearken, at intervals, as if they heard the rattle of musketry or the shout of Indians; a scouting-party shall be driven in, with two or three faint and bloody men among them. And, in spite of these disturbances, business goes on briskly in the market of the wilderness.

It must not be supposed that the martial character of the times interrupted all pursuits except those connected with war. On the contrary, there appears to have been a general vigor and vivacity diffused into the whole round of colonial life. During the winter of 1759, it was computed that about a thousand sled-loads of country produce were daily brought into Boston market. It was a symptom of an irregular and unquiet course of affairs, that innumerable lotteries were projected, ostensibly for the purpose of public improvements, such as roads and bridges. Many females seized the opportunity to engage in business: as, among others, Alice Quick, who dealt in crockery and hosiery, next door to Deacon Beautineau's; Mary Jackson, who sold butter, at the Brazen-Head, in Cornhill; Abigail Hiller, who taught ornamental work, near the Orange-Tree, where also were to be seen the King and Queen, in wax-work; Sarah Morehead, an instructor in glass-painting, drawing, and japanning; Mary Salmon, who shod horses, at the South

End; Harriet Pain, at the Buck and Glove, and Mrs.
Henrietta Maria Caine, at the Golden Fan, both fashionable milliners; Anna Adams, who advertises Quebec
and Garrick bonnets, Prussian cloaks, and scarlet cardi-
nals, opposite the old brick meeting-house; besides a
lady at the head of a wine and spirit establishment.
Little did these good dames expect to reappear before the
public, so long after they had made their last courtesies
behind the counter. Our great-grandmothers were a
stirring sisterhood, and seem not to have been utterly
despised by the gentlemen at the British coffee-house;
at least, some gracious bachelor, there resident, gives
public notice of his willingness to take a wife, provided
she be not above twenty-three, and possess brown hair,
regular features, a brisk eye, and a fortune. Now, this
was great condescension towards the ladies of Massachusetts Bay, in a threadbare lieutenant of foot.

Polite literature was beginning to make its appearance.
Few native works were advertised, it is true, except sermons and treatises of controversial divinity; nor were
the English authors of the day much known on this
side of the Atlantic. But catalogues were frequently
offered at auction or private sale, comprising the standard English books, history, essays, and poetry, of Queen
Anne's age, and the preceding century. We see nothing
in the nature of a novel, unless it be " The Two Mothers,
price four coppers." There was an American poet, however, of whom Mr. Kettell has preserved no specimen,
— the author of " War, an Heroic Poem "; he publishes
by subscription, and threatens to prosecute his patrons
for not taking their books. We have discovered a peri-
odical, also, and one that has a peculiar claim to be recorded here, since it bore the title of " THE NEW ENG-
LAND MAGAZINE," a forgotten predecessor, for which

we should have a filial respect, and take its excellence on trust. The fine arts, too, were budding into existence. At the " old glass and picture shop," in Cornhill, various maps, plates, and views are advertised, and among them a " Prospect of Boston," a copperplate engraving of Quebec, and the effigies of all the New England ministers ever done in mezzotinto. All these must have been very salable articles. Other ornamental wares were to be found at the same shop; such as violins, flutes, hautboys, musical books, English and Dutch toys, and London babies. About this period, Mr. Dipper gives notice of a concert of vocal and instrumental music. There had already been an attempt at theatrical exhibitions.

There are tokens, in every newspaper, of a style of luxury and magnificence which we do not usually associate with our ideas of the times. When the property of a deceased person was to be sold, we find, among the household furniture, silk beds and hangings, damask table-cloths, Turkey carpets, pictures, pier-glasses, massive plate, and all things proper for a noble mansion. Wine was more generally drunk than now, though by no means to the neglect of ardent spirits. For the apparel of both sexes, the mercers and milliners imported good store of fine broadcloths, especially scarlet, crimson, and sky-blue, silks, satins, lawns, and velvets, gold brocade, and gold and silver lace, and silver tassels, and silver spangles, until Cornhill shone and sparkled with their merchandise. The gaudiest dress permissible by modern taste fades into a Quaker-like sobriety, compared with the deep, rich, glowing splendor of our ancestors. Such figures were almost too fine to go about town on foot; accordingly, carriages were so numerous as to require a tax; and it is recorded that, when Governor

8

Bernard came to the province, he was met between Dedham and Boston by a multitude of gentlemen in their coaches and chariots.

Take my arm, gentle reader, and come with me into some street, perhaps trodden by your daily footsteps, but which now has such an aspect of half-familiar strangeness, that you suspect yourself to be walking abroad in a dream. True, there are some brick edifices which you remember from childhood, and which your father and grandfather remembered as well; but you are perplexed by the absence of many that were here only an hour or two since; and still more amazing is the presence of whole rows of wooden and plastered houses, projecting over the sidewalks, and bearing iron figures on their fronts, which prove them to have stood on the same sites above a century. Where have your eyes been that you never saw them before? Along the ghostly street, — for, at length, you conclude that all is unsubstantial, though it be so good a mockery of an antique town, — along the ghostly street, there are ghostly people too. Every gentleman has his three-cornered hat, either on his head or under his arm; and all wear wigs in infinite variety, — the Tie, the Brigadier, the Spencer, the Albemarle, the Major, the Ramillies, the grave Full-bottom, or the giddy Feather-top. Look at the elaborate lace-ruffles, and the square-skirted coats of gorgeous hues, bedizened with silver and gold! Make way for the phantom-ladies, whose hoops require such breadth of passage, as they pace majestically along, in silken gowns, blue, green, or yellow, brilliantly embroidered, and with small satin hats surmounting their powdered hair. Make way; for the whole spectral show will vanish, if your earthly garments brush against their robes. Now that the scene is brightest, and the whole street glitters with imaginary sun-

shine, — now hark to the bells of the Old South and the
Old North, ringing out with a sudden and merry peal,
while the cannon of Castle William thunder below the
town, and those of the Diana frigate repeat the sound,
and the Charlestown batteries reply with a nearer roar!
You see the crowd toss up their hats in visionary joy.
You hear of illuminations and fire-works, and of bonfires,
built on scaffolds, raised several stories above the ground,
that are to blaze all night in King Street and on Beacon
Hill. And here come the trumpets and kettle-drums,
and the tramping hoofs of the Boston troop of horse-
guards, escorting the governor to King's Chapel, where
he is to return solemn thanks for the surrender of Quebec.
March on, thou shadowy troop! and vanish, ghostly
crowd! and change again, old street! for those stirring
times are gone.

Opportunely for the conclusion of our sketch, a fire
broke out, on the twentieth of March, 1760, at the
Brazen-Head, in Cornhill, and consumed nearly four
hundred buildings. Similar disasters have always been
epochs in the chronology of Boston. That of 1711 had
hitherto been termed the Great Fire, but now resigned
its baleful dignity to one which has ever since retained
it. Did we desire to move the reader's sympathies on
this subject, we would not be grandiloquent about the
sea of billowy flame, the glowing and crumbling streets,
the broad, black firmament of smoke, and the blast of
wind that sprang up with the conflagration and roared
behind it. It would be more effective to mark out a
single family at the moment when the flames caught
upon an angle of their dwelling: then would ensue the
removal of the bedridden grandmother, the cradle with
the sleeping infant, and, most dismal of all, the dying
man just at the extremity of a lingering disease. Do

but imagine the confused agony of one thus awfully disturbed in his last hour; his fearful glance behind at the consuming fire raging after him, from house to house, as its devoted victim; and, finally, the almost eagerness with which he would seize some calmer interval to die! The Great Fire must have realized many such a scene.

Doubtless posterity has acquired a better city by the calamity of that generation. None will be inclined to lament it at this late day, except the lover of antiquity, who would have been glad to walk among those streets of venerable houses, fancying the old inhabitants still there, that he might commune with their shadows, and paint a more vivid picture of their times.

III. THE OLD TORY.

AGAIN we take a leap of about twenty years, and alight in the midst of the Revolution. Indeed, having just closed a volume of colonial newspapers, which represented the period when monarchical and aristocratic sentiments were at the highest, — and now opening another volume printed in the same metropolis, after such sentiments had long been deemed a sin and shame, — we feel as if the leap were more than figurative. Our late course of reading has tinctured us, for the moment, with antique prejudices; and we shrink from the strangely contrasted times into which we emerge, like one of those immutable old Tories, who acknowledge no oppression in the Stamp Act. It may be the most effective method of going through the present file of papers, to follow out this idea, and transform ourself, perchance, from a modern Tory into such a sturdy King-man as once wore that pliable nickname.

Well, then, here we sit, an old, gray, withered, sour-visaged, threadbare sort of gentleman, erect enough, here in our solitude, but marked out by a depressed and distrustful mien abroad, as one conscious of a stigma upon his forehead, though for no crime. We were already in the decline of life when the first tremors of the earthquake that has convulsed the continent were felt. Our mind had grown too rigid to change any of its opinions, when the voice of the people demanded that all should be changed. We are an Episcopalian, and sat under the High-Church doctrines of Dr. Caner; we have been a captain of the provincial forces, and love our king the better for the blood that we shed in his cause on the Plains of Abraham. Among all the refugees, there is not one more loyal to the backbone than we. Still we lingered behind when the British army evacuated Boston, sweeping in its train most of those with whom we held communion; the old, loyal gentlemen, the aristocracy of the colonies, the hereditary Englishman, imbued with more than native zeal and admiration for the glorious island and its monarch, because the far-intervening ocean threw a dim reverence around them. When our brethren departed, we could not tear our aged roots out of the soil. We have remained, therefore, enduring to be outwardly a freeman, but idolizing King George in secrecy and silence, — one true old heart amongst a host of enemies. We watch, with a weary hope, for the moment when all this turmoil shall subside, and the impious novelty that has distracted our latter years, like a wild dream, give place to the blessed quietude of royal sway, with the king's name in every ordinance, his prayer in the church, his health at the board, and his love in the people's heart. Meantime, our old age finds little honor. Hustled have we been, till driven from town-meetings; dirty water has been cast upon our ruffles by a Whig chambermaid; John Hancock's coachman seizes every opportunity to bespatter us with mud; daily are we hooted by the unbreeched rebel brats; and narrowly, once, did our gray hairs escape the ignominy of tar and feathers. Alas! only that we cannot bear to die till the next royal governor comes over, we would fain be in our quiet grave.

Such an old man among new things are we who now hold at arm's-length the rebel newspaper of the day. The very figure-head, for the thousandth time, elicits a groan of spiteful lamentation. Where are the united heart and crown, the loyal emblem, that used to hallow the sheet on which it was impressed, in our younger days? In its stead we find a continental officer, with the Declaration of Independence in one hand, a drawn sword in the other, and above his head a scroll, bearing the motto, "WE APPEAL TO HEAVEN." Then say we, with a prospective triumph, let Heaven judge, in its own good time! The material of the sheet attracts our scorn. It is a fair specimen of rebel manufacture, thick and coarse, like wrapping-paper, all overspread with little knobs; and of such a deep, dingy blue color, that we wipe our spectacles thrice before we can distinguish a letter of the wretched print. Thus, in all points, the newspaper is a type of the times, far more fit for the rough hands of a democratic mob, than for our own delicate, though bony fingers. Nay; we will not handle it without our gloves!

Glancing down the page, our eyes are greeted everywhere by the offer of lands at auction, for sale or to be

leased, not by the rightful owners, but a rebel committee; notices of the town constable, that he is authorized
to receive the taxes on such an estate, in default of
which, that also is to be knocked down to the highest
bidder; and notifications of complaints filed by the at-
torney-general against certain traitorous absentees, and
of confiscations that are to ensue. And who are these
traitors? Our own best friends; names as old, once as
honored, as any in the land where they are no longer to
have a patrimony, nor to be remembered as good men
who have passed away. We are ashamed of not relin-
quishing our little property, too; but comfort ourselves
because we still keep our principles, without gratifying
the rebels with our plunder. Plunder, indeed, they are
seizing everywhere, — by the strong hand at sea, as well
as by legal forms on shore. Here are prize-vessels for
sale; no French nor Spanish merchantmen, whose wealth
is the birthright of British subjects, but hulls of British
oak, from Liverpool, Bristol, and the Thames, laden with
the king's own stores, for his army in New York. And
what a fleet of privateers — pirates, say we -- are fitting
out for new ravages, with rebellion in their very names!
The Free Yankee, the General Green, the Saratoga, the
Lafayette, and the Grand Monarch! Yes, the Grand
Monarch; so is a French king styled, by the sons of
Englishmen. And here we have an ordinance from the
Court of Versailles, with the Bourbon's own signature
affixed, as if New England were already a French province. Everything is French, — French soldiers, French
sailors, French surgeons, and French diseases too, I
trow; besides French dancing-masters and French milliners, to debauch our daughters with French fashions!
Everything in America is French, except the Canadas,
the loyal Canadas, which we helped to wrest from

France. And to that old French province the English-man of the colonies must go to find his country!

O, the misery of seeing the whole system of things changed in my old days, when I would be loath to change even a pair of buckles! The British coffee-house, where oft we sat, brimful of wine and loyalty, with the gallant gentlemen of Amherst's army, when we wore a red-coat too, — the British coffee-house, forsooth, must now be styled the American, with a golden eagle instead of the royal arms above the door. Even the street it stands in is no longer King Street! Nothing is the king's, except this heavy heart in my old bosom. Wherever I glance my eyes, they meet something that pricks them like a needle. This soap-maker, for instance, this Robert Hewes, has conspired against my peace, by notifying that his shop is situated near Liberty Stump. But when will their misnamed liberty have its true emblem in that Stump, hewn down by British steel?

Where shall we buy our next year's almanac? Not this of Weatherwise's, certainly; for it contains a likeness of George Washington, the upright rebel, whom we most hate, though reverentially, as a fallen angel, with his heavenly brightness undiminished, evincing pure fame in an unhallowed cause. And here is a new book for my evening's recreation, — a History of the War till the close of the year 1779, with the heads of thirteen distinguished officers, engraved on copperplate. A plague upon their heads! We desire not to see them till they grin at us from the balcony before the town-house, fixed on spikes, as the heads of traitors. How bloody-minded the villains make a peaceable old man! What next? An Oration, on the Horrid Massacre of 1770. When that blood was shed, — the first that the British soldier ever drew from the bosoms of our countrymen, — we turned sick at heart, and do so still, as often as they make it reek anew from among the stones in King Street. The pool that we saw that night has swelled into a lake, — English blood and American, — no! all British, all blood of my brethren. And here come down tears. Shame on me, since half of them are shed for rebels! Who are not rebels now! Even the women are thrusting their white hands into the war, and come out in this very paper with proposals to form a society — the lady of George Washington at their head — for clothing the continental troops. They will strip off their stiff petticoats to cover the ragged rascals, and then enlist in the ranks themselves.

What have we here? Burgoyne's proclamation turned into Hudibrastic rhyme! And here, some verses against the king, in which the scribbler leaves a blank for the name of George, as if his doggerel might yet exalt him to the pillory. Such, after years of rebellion, is the heart's unconquerable reverence for the Lord's anointed! In the next column, we have scripture parodied in a squib against his sacred Majesty. What would our Puritan-great-grandsires have said to that? They never laughed at God's word, though they cut off a king's head.

Yes; it was for us to prove how disloyalty goes hand in hand with irreligion, and all other vices come trooping in the train. Nowadays men commit robbery and sacrilege for the mere luxury of wickedness, as this advertisement testifies. Three hundred pounds reward for the detection of the villains who stole and destroyed the cushions and pulpit drapery of the Brattle Street and Old South churches. Was it a crime? I can scarcely think our temples hallowed, since the king ceased to be prayed for. But it is not temples only that they rob. Here a man offers a thousand dollars — a thousand dollars, in

8 *   L

Continental rags! — for the recovery of his stolen cloak, and other articles of clothing. Horse-thieves are innumerable. Now is the day when every beggar gets on horseback. And is not the whole land like a beggar on horseback riding post to the Devil? Ha! here is a murder, too. A woman slain at midnight, by an unknown ruffian, and found cold, stiff, and bloody, in her violated bed! Let the hue-and-cry follow hard after the man in the uniform of blue and buff who last went by that way. My life on it, he is the blood-stained ravisher! These deserters whom we see proclaimed in every column, — proof that the banditti are as false to their Stars and Stripes as to the Holy Red Cross, — they bring the crimes of a rebel camp into a soil well suited to them; the bosom of a people, without the heart that kept them virtuous, — their king!

Here, flaunting down a whole column, with official seal and signature, here comes a proclamation. By whose authority? Ah! the United States, — these thirteen little anarchies, assembled in that one grand anarchy, their Congress. And what the import? A general Fast. By Heaven! for once the traitorous blockheads have legislated wisely! Yea; let a misguided people kneel down in sackcloth and ashes, from end to end, from border to border, of their wasted country. Well may they fast where there is no food, and cry aloud for whatever remnant of God's mercy their sins may not have exhausted. We too will fast, even at a rebel summons. Pray others as they will, there shall be at least an old man kneeling for the righteous cause. Lord, put down the rebels! God save the king!

Peace to the good old Tory! One of our objects has been to exemplify, without softening a single prejudice proper to the character which we assumed, that the

Americans who clung to the losing side in the Revolution were men greatly to be pitied and often worthy of our sympathy. It would be difficult to say whose lot was most lamentable, that of the active Tories, who gave up their patrimonies for a pittance from the British pension-roll, and their native land for a cold reception in their miscalled home, or the passive ones who remained behind to endure the coldness of former friends, and the public opprobrium, as despised citizens, under a government which they abhorred. In justice to the old gentleman who has favored us with his discontented musings, we must remark that the state of the country, so far as can be gathered from these papers, was of dismal augury for the tendencies of democratic rule. It was pardonable in the conservative of that day to mistake the temporary evils of a change for permanent diseases of the system which that change was to establish. A revolution, or anything that interrupts social order, may afford opportunities for the individual display of eminent virtues; but its effects are pernicious to general morality. Most people are so constituted that they can be virtuous only in a certain routine; and an irregular course of public affairs demoralizes them. One great source of disorder was the multitude of disbanded troops, who were continually returning home, after terms of service just long enough to give them a distaste to peaceable occupations; neither citizens nor soldiers, they were very liable to become ruffians. Almost all our impressions in regard to this period are unpleasant, whether referring to the state of civil society, or to the character of the contest, which, especially where native Americans were opposed to each other, was waged with the deadly hatred of fraternal enemies. It is the beauty of war, for men to commit mutual havoc with undisturbed good-humor.

The present volume of newspapers contains fewer characteristic traits than any which we have looked over. Except for the peculiarities attendant on the passing struggle, manners seem to have taken a modern cast. Whatever antique fashions lingered into the War of the Revolution, or beyond it, they were not so strongly marked as to leave their traces in the public journals. Moreover, the old newspapers had an indescribable picturesqueness, not to be found in the later ones. Whether it be something in the literary execution, or the ancient print and paper, and the idea that those same musty pages have been handled by people once alive and bustling amid the scenes there recorded, yet now in their graves beyond the memory of man; so it is, that in those elder volumes we seem to find the life of a past age preserved between the leaves, like a dry specimen of foliage. It is so difficult to discover what touches are really picturesque, that we doubt whether our attempts have produced any similar effect.

THE MAN OF ADAMANT:

AN APOLOGUE.

IN the old times of religious gloom and intolerance lived Richard Digby, the gloomiest and most intolerant of a stern brotherhood. His plan of salvation was so narrow, that, like a plank in a tempestuous sea, it could avail no sinner but himself, who bestrode it triumphantly, and hurled anathemas against the wretches whom he saw struggling with the billows of eternal death. In his view of the matter, it was a most abominable crime — as, indeed, it is a great folly — for men to trust to their own strength, or even to grapple to any other fragment of the wreck, save this narrow plank, which, moreover, he took special care to keep out of their reach. In other words, as his creed was like no man's else, and being well pleased that Providence had intrusted him alone, of mortals, with the treasure of a true faith, Richard Digby determined to seclude himself to the sole and constant enjoyment of his happy fortune.

"And verily," thought he, "I deem it a chief condition of Heaven's mercy to myself, that I hold no communion with those abominable myriads which it hath cast off to perish. Peradventure, were I to tarry longer in the tents of Kedar, the gracious boon would be revoked, and I also be swallowed up in the deluge of wrath, or consumed in the storm of fire and brimstone, or involved in whatever new kind of ruin is ordained for the horrible perversity of this generation."

So Richard Digby took an axe, to hew space enough for a tabernacle in the wilderness, and some few other necessaries, especially a sword and gun, to smite and slay any intruder upon his hallowed seclusion; and plunged into the dreariest depths of the forest. On its verge, however, he paused a moment, to shake off the dust of his feet against the village where he had dwelt, and to invoke a curse on the meeting-house, which he regarded as a temple of heathen idolatry. He felt a curiosity, also, to see whether the fire and brimstone would not rush down from Heaven at once, now that the one righteous man had provided for his own safety. But, as the sunshine continued to fall peacefully on the cottages and fields, and the husbandmen labored and children played, and as there were many tokens of present happiness, and nothing ominous of a speedy judgment, he turned away, somewhat disappointed. The farther he went, however, and the lonelier he felt himself, and the thicker the trees stood along his path, and the darker the shadow overhead, so much the more did Richard Digby exult. He talked to himself, as he strode onward; he read his Bible to himself, as he sat beneath the trees: and, as the gloom of the forest hid the blessed sky, I had almost added, that, at morning, noon, and eventide, he prayed to himself. So congenial was this mode of life to his disposition, that he often laughed to himself, but was displeased when an echo tossed him back the long loud roar.

In this manner, he journeyed onward three days and

two nights, and came, on the third evening, to the mouth
of a cave, which, at first sight, reminded him of Elijah's
cave at Horeb, though perhaps it more resembled Abraham's sepulchral cave at Machpelah. It entered into
the heart of a rocky hill. There was so dense a veil of
tangled foliage about it, that none but a sworn lover
of gloomy recesses would have discovered the low arch
of its entrance, or have dared to step within its vaulted
chamber, where the burning eyes of a panther might
encounter him. If Nature meant this remote and dismal
cavern for the use of man, it could only be to bury in its
gloom the victims of a pestilence, and then to block up
its mouth with stones, and avoid the spot forever after.
There was nothing bright nor cheerful near it, except
a bubbling fountain, some twenty paces off, at which
Richard Digby hardly threw away a glance. But he
thrust his head into the cave, shivered, and congratulated
himself.

"The finger of Providence hath pointed my way!"
cried he, aloud, while the tomb-like den returned a
strange echo, as if some one within were mocking him.
"Here my soul will be at peace; for the wicked will not
find me. Here I can read the Scriptures, and be no more
provoked with lying interpretations. Here I can offer
up acceptable prayers, because my voice will not be mingled with the sinful supplications of the multitude. Of
a truth, the only way to heaven leadeth through the
narrow entrance of this cave, — and I alone have found
it!"

In regard to this cave it was observable that the roof,
so far as the imperfect light permitted it to be seen, was
hung with substances resembling opaque icicles; for the
damps of unknown centuries, dripping down continually,
had become as hard as adamant; and wherever that

moisture fell, it seemed to possess the power of converting what it bathed to stone. The fallen leaves and sprigs
of foliage, which the wind had swept into the cave, and
the little feathery shrubs, rooted near the threshold, were
not wet with a natural dew, but had been embalmed by
this wondrous process. And here I am put in mind
that Richard Digby, before he withdrew himself from the
world, was supposed by skilful physicians to have contracted a disease for which no remedy was written in
their medical books. It was a deposition of calculous
particles within his heart, caused by an obstructed circu-
lation of the blood; and, unless a miracle should be
wrought for him, there was danger that the malady might
act on the entire substance of the organ, and change his
fleshy heart to stone. Many, indeed, affirmed that the
process was already near its consummation. Richard
Digby, however, could never be convinced that any such
direful work was going on within him; nor when he saw
the sprigs of marble foliage, did his heart even throb the
quicker, at the similitude suggested by these once tender herbs. It may be that this same insensibility was a
symptom of the disease.

Be that as it might, Richard Digby was well contented
with his sepulchral cave. So dearly did he love this congenial spot, that, instead of going a few paces to the
bubbling spring for water, he allayed his thirst with now
and then a drop of moisture from the roof, which, had it
fallen anywhere but on his tongue, would have been con-
gealed into a pebble. For a man predisposed to stoni-
ness of the heart, this surely was unwholesome liquor.
But there he dwelt, for three days more eating herbs
and roots, drinking his own destruction, sleeping, as it
were, in a tomb, and awaking to the solitude of death,
yet esteeming this horrible mode of life as hardly inferior

to celestial bliss. Perhaps superior; for, above the sky, there would be angels to disturb him. At the close of the third day, he sat in the portal of his mansion, reading the Bible aloud, because no other ear could profit by it, and reading it amiss, because the rays of the setting sun did not penetrate the dismal depth of shadow round about him, nor fall upon the sacred page. Suddenly, however, a faint gleam of light was thrown over the volume, and, raising his eyes, Richard Digby saw that a young woman stood before the mouth of the cave, and that the sunbeams bathed her white garment, which thus seemed to possess a radiance of its own.

"Good evening, Richard," said the girl; "I have come from afar to find thee."

The slender grace and gentle loveliness of this young woman were at once recognized by Richard Digby. Her name was Mary Goffe. She had been a convert to his preaching of the word in England, before he yielded himself to that exclusive bigotry which now enfolded him with such an iron grasp that no other sentiment could reach his bosom. When he came a pilgrim to America, she had remained in her father's hall: but now, as it appeared, had crossed the ocean after him, impelled by the same faith that led other exiles hither, and perhaps by love almost as holy. What else but faith and love united could have sustained so delicate a creature, wandering thus far into the forest, with her golden hair dishevelled by the boughs, and her feet wounded by the thorns? Yet, weary and faint though she must have been, and affrighted at the dreariness of the cave, she looked on the lonely man with a mild and pitying expression, such as might beam from an angel's eyes, towards an afflicted mortal. But the recluse, frowning sternly upon her, and keeping his finger between the leaves of his half-closed Bible, motioned her away with his hand.

"Off!" cried he. "I am sanctified, and thou art sinful. Away!"

"O Richard," said she, earnestly, "I have come this weary way because I heard that a grievous distemper had seized upon thy heart; and a great Physician hath given me the skill to cure it. There is no other remedy than this which I have brought thee. Turn me not away, therefore, nor refuse my medicine; for then must this dismal cave be thy sepulchre."

"Away!" replied Richard Digby, still with a dark frown. "My heart is in better condition than thine own. Leave me, earthly one; for the sun is almost set; and when no light reaches the door of the cave, then is my prayer-time."

Now, great as was her need, Mary Goffe did not plead with this stony-hearted man for shelter and protection, nor ask anything whatever for her own sake. All her zeal was for his welfare.

"Come back with me!" she exclaimed, clasping her hands, — "come back to thy fellow-men; for they need thee, Richard, and thou hast tenfold need of them. Stay not in this evil den; for the air is chill, and the damps are fatal; nor will any that perish within it ever find the path to heaven. Hasten hence, I entreat thee, for thine own soul's sake; for either the roof will fall upon thy head, or some other speedy destruction is at hand."

"Perverse woman!" answered Richard Digby, laughing aloud, — for he was moved to bitter mirth by her foolish vehemence, — "I tell thee that the path to heaven leadeth straight through this narrow portal where I sit. And, moreover, the destruction thou speakest of is

ordained, not for this blessed cave, but for all other habitations of mankind, throughout the earth. Get thee
hence speedily, that thou mayst have thy share!"

So saying, he opened his Bible again, and fixed his
eyes intently on the page, being resolved to withdraw
his thoughts from this child of sin and wrath, and to
waste no more of his holy breath upon her. The shadow
had now grown so deep, where he was sitting, that he
made continual mistakes in what he read, converting all
that was gracious and merciful to denunciations of vengeance and unutterable woe on every created being but
himself. Mary Goffe, meanwhile, was leaning against
a tree, beside the sepulchral cave, very sad, yet with
something heavenly and ethereal in her unselfish sorrow.
The light from the setting sun still glorified her form,
and was reflected a little way within the darksome den,
discovering so terrible a gloom that the maiden shuddered for its self-doomed inhabitant. Espying the bright
fountain near at hand, she hastened thither, and scooped
up a portion of its water, in a cup of birchen bark. A
few tears mingled with the draught, and perhaps gave it
all its efficacy. She then returned to the mouth of the
cave, and knelt down at Richard Digby's feet.

"Richard," she said, with passionate fervor, yet a
gentleness in all her passion, "I pray thee, by thy hope
of heaven, and as thou wouldst not dwell in this tomb
forever, drink of this hallowed water, be it but a single
drop! Then, make room for me by thy side, and let us
read together one page of that blessed volume; and,
lastly, kneel down with me and pray! Do this, and thy
stony heart shall become softer than a babe's, and all be
well."

But Richard Digby, in utter abhorrence of the proposal, cast the Bible at his feet, and eyed her with such

a fixed and evil frown, that he looked less like a living man than a marble statue, wrought by some dark-imagined sculptor to express the most repulsive mood that human features could assume. And, as his look grew even devilish, so, with an equal change did Mary Goffe become more sad, more mild, more pitiful, more like a sorrowing angel. But, the more heavenly she was, the more hateful did she seem to Richard Digby, who at length raised his hand, and smote down the cup of hallowed water upon the threshold of the cave, thus rejecting the only medicine that could have cured his stony heart. A sweet perfume lingered in the air for a moment, and then was gone.

"Tempt me no more, accursed woman," exclaimed he, still with his marble frown, "lest I smite thee down also! What hast thou to do with my Bible? — what with my prayers? — what with my heaven?"

No sooner had he spoken these dreadful words, than Richard Digby's heart ceased to beat; while — so the legend says — the form of Mary Goffe melted into the last sunbeams, and returned from the sepulchral cave to heaven. For Mary Goffe had been buried in an English churchyard, months before; and either it was her ghost that haunted the wild forest, or else a dream-like spirit, typifying pure Religion.

Above a century afterwards, when the trackless forest of Richard Digby's day had long been interspersed with settlements, the children of a neighboring farmer were playing at the foot of a hill. The trees, on account of the rude and broken surface of this acclivity, had never been felled, and were crowded so densely together as to hide all but a few rocky prominences, wherever their roots could grapple with the soil. A little boy and girl, to conceal themselves from their playmates, had crept

into the deepest shade, where not only the darksome
pines, but a thick veil of creeping plants suspended from
an overhanging rock, combined to make a twilight at
noonday, and almost a midnight at all other seasons.
There the children hid themselves, and shouted, repeating the cry at intervals, till the whole party of pursuers were drawn thither, and pulling aside the mat-
ted foliage, let in a doubtful glimpse of daylight. But
scarcely was this accomplished, when the little group
uttered a simultaneous shriek, and tumbled headlong
down the hill, making the best of their way homeward,
without a second glance into the gloomy recess. Their
father, unable to comprehend what had so startled them,
took his axe, and, by felling one or two trees, and tear-
ing away the creeping plants, laid the mystery open to
the day. He had discovered the entrance of a cave,
closely resembling the mouth of a sepulchre, within
which sat the figure of a man, whose gesture and attitude warned the father and children to stand back, while
his visage wore a most forbidding frown. This repulsive personage seemed to have been carved in the same
gray stone that formed the walls and portal of the cave.
On minuter inspection, indeed, such blemishes were observed, as made it doubtful whether the figure were
really a statue, chiselled by human art, and somewhat
worn and defaced by the lapse of ages, or a freak of
Nature, who might have chosen to imitate, in stone,
her usual handiwork of flesh. Perhaps it was the least
unreasonable idea, suggested by this strange spectacle,
that the moisture of the cave possessed a petrifying
quality, which had thus awfully embalmed a human
corpse.

There was something so frightful in the aspect of this
Man of Adamant, that the farmer, the moment that he

recovered from the fascination of his first gaze, began to
heap stones into the mouth of the cavern. His wife,
who had followed him to the hill, assisted her husband's
efforts. The children, also, approached as near as they
durst, with their little hands full of pebbles, and cast
them on the pile. Earth was then thrown into the
crevices, and the whole fabric overlaid with sods. Thus
all traces of the discovery were obliterated, leaving only
a marvellous legend, which grew wilder from one generation to another, as the children told it to their grandchildren, and they to their posterity, till few believed
that there had ever been a cavern or a statue, where
now they saw but a grassy patch on the shadowy hillside. Yet, grown people avoid the spot, nor do children
play there. Friendship, and Love, and Piety, all human
and celestial sympathies, should keep aloof from that
hidden cave; for there still sits, and, unless an earthquake crumble down the roof upon his head, shall sit
forever, the shape of Richard Digby, in the attitude of
repelling the whole race of mortals, — not from heaven,
— but from the horrible loneliness of his dark, cold
sepulchre !

THE DEVIL IN MANUSCRIPT.

ON a bitter evening of December, I arrived by mail in a large town, which was then the residence of an intimate friend, one of those gifted youths who cultivate poetry and the belles-lettres, and call themselves students at law. My first business, after supper, was to visit him at the office of his distinguished instructor. As I have said, it was a bitter night, clear starlight, but cold as Nova Zembla, — the shop-windows along the street being frosted, so as almost to hide the lights, while the wheels of coaches thundered equally loud over frozen earth and pavements of stone. There was no snow, either on the ground or the roofs of the houses. The wind blew so violently, that I had but to spread my cloak like a main-sail, and scud along the street at the rate of ten knots, greatly envied by other navigators, who were beating slowly up, with the gale right in their teeth. One of these I capsized, but was gone on the wings of the wind before he could even vociferate an oath.

After this picture of an inclement night, behold us seated by a great blazing fire, which looked so comfortable and delicious that I felt inclined to lie down and roll among the hot coals. The usual furniture of a lawyer's office was around us, — rows of volumes in sheep-skin, and a multitude of writs, summonses, and other legal papers, scattered over the desks and tables. But there were certain objects which seemed to intimate that we had little dread of the intrusion of clients, or of the learned counsellor himself, who, indeed, was attending court in a distant town. A tall, decanter-shaped bottle stood on the table, between two tumblers, and beside a pile of blotted manuscripts, altogether dissimilar to any law documents recognized in our courts. My friend, whom I shall call Oberon, — it was a name of fancy and friendship between him and me, — my friend Oberon looked at these papers with a peculiar expression of disquietude.

" I do believe," said he, soberly, "or, at least, I could believe, if I chose, that there is a devil in this pile of blotted papers. You have read them, and know what I mean, — that conception in which I endeavored to embody the character of a fiend, as represented in our traditions and the written records of witchcraft. O, I have a horror of what was created in my own brain, and shudder at the manuscripts in which I gave that dark idea a sort of material existence! Would they were out of my sight ! "

" And of mine, too," thought I.

" You remember," continued Oberon, " how the hellish thing used to suck away the happiness of those who, by a simple concession that seemed almost innocent, subjected themselves to his power. Just so my peace is gone, and all by these accursed manuscripts. Have you felt nothing of the same influence ? "

" Nothing," replied I, " unless the spell be hid in a desire to turn novelist, after reading your delightful tales."

" Novelist ! " exclaimed Oberon, half seriously. " Then,

indeed, my devil has his claw on you! You are gone! You cannot even pray for deliverance! But we will be the last and only victims; for this night I mean to burn the manuscripts, and commit the fiend to his retribution in the flames."

"Burn your tales!" repeated I, startled at the desperation of the idea.

"Even so," said the author, despondingly. "You cannot conceive what an effect the composition of these tales has had on me. I have become ambitious of a bubble, and careless of solid reputation. I am surrounding myself with shadows, which bewilder me, by aping the realities of life. They have drawn me aside from the beaten path of the world, and led me into a strange sort of solitude, — a solitude in the midst of men, — where nobody wishes for what I do, nor thinks nor feels as I do. The tales have done all this. When they are ashes, perhaps I shall be as I was before they had existence. Moreover, the sacrifice is less than you may suppose; since nobody will publish them."

"That does make a difference, indeed," said I.

"They have been offered, by letter," continued Oberon, reddening with vexation, "to some seventeen booksellers. It would make you stare to read their answers; and read them you should, only that I burnt them as fast as they arrived. One man publishes nothing but school-books; another has five novels already under examination."

"What a voluminous mass the unpublished literature of America must be!" cried I.

"O, the Alexandrian manuscripts were nothing to it!" said my friend. "Well, another gentleman is just giving up business, on purpose, I verily believe, to escape publishing my book. Several, however, would not abso-

lutely decline the agency, on my advancing half the cost
of an edition, and giving bonds for the remainder, besides
a high percentage to themselves, whether the book sells
or not.   Another advises a subscription."

"The villain!" exclaimed I.

"A fact!" said Oberon.   "In short, of all the seventeen booksellers, only one has vouchsafed even to read
my tales; and he — a literary dabbler himself, I should
judge — has the impertinence to criticise them, proposing
what he calls vast improvements, and concluding, after a
general sentence of condemnation, with the definitive as-
surance that he will not be concerned on any terms.

"It might not be amiss to pull that fellow's nose,"
remarked I.

"If the whole 'trade' had one common nose, there
would be some satisfaction in pulling it," answered the
author.   "But, there does seem to be one honest man
among these seventeen unrighteous ones; and he tells
me fairly, that no American publisher will meddle with
an American work, — seldom if by a known writer, and
never if by a new one, — unless at the writer's risk."

"The paltry rogues!" cried I.   "Will they live by
literature, and yet risk nothing for its sake?   But, after
all, you might publish on your own account."

"And so I might," replied Oberon.   "But the devil
of the business is this.   These people have put me so
out of conceit with the tales, that I loathe the very
thought of them, and actually experience a physical sickness of the stomach, whenever I glance at them on the
table.   I tell you there is a demon in them!   I antici-
pate a wild enjoyment in seeing them in the blaze; such
as I should feel in taking vengeance on an enemy, or
destroying something noxious."

I did not very strenuously oppose this determination,

being privately of opinion, in spite of my partiality for the author, that his tales would make a more brilliant appearance in the fire than anywhere else. Before proceeding to execution, we broached the bottle of champagne, which Oberon had provided for keeping up his spirits in this doleful business. We swallowed each a tumblerful, in sparkling commotion; it went bubbling down our throats, and brightened my eyes at once, but left my friend sad and heavy as before. He drew the tales towards him, with a mixture of natural affection and natural disgust, like a father taking a deformed infant into his arms.

"Pooh! Pish! Pshaw!" exclaimed he, holding them at arm's-length. "It was Gray's idea of heaven, to lounge on a sofa and read new novels. Now, what more appropriate torture would Dante himself have contrived, for the sinner who perpetrates a bad book, than to be continually turning over the manuscript?"

"It would fail of effect," said I, "because a bad author is always his own great admirer."

"I lack that one characteristic of my tribe, — the only desirable one," observed Oberon. "But how many recollections throng upon me, as I turn over these leaves! This scene came into my fancy as I walked along a hilly road, on a starlight October evening; in the pure and bracing air, I became all soul, and felt as if I could climb the sky, and run a race along the Milky-Way. Here is another tale, in which I wrapt myself during a dark and dreary night-ride in the month of March, till the rattling of the wheels and the voices of my companions seemed like faint sounds of a dream, and my visions a bright reality. That scribbled page describes shadows which I summoned to my bedside at midnight: they would not depart when I bade them;

the gray dawn came, and found me wide awake and feverish, the victim of my own enchantments!".

"There must have been a sort of happiness in all this," said I, smitten with a strange longing to make proof of it.

"There may be happiness in a fever fit," replied the author. "And then the various moods in which I wrote! Sometimes my ideas were like precious stones under the earth, requiring toil to dig them up, and care to polish and brighten them; but often, a delicious stream of thought would gush out upon the page at once, like water sparkling up suddenly in the desert; and when it had passed, I gnawed my pen hopelessly, or blundered on with cold and miserable toil, as if there were a wall of ice between me and my subject."

"Do you now perceive a corresponding difference," inquired I, "between the passages which you wrote so coldly, and those fervid flashes of the mind?"

"No," said Oberon, tossing the manuscripts on the table. "I find no traces of the golden pen, with which I wrote in characters of fire. My treasure of fairy coin is changed to worthless dross. My picture, painted in what seemed the loveliest hues, presents nothing but a faded and indistinguishable surface. I have been eloquent and poetical and humorous in a dream, — and behold! it is all nonsense, now that I am awake."

My friend now threw sticks of wood and dry chips upon the fire, and seeing it blaze like Nebuchadnezzar's furnace, seized the champagne-bottle, and drank two or three brimming bumpers, successively. The heady liquor combined with his agitation to throw him into a species of rage. He laid violent hands on the tales. In one instant more, their faults and beauties would alike have vanished in a glowing purgatory. But, all at once, I remembered passages of high imagination, deep pathos, original thoughts, and points of such varied excellence, that the vastness of the sacrifice struck me most forcibly. I caught his arm.

"Surely, you do not mean to burn them!" I exclaimed.

"Let me alone!" cried Oberon, his eyes flashing fire. "I will burn them! Not a scorched syllable shall escape! Would you have me a damned author?—To undergo sneers, taunts, abuse, and cold neglect, and faint praise, bestowed, for pity's sake, against the giver's conscience! A hissing and a laughing-stock to my own traitorous thoughts! An outlaw from the protection of the grave,—one whose ashes every careless foot might spurn, unhonored in life, and remembered scornfully in death! Am I to bear all this, when yonder fire will insure me from the whole? No! There go the tales! May my hand wither when it would write another!"

The deed was done. He had thrown the manuscripts into the hottest of the fire, which at first seemed to shrink away, but soon curled around them, and made them a part of its own fervent brightness. Oberon stood gazing at the conflagration, and shortly began to soliloquize, in the wildest strain, as if Fancy resisted and became riotous, at the moment when he would have compelled her to ascend that funeral pile. His words described objects which he appeared to discern in the fire, fed by his own precious thoughts; perhaps the thousand visions which the writer's magic had incorporated with these pages became visible to him in the dissolving heat, brightening forth ere they vanished forever; while the smoke, the vivid sheets of flame, the ruddy and whitening coals, caught the aspect of a varied scenery.

"They blaze," said he, "as if I had steeped them in

the intensest spirit of genius. There I see my lovers
clasped in each other's arms. How pure the flame that
bursts from their glowing hearts! And yonder the
features of a villain writhing in the fire that shall torment him to eternity. My holy men, my pious and
angelic women, stand like martyrs amid the flames, their
mild eyes lifted heavenward. Ring out the bells! A
city is on fire. See! — destruction roars through my
dark forests, while the lakes boil up in steaming billows,
and the mountains are volcanoes, and the sky kindles
with a lurid brightness! All elements are but one pervading flame! Ha! The fiend!"

I was somewhat startled by this latter exclamation.
The tales were almost consumed, but just then threw
forth a broad sheet of fire, which flickered as with laughter, making the whole room dance in its brightness, and
then roared portentously up the chimney.

"You saw him? You must have seen him!" cried
Oberon. "How he 'glared at me and laughed, in that
last sheet of flame, with just the features that I imagined
for him! Well! The tales are gone."

The papers were indeed reduced to a heap of black
cinders, with a multitude of sparks hurrying confusedly
among them, the traces of the pen being now represented
by white lines, and the whole mass fluttering to and fro,
in the draughts of air. The destroyer knelt down to
look at them.

"What is more potent than fire!" said he, in his
gloomiest tone. "Even thought, invisible and incorpo-
real as it is, cannot escape it. In this little time, it has
annihilated the creations of long nights and days, which
I could no more reproduce, in their first glow and freshness, than cause ashes and whitened bones to rise up and
live. There, too, I sacrificed the unborn children of my

mind. All that I had accomplished — all that I planned
for future years — has perished by one common ruin, and
left only this heap of embers! The deed has been my
fate. And what remains? A weary and aimless life, —
a long repentance of this hour, — and at last an obscure
grave, where they will bury and forget me!"

As the author concluded his dolorous moan, the extinguished embers arose and settled down and arose again,
and finally flew up the chimney, like a demon with sable
wings. Just as they disappeared, there was a loud and
solitary cry in the street below us. "Fire! Fire!"
Other voices caught up that terrible word, and it speedily
became the shout of a multitude. Oberon started to his
feet, in fresh excitement.

"A fire on such a night!" cried he. "The wind
blows a gale, and wherever it whirls the flames, the roofs
will flash up like gunpowder. Every pump is frozen up,
and boiling water would turn to ice the moment it was
flung from the engine. In an hour, this wooden town
will be one great bonfire! What a glorious scene for my
next — Pshaw!"

The street was now all alive with footsteps, and the
air full of voices. We heard one engine thundering
round a corner, and another rattling from a distance over
the pavements. The bells of three steeples clanged out
at once, spreading the alarm to many a neighboring
town, and expressing hurry, confusion, and terror, so
inimitably that I could almost distinguish in their peal
the burden of the universal cry, — "Fire! Fire! Fire!"

"What is so eloquent as their iron tongues!" exclaimed Oberon. "My heart leaps and trembles, but
not with fear. And that other sound, too, – deep and
awful as a mighty organ, — the roar and thunder of the
multitude on the pavement below! Come! We are

losing time. I will cry out in the loudest of the uproar, and mingle my spirit with the wildest of the confusion, and be a bubble on the top of the ferment!"

From the first outcry, my forebodings had warned me of the true object and centre of alarm. There was nothing now but uproar, above, beneath, and around us; footsteps stumbling pell-mell up the public staircase, eager shouts and heavy thumps at the door, the whiz and dash of water from the engines, and the crash of furniture thrown upon the pavement. At once, the truth flashed upon my friend. His frenzy took the hue of joy, and, with a wild gesture of exultation, he leaped almost to the ceiling of the chamber.

"My tales!" cried Oberon. "The chimney! The roof! The Fiend has gone forth by night, and startled thousands in fear and wonder from their beds! Here I stand, — a triumphant author! Huzza! Huzza! My brain has set the town on fire! Huzza!"

JOHN INGLEFIELD'S THANKSGIVING.

ON the evening of Thanksgiving day, John Inglefield, the blacksmith, sat in his elbow-chair, among those who had been keeping festival at his board. Being the central figure of the domestic circle, the fire threw its strongest light on his massive and sturdy frame, reddening his rough visage, so that it looked like the head of an iron statue, all aglow, from his own forge, and with its features rudely fashioned on his own anvil. At John Inglefield's right hand was an empty chair. The other places round the hearth were filled by the members of the family, who all sat quietly, while, with a semblance of fantastic merriment, their shadows danced on the wall behind them. One of the group was John Inglefield's son, who had been bred at college, and was now a student of theology at Andover. There was also a daughter of sixteen, whom nobody could look at without thinking of a rosebud almost blossomed. The only other person at the fireside was Robert Moore, formerly an apprentice of the blacksmith, but now his journeyman, and who seemed more like an own son of John Inglefield than did the pale and slender student.

Only these four had kept New England's festival beneath that roof. The vacant chair at John Inglefield's right hand was in memory of his wife, whom death had snatched from him since the previous Thanksgiving. With a feeling that few would have looked for in his rough nature, the bereaved husband had himself set the chair in its place next his own; and often did his eye glance thitherward, as if he deemed it possible that the cold grave might send back its tenant to the cheerful fireside, at least for that one evening. Thus did he cherish the grief that was dear to him. But there was another grief which he would fain have torn from his heart; or, since that could never be, have buried it too deep for others to behold, or for his own remembrance. Within the past year another member of his household had gone from him, but not to the grave. Yet they kept no vacant chair for her.

While John Inglefield and his family were sitting round the hearth with the shadows dancing behind them on the wall, the outer door was opened, and a light footstep came along the passage. The latch of the inner door was lifted by some familiar hand, and a young girl came in, wearing a cloak and hood, which she took off, and laid on the table beneath the looking-glass. Then, after gazing a moment at the fireside circle, she approached, and took the seat at John Inglefield's right hand, as if it had been reserved on purpose for her.

"Here I am, at last, father," said she. "You ate your Thanksgiving dinner without me, but I have come back to spend the evening with you."

Yes, it was Prudence Inglefield. She wore the same neat and maidenly attire which she had been accustomed to put on when the household work was over for the day, and her hair was parted from her brow, in the simple and modest fashion that became her best of all. If her cheek might otherwise have been pale, yet the glow of the fire suffused it with a healthful bloom. If she had spent the many months of her absence in guilt and infamy, yet they seemed to have left no traces on her gentle aspect. She could not have looked less altered, had she merely stepped away from her father's fireside for half an hour, and returned while the blaze was quivering upwards from the same brands that were burning at her departure. And to John Inglefield she was the very image of his buried wife, such as he remembered her on the first Thanksgiving which they had passed under their own roof. Therefore, though naturally a stern and rugged man, he could not speak unkindly to his sinful child, nor yet could he take her to his bosom.

"You are welcome home, Prudence," said he, glancing sideways at her, and his voice faltered. "Your mother would have rejoiced to see you, but she has been gone from us these four months."

"I know it, father, I know it," replied Prudence, quickly. "And yet, when I first came in, my eyes were so dazzled by the firelight, that she seemed to be sitting in this very chair!"

By this time the other members of the family had begun to recover from their surprise, and became sensible that it was no ghost from the grave, nor vision of their vivid recollections, but Prudence, her own self. Her brother was the next that greeted her. He advanced and held out his hand affectionately, as a brother should; yet not entirely like a brother, for, with all his kindness, he was still a clergyman, and speaking to a child of sin.

"Sister Prudence," said he, earnestly, "I rejoice that a merciful Providence hath turned your steps homeward, in time for me to bid you a last farewell. In a few weeks, sister, I am to sail as a missionary to the far islands of the Pacific. There is not one of these beloved faces that I shall ever hope to behold again on this earth. O, may I see all of them — yours and all — beyond the grave!"

A shadow flitted across the girl's countenance.

"The grave is very dark, brother," answered she, withdrawing her hand somewhat hastily from his grasp. "You must look your last at me by the light of this fire."

While this was passing, the twin-girl — the rosebud that had grown on the same stem with the castaway — stood gazing at her sister, longing to fling herself upon her bosom, so that the tendrils of their hearts might intertwine again. At first she was restrained by mingled grief and shame, and by a dread that Prudence was too much changed to respond to her affection, or that her own purity would be felt as a reproach by the lost one. But, as she listened to the familiar voice, while the face grew more and more familiar, she forgot everything save that Prudence had come back. Springing forward, she would have clasped her in a close embrace. At that very instant, however, Prudence started from her chair, and held out both her hands, with a warning gesture.

"No, Mary, — no, my sister," cried she, "do not you touch me. Your bosom must not be pressed to mine!"

Mary shuddered and stood still, for she felt that something darker than the grave was between Prudence and herself, though they seemed so near each other in the light of their father's hearth, where they had grown up together. Meanwhile Prudence threw her eyes around the room, in search of one who had not yet bidden her welcome. He had withdrawn from his seat by the fireside, and was standing near the door, with his face averted, so that his features could be discerned only by

the flickering shadow of the profile upon the wall.   But
Prudence called to him, in a cheerful and kindly tone : —

"Come, Robert," said she, "won't you shake hands
with your old friend ? "

Robert Moore held back for a moment, but affection
struggled powerfully, and overcame his pride and resent-
ment ; he rushed towards Prudence, seized her hand,
and pressed it to his bosom.

"There, there, Robert ! " said she, smiling sadly, as
she withdrew her hand, "you must not give me too
warm a welcome."

And now, having exchanged greetings with each member of the family, Prudence again seated herself in the
chair at John Inglefield's right hand.   She was naturally a girl of quick and tender sensibilities, gladsome
in her general mood, but with a bewitching pathos inter-
fused among her merriest words and deeds.   It was
remarked of her, too, that she had a faculty, even from
childhood, of throwing her own feelings, like a spell, over
her companions.   Such as she had been in her days of
innocence, so did she appear this evening.   Her friends,
in the surprise and bewilderment of her return, almost
forgot that she had ever left them, or that she had for-
feited any of her claims to their affection.   In the morning, perhaps, they might have looked at her with altered
eyes, but by the Thanksgiving fireside they felt only
that their own Prudence had come back to them, and
were thankful.   John Inglefield's rough visage brightened with the glow of his heart, as it grew warm and
merry within him ; once or twice, even, he laughed
till the room rang again, yet seemed startled by the
echo of his own mirth.   The grave young minister
became as frolicsome as a school-boy.   Mary, too, the
rosebud, forgot that her twin-blossom had ever been

torn from the stem, and trampled in the dust. And as for Robert Moore, he gazed at Prudence with the bashful earnestness of love new-born, while she, with sweet maiden coquetry, half smiled upon and half discouraged him.

In short, it was one of those intervals when sorrow vanishes in its own depth of shadow, and joy starts forth in transitory brightness. When the clock struck eight, Prudence poured out her father's customary draught of herb-tea, which had been steeping by the fireside ever since twilight.

"God bless you, child!" said John Inglefield, as he took the cup from her hand; "you have made your old father happy again. But we miss your mother sadly, Prudence, sadly. It seems as if she ought to be here now."

"Now, father, or never," replied Prudence.

It was now the hour for domestic worship. But while the family were making preparations for this duty, they suddenly perceived that Prudence had put on her cloak and hood, and was lifting the latch of the door.

"Prudence, Prudence! where are you going?" cried they all, with one voice.

As Prudence passed out of the door, she turned towards them, and flung back her hand with a gesture of farewell. But her face was so changed that they hardly recognized it. Sin and evil passions glowed through its comeliness, and wrought a horrible deformity; a smile gleamed in her eyes, as of triumphant mockery, at their surprise and grief.

"Daughter," cried John Inglefield, between wrath and sorrow, "stay and be your father's blessing, or take his curse with you!"

For an instant Prudence lingered and looked back into

the fire-lighted room, while her countenance wore almost the expression as if she were struggling with a fiend, who had power to seize his victim even within the hallowed precincts of her father's hearth. The fiend prevailed; and Prudence vanished into the outer darkness. When the family rushed to the door, they could see nothing, but heard the sound of wheels rattling over the frozen ground.

That same night, among the painted beauties at the theatre of a neighboring city, there was one whose dissolute mirth seemed inconsistent with any sympathy for pure affections, and for the joys and griefs which are hallowed by them. Yet this was Prudence Inglefield. Her visit to the Thanksgiving fireside was the realization of one of those waking dreams in which the guilty soul will sometimes stray back to its innocence. But Sin, alas! is careful of her bond-slaves; they hear her voice, perhaps, at the holiest moment, and are constrained to go whither she summons them. The same dark power that drew Prudence Inglefield from her father's hearth — the same in its nature, though heightened then to a dread necessity — would snatch a guilty soul from the gate of heaven, and make its sin and its punishment alike eternal.

OLD TICONDEROGA.

A PICTURE OF THE PAST.

THE greatest attraction, in this vicinity, is the famous old fortress of Ticonderoga, the remains of which are visible from the piazza of the tavern, on a swell of land that shuts in the prospect of the lake. Those celebrated heights, Mount Defiance and Mount Independence, familiar to all Americans in history, stand too prominent not to be recognized, though neither of them precisely corresponds to the images excited by their names. In truth, the whole scene, except the interior of the fortress, disappointed me. Mount Defiance, which one pictures as a steep, lofty, and rugged hill, of most formidable aspect, frowning down with the grim visage of a precipice on old Ticonderoga, is merely a long and wooded ridge; and bore, at some former period, the gentle name of Sugar Hill. The brow is certainly difficult to climb, and high enough to look into every corner of the fortress. St. Clair's most probable reason, however, for neglecting to occupy it, was the deficiency of troops to man the works already constructed, rather than the supposed inaccessibility of Mount Defiance. It is singular that the French never fortified this height, standing, as it does, in the quarter whence they must have looked for the advance of a British army.

In my first view of the ruins, I was favored with the scientific guidance of a young lieutenant of engineers, recently from West Point, where he had gained credit for great military genius. I saw nothing but confusion in what chiefly interested him; straight lines and zigzags, defence within defence, wall opposed to wall, and ditch intersecting ditch; oblong squares of masonry below the surface of the earth, and huge mounds, or turf-covered hills of stone, above it. On one of these artificial hillocks, a pine-tree has rooted itself, and grown tall and strong, since the banner-staff was levelled. But where my unmilitary glance could trace no regularity, the young lieutenant was perfectly at home. He fathomed the meaning of every ditch, and formed an entire plan of the fortress from its half-obliterated lines. His description of Ticonderoga would be as accurate as a geometrical theorem, and as barren of the poetry that has clustered round its decay. I viewed Ticonderoga as a place of ancient strength, in ruins for half a century: where the flags of three nations had successively waved, and none waved now; where armies had struggled, so long ago that the bones of the slain were mouldered; where Peace had found a heritage in the forsaken haunts of War. Now the young West-Pointer, with his lectures on ravelins, counterscarps, angles, and covered ways, made it an affair of brick and mortar and hewn stone, arranged on certain regular principles, having a good deal to do with mathematics, but nothing at all with poetry.

I should have been glad of a hoary veteran to totter by my side, and tell me, perhaps, of the French garrisons and their Indian allies, — of Abercrombie, Lord Howe, and Amherst, — of Ethan Allen's triumph and St. Clair's surrender. The old soldier and the old fortress would be emblems of each other. His reminiscences, though

N

vivid as the image of Ticonderoga in the lake, would
harmonize with the gray influence of the scene. A survivor of the long-disbanded garrisons, though but a
private soldier, might have mustered his dead chiefs and
comrades, — some from Westminster Abbey, and English churchyards, and battle-fields in Europe, — others
from their graves here in America, — others, not a few,
who lie sleeping round the fortress; he might have
mustered them all, and bid them march through the
ruined gateway, turning their old historic faces on me, as
they passed. Next to such a companion, the best is one's
own fancy.

At another visit I was alone, and, after rambling all
over the ramparts, sat down to rest myself in one of the
roofless barracks. These are old French structures, and
appear to have occupied three sides of a large area, now
overgrown with grass, nettles, and thistles. The one in
which I sat was long and narrow, as all the rest had
been, with peaked gables. The exterior walls were
nearly entire, constructed of gray, flat, unpicked stones,
the aged strength of which promised long to resist the
elements, if no other violence should precipitate their
fall. The roof, floors, partitions, and the rest of the
wood-work had probably been burnt, except some bars
of stanch old oak, which were blackened with fire, but
still remained imbedded into the window-sills and over
the doors. There were a few particles of plastering near
the chimney, scratched with rude figures, perhaps by a
soldier's hand. A most luxuriant crop of weeds had
sprung up within the edifice, and hid the scattered fragments of the wall. Grass and weeds grew in the windows, and in all the crevices of the stone, climbing, step
by step, till a tuft of yellow flowers was waving on the
highest peak of the gable. Some spicy herb diffused a

pleasant odor through the ruin. A verdant heap of vegetation had covered the hearth of the second floor, clustering on the very spot where the huge logs had mouldered to glowing coals, and flourished beneath the broad flue, which had so often puffed the smoke over a circle of French or English soldiers. I felt that there was no other token of decay so impressive as that bed of weeds in the place of the backlog.

Here I sat, with those roofless walls about me, the clear sky over my head, and the afternoon sunshine falling gently bright through the window-frames and doorway. I heard the tinkling of a cow-bell, the twittering of birds, and the pleasant hum of insects. Once a gay butterfly, with four gold-speckled wings, came and fluttered about my head, then flew up and lighted on the highest tuft of yellow flowers, and at last took wing across the lake. Next a bee buzzed through the sunshine, and found much sweetness among the weeds. After watching him till he went off to his distant hive, I closed my eyes on Ticonderoga in ruins, and cast a dream-like glance over pictures of the past, and scenes of which this spot had been the theatre.

At first, my fancy saw only the stern hills, lonely lakes, and venerable woods. Not a tree, since their seeds were first scattered over the infant soil, had felt the axe, but had grown up and flourished through its long generation, had fallen beneath the weight of years, been buried in green moss, and nourished the roots of others as gigantic. Hark! A light paddle dips into the lake, a birch canoe glides round the point, and an Indian chief has passed, painted and feather-crested, armed with a bow of hickory, a stone tomahawk, and flint-headed arrows. But the ripple had hardly vanished from the water, when a white flag caught the breeze, over a castle in the wilderness, with frowning ramparts and a hundred cannon. There stood a French chevalier, commandant of the fortress, paying court to a copper-colored lady, the princess of the land, and winning her wild love by the arts which had been successful with Parisian dames. A war-party of French and Indians were issuing from the gate to lay waste some village of New England. Near the fortress there was a group of dancers. The merry soldiers footing it with the swart savage maids; deeper in the wood, some red men were growing frantic around a keg of the fire-water; and elsewhere a Jesuit preached the faith of high cathedrals beneath a canopy of forest boughs, and distributed crucifixes to be worn beside English scalps.

I tried to make a series of pictures from the old French war, when fleets were on the lake and armies in the woods, and especially of Abercrombie's disastrous repulse, where thousands of lives were utterly thrown away; but, being at a loss how to order the battle, I chose an evening scene in the barracks, after the fortress had surrendered to Sir Jeffrey Amherst. What an immense fire blazes on that hearth, gleaming on swords, bayonets, and musket-barrels, and blending with the hue of the scarlet coats till the whole barrack-room is quivering with ruddy light! One soldier has thrown himself down to rest, after a deer-hunt, or perhaps a long run through the woods with Indians on his trail. Two stand up to wrestle, and are on the point of coming to blows. A fifer plays a shrill accompaniment to a drummer's song, — a strain of light love and bloody war, with a chorus thundered forth by twenty voices. Meantime, a veteran in the corner is prosing about Dettingen and Fontenoye, and relates camp-traditions of Marlborough's battles, till his pipe, having been roguishly charged with gunpowder, makes a terrible explosion under his nose. And now they all vanish in a puff of smoke from the chimney.

I merely glanced at the ensuing twenty years, which glided peacefully over the frontier fortress, till Ethan Allen's shout was heard, summoning it to surrender "in the name of the great Jehovah and of the Continental Congress." Strange allies! thought the British captain. Next came the hurried muster of the soldiers of liberty, when the cannon of Burgoyne, pointing down upon their stronghold from the brow of Mount Defiance, announced a new conqueror of Ticonderoga. No virgin fortress, this! Forth rushed the motley throng from the barracks, one man wearing the blue and buff of the Union, another the red coat of Britain, a third a dragoon's jacket, and a fourth a cotton frock; here was a pair of leather breeches, and striped trousers there; a grenadier's cap on one head, and a broad-brimmed hat, with a tall feather, on the next; this fellow shouldering a king's arm, that might throw a bullet to Crown Point, and his comrade a long fowling-piece, admirable to shoot ducks on the lake. In the midst of the bustle, when the fortress was all alive with its last warlike scene, the ringing of a bell on the lake made me suddenly unclose my eyes, and behold only the gray and weed-grown ruins. They were as peaceful in the sun as a warrior's grave.

Hastening to the rampart, I perceived that the signal had been given by the steamboat Franklin, which landed a passenger from Whitehall at the tavern, and resumed its progress northward, to reach Canada the next morning. A sloop was pursuing the same track; a little skiff had just crossed the ferry; while a scow, laden with lumber, spread its huge square sail, and went up the lake. The whole country was a cultivated farm. Within musket-shot of the ramparts lay the neat villa of Mr. Pell, who, since the Revolution, has become proprietor of a spot for which France, England, and America have so often struggled. How forcibly the lapse of time and change of circumstances came home to my apprehension. Banner would never wave again, nor cannon roar, nor blood be shed, nor trumpet stir up a soldier's heart, in this old fort of Ticonderoga. Tall trees have grown upon its ramparts, since the last garrison marched out, to return no more, or only at some dreamer's summons, gliding from the twilight past to vanish among realites.

THE WIVES OF THE DEAD.

HE following story, the simple and domestic in-
cidents of which may be deemed scarcely worth
relating, after such a lapse of time, awakened
some degree of interest, a hundred years ago, in a principal seaport of the Bay Province. The rainy twilight of
an autumn day, — a parlor on the second floor of a small
house, plainly furnished, as beseemed the middling circumstances of its inhabitants, yet decorated with little
curiosities from beyond the sea, and a few delicate specimens of Indian manufacture, — these are the only partic-
ulars to be premised in regard to scene and season. Two
young and comely women sat together by the fireside,
nursing their mutual and peculiar sorrows. They were
the recent brides of two brothers, a sailor and a landsman,
and two successive days had brought tidings of the death
of each, by the chances of Canadian warfare and the tempestuous Atlantic. The universal sympathy excited by
this bereavement drew numerous condoling guests to the
habitation of the widowed sisters. Several, among whom
was the minister, had remained till the verge of evening;
when, one by one, whispering many comfortable passages of Scripture, that were answered by more abundant
tears, they took their leave, and departed to their own
happier homes. The mourners, though not insensible to

the kindness of their friends, had yearned to be left alone. United, as they had been, by the relationship of the living, and now more closely so by that of the dead, each felt as if whatever consolation her grief admitted were to be found in the bosom of the other. They joined their hearts, and wept together silently. But after an hour of such indulgence, one of the sisters, all of whose emotions were influenced by her mild, quiet, yet not feeble character, began to recollect the precepts of resignation and endurance which piety had taught her, when she did not think to need them. Her misfortune, besides, as earliest known, should earliest cease to interfere with her regular course of duties; accordingly, having placed the table before the fire, and arranged a frugal meal, she took the hand of her companion.

"Come, dearest sister; you have eaten not a morsel to-day," she said. "Arise, I pray you, and let us ask a blessing on that which is provided for us."

Her sister-in-law was of a lively and irritable temperament, and the first pangs of her sorrow had been expressed by shrieks and passionate lamentation. She now shrunk from Mary's words, like a wounded sufferer from a hand that revives the throb.

"There is no blessing left for me, neither will I ask it!" cried Margaret, with a fresh burst of tears. "Would it were His will that I might never taste food more!"

Yet she trembled at these rebellious expressions, almost as soon as they were uttered, and, by degrees, Mary succeeded in bringing her sister's mind nearer to the situation of her own. Time went on, and their usual hour of repose arrived. The brothers and their brides, entering the married state with no more than the slender means which then sanctioned such a step, had confederated themselves in one household, with equal rights to the parlor, and claiming exclusive privileges in two sleeping-rooms contiguous to it. Thither the widowed ones retired, after heaping ashes upon the dying embers of their fire, and placing a lighted lamp upon the hearth. The doors of both chambers were left open, so that a part of the interior of each, and the beds with their unclosed curtains, were reciprocally visible. Sleep did not steal upon the sisters at one and the same time. Mary experienced the effect often consequent upon grief quietly borne, and soon sunk into temporary forgetfulness, while Margaret became more disturbed and feverish, in proportion as the night advanced with its deepest and stillest hours. She lay listening to the drops of rain, that came down in monotonous succession, unswayed by a breath of wind; and a nervous impulse continually caused her to lift her head from the pillow, and gaze into Mary's chamber and the intermediate apartment. The cold light of the lamp threw the shadows of the furniture up against the wall, stamping them immovably there, except when they were shaken by a sudden flicker of the flame. Two vacant arm-chairs were in their old positions on opposite sides of the hearth, where the brothers had been wont to sit in young and laughing dignity, as heads of families; two humbler seats were near them, the true thrones of that little empire, where Mary and herself had exercised in love a power that love had won. The cheerful radiance of the fire had shone upon the happy circle, and the dead glimmer of the lamp might have befitted their reunion now. While Margaret groaned in bitterness, she heard a knock at the street-door.

"How would my heart have leapt at that sound but yesterday!" thought she, remembering the anxiety with which she had long awaited tidings from her husband.

10

"I care not for it now; let them begone, for I will not arise."

But even while a sort of childish fretfulness made her thus resolve, she was breathing hurriedly, and straining her ears to catch a repetition of the summons. It is difficult to be convinced of the death of one whom we have deemed another self. The knocking was now renewed in slow and regular strokes, apparently given with the soft end of a doubled fist, and was accompanied by words, faintly heard through several thicknesses of wall. Margaret looked to her sister's chamber, and beheld her still lying in the depths of sleep. She arose, placed her foot upon the floor, and slightly arrayed herself, trembling between fear and eagerness as she did so.

"Heaven help me!" sighed she. "I have nothing left to fear, and methinks I am ten times more a coward than ever."

Seizing the lamp from the hearth, she hastened to the window that overlooked the street-door. It was a lattice, turning upon hinges; and having thrown it back, she stretched her head a little way into the moist atmosphere. A lantern was reddening the front of the house, and melting its light in the neighboring puddles, while a deluge of darkness overwhelmed every other object. As the window grated on its hinges, a man in a broad-brimmed hat and blanket-coat stepped from under the shelter of the projecting story, and looked upward to discover whom his application had aroused. Margaret knew him as a friendly innkeeper of the town.

"What would you have, Goodman Parker?" cried the widow.

"Lackaday, is it you, Mistress Margaret?" replied the innkeeper. "I was afraid it might be your sister

Mary; for I hate to see a young woman in trouble, when I have n't a word of comfort to whisper her."

"For Heaven's sake, what news do you bring?" screamed Margaret.

"Why, there has been an express through the town within this half-hour," said Goodman Parker, "travelling from the eastern jurisdiction with letters from the governor and council. He tarried at my house to refresh himself with a drop and a morsel, and I asked him what tidings on the frontiers. He tells me we had the better in the skirmish you wot of, and that thirteen men reported slain are well and sound, and your husband among them. Besides, he is appointed of the escort to bring the captivated Frenchers and Indians home to the province jail. I judged you would n't mind being broke of your rest, and so I stepped over to tell you. Good night."

So saying, the honest man departed; and his lantern gleamed along the street, bringing to view indistinct shapes of things, and the fragments of a world, like order glimmering through chaos, or memory roaming over the past. But Margaret stayed not to watch these picturesque effects. Joy flashed into her heart, and lighted it up at once; and breathless, and with winged steps, she flew to the bedside of her sister. She paused, however, at the door of the chamber, while a thought of pain broke in upon her.

"Poor Mary!" said she to herself. "Shall I waken her, to feel her sorrow sharpened by my happiness? No; I will keep it within my own bosom till the morrow."

She approached the bed, to discover if Mary's sleep were peaceful. Her face was turned partly inward to the pillow, and had been hidden there to weep; but a look of motionless contentment was now visible upon it,

as if her heart, like a deep lake, had grown calm because
its dead had sunk down so far within.   Happy is it, and
strange, that the lighter sorrows are those from which
dreams are chiefly fabricated.   Margaret shrunk from
disturbing her sister-in-law, and felt as if her own better
fortune had rendered her involuntarily unfaithful, and
as if altered and diminished affection must be the consequence of the disclosure she had to make.   With a
sudden step she turned away.   But joy could not long
be repressed, even by circumstances that would have
excited heavy grief at another moment.   Her mind was
thronged with delightful thoughts, till sleep stole on, and
transformed them to visions, more delightful and more
wild, like the breath of winter (but what a cold comparison!) working fantastic tracery upon a window.

When the night was far advanced, Mary awoke with
a sudden start.   A vivid dream had latterly involved
her in its unreal life, of which, however, she could only
remember that it had been broken in upon at the most
interesting point.   For a little time, slumber hung about
her like a morning mist, hindering her from perceiving
the distinct outline of her situation.   She listened with
imperfect consciousness to two or three volleys of a rapid
and eager knocking; and first she deemed the noise a
matter of course, like the breath she drew; next, it
appeared a thing in which she had no concern; and
lastly, she became aware that it was a summons necessary to be obeyed.   At the same moment, the pang of
recollection darted into her mind; the pall of sleep was
thrown back from the face of grief; the dim light of the
chamber, and the objects therein revealed, had retained
all her suspended ideas, and restored them as soon as
she unclosed her eyes.   Again there was a quick peal
upon the street-door.   Fearing that her sister would also

be disturbed, Mary wrapped herself in a cloak and hood, took the lamp from the hearth, and hastened to the window. By some accident, it had been left unhasped, and yielded easily to her hand.

"Who's there?" asked Mary, trembling as she looked forth.

The storm was over, and the moon was up; it shone upon broken clouds above, and below upon houses black with moisture, and upon little lakes of the fallen rain, curling into silver beneath the quick enchantment of a breeze. A young man in a sailor's dress, wet as if he had come out of the depths of the sea, stood alone under the window. Mary recognized him as one whose livelihood was gained by short voyages along the coast; nor did she forget that, previous to her marriage, he had been an unsuccessful wooer of her own.

"What do you seek here, Stephen?" said she.

"Cheer up, Mary, for I seek to comfort you," answered the rejected lover. "You must know I got home not ten minutes ago, and the first thing my good mother told me was the news about your husband. So, without saying a word to the old woman, I clapped on my hat, and ran out of the house. I could n't have slept a wink before speaking to you, Mary, for the sake of old times."

"Stephen, I thought better of you!" exclaimed the widow, with gushing tears and preparing to close the lattice; for she was no whit inclined to imitate the first wife of Zadig.

"But stop, and hear my story out," cried the young sailor. "I tell you we spoke a brig yesterday afternoon, bound in from Old England. And who do you think I saw standing on deck, well and hearty, only a bit thinner than he was five months ago?"

Mary leaned from the window, but could not speak.

"Why, it was your husband himself," continued the generous seaman. "He and three others saved themselves on a spar, when the Blessing turned bottom upwards. The brig will beat into the bay by daylight, with this wind, and you'll see him here to-morrow. There's the comfort I bring you, Mary, and so good night."

He hurried away, while Mary watched him with a doubt of waking reality, that seemed stronger or weaker as he alternately entered the shade of the houses, or emerged into the broad streaks of moonlight. Gradually, however, a blessed flood of conviction swelled into her heart, in strength enough to overwhelm her, had its increase been more abrupt. Her first impulse was to rouse her sister-in-law, and communicate the new-born gladness. She opened the chamber-door, which had been closed in the course of the night, though not latched, advanced to the bedside, and was about to lay her hand upon the slumberer's shoulder. But then she remembered that Margaret would awake to thoughts of death and woe, rendered not the less bitter by their contrast with her own felicity. She suffered the rays of the lamp to fall upon the unconscious form of the bereaved one. Margaret lay in unquiet sleep, and the drapery was displaced around her; her young cheek was rosy-tinted, and her lips half opened in a vivid smile; an expression of joy, debarred its passage by her sealed eyelids, struggled forth like incense from the whole countenance.

"My poor sister! you will waken too soon from that happy dream," thought Mary.

Before retiring, she set down the lamp, and endeavored to arrange the bedclothes so that the chill air might not do harm to the feverish slumberer. But her hand trembled against Margaret's neck, a tear also fell upon her cheek, and she suddenly awoke.

LITTLE DAFFYDOWNDILLY.

DAFFYDOWNDILLY was so called because in his nature he resembled a flower, and loved to do only what was beautiful and agreeable, and took no delight in labor of any kind. But, while Daffydowndilly was yet a little boy, his mother sent him away from his pleasant home, and put him under the care of a very strict schoolmaster, who went by the name of Mr. Toil. Those who knew him best affirmed that this Mr. Toil was a very worthy character; and that he had done more good, both to children and grown people, than anybody else in the world. Certainly he had lived long enough to do a great deal of good; for, if all stories be true, he had dwelt upon earth ever since Adam was driven from the garden of Eden.

Nevertheless, Mr. Toil had a severe and ugly countenance, especially for such little boys or big men as were inclined to be idle; his voice, too, was harsh; and all his ways and customs seemed very disagreeable to our friend Daffydowndilly. The whole day long, this terrible old schoolmaster sat at his desk overlooking the scholars, or stalked about the school-room with a certain awful birch rod in his hand. Now came a rap over the shoulders of a boy whom Mr. Toil had caught at play; now he punished a whole class who were behindhand

with their lessons; and, in short, unless a lad chose to
attend quietly and constantly to his book, he had no
chance of enjoying a quiet moment in the school-room
of Mr. Toil.

"This will never do for me," thought Daffydowndilly.

Now, the whole of Daffydowndilly's life had hitherto
been passed with his dear mother, who had a much
sweeter face than old Mr. Toil, and who had always
been very indulgent to her little boy.   No wonder,
therefore, that poor Daffydowndilly found it a woful
change, to be sent away from the good lady's side, and
put under the care of this ugly-visaged schoolmaster,
who never gave him any apples or cakes, and seemed
to think that little boys were created only to get lessons.

"I can't bear it any longer," said Daffydowndilly to
himself, when he had been at school about a week.   "I'll
run away, and try to find my dear mother; and, at any
rate, I shall never find anybody half so disagreeable as
this old Mr. Toil!"

So, the very next morning, off started poor Daffydowndilly, and began his rambles about the world, with only
some bread and cheese for his breakfast, and very little
pocket-money to pay his expenses.   But he had gone
only a short distance, when he overtook a man of grave
and sedate appearance, who was trudging at a moderate
pace along the road.

"Good morning, my fine lad," said the stranger; and
his voice seemed hard and severe, but yet had a sort
of kindness in it; "whence do you come so early, and
whither are you going?"

Little Daffydowndilly was a boy of very ingenuous disposition, and had never been known to tell a lie in all
his life.   Nor did he tell one now.   He hesitated a
moment or two, but finally confessed that he had run

away from school, on account of his great dislike to
Mr. Toil; and that he was resolved to find some place
in the world where he should never see or hear of the
old schoolmaster again.

"O, very well, my little friend!" answered the stranger. "Then we will go together; for I, likewise, have
had a good deal to do with Mr. Toil, and should be glad
to find some place where he was never heard of."

Our friend Daffydowndilly would have been better
pleased with a companion of his own age, with whom
he might have gathered flowers along the roadside, or
have chased butterflies, or have done many other things
to make the journey pleasant. But he had wisdom
enough to understand that he should get along through
the world much easier by having a man of experience
to show him the way. So he accepted the stranger's
proposal, and they walked on very sociably together.

They had not gone far, when the road passed by a
field where some haymakers were at work, mowing
down the tall grass, and spreading it out in the sun
to dry. Daffydowndilly was delighted with the sweet
smell of the new-mown grass, and thought how much
pleasanter it must be to make hay in the sunshine, under
the blue sky, and with the birds singing sweetly in the
neighboring trees and bushes, than to be shut up in a
dismal school-room, learning lessons all day long, and
continually scolded by old Mr. Toil. But, in the midst
of these thoughts, while he was stopping to peep over
the stone wall, he started back and caught hold of his
companion's hand.

"Quick, quick!" cried he. "Let us run away, or he
will catch us!"

"Who will catch us?" asked the stranger.

"Mr. Toil, the old schoolmaster!" answered Daffy-

10 *   o

downdilly. "Don't you see him amongst the hay-makers?"

And Daffydowndilly pointed to an elderly man, who seemed to be the owner of the field, and the employer of the men at work there. He had stripped off his coat and waistcoat, and was busily at work in his shirt-sleeves. The drops of sweat stood upon his brow; but he gave himself not a moment's rest, and kept crying out to the haymakers to make hay while the sun shone. Now, strange to say, the figure and features of this old farmer were precisely the same as those of old Mr. Toil, who, at that very moment, must have been just entering his school-room.

"Don't be afraid," said the stranger. "This is not Mr. Toil the schoolmaster, but a brother of his, who was bred a farmer; and people say he is the most disagreeable man of the two. However, he won't trouble you, unless you become a laborer on the farm."

Little Daffydowndilly believed what his companion said, but was very glad, nevertheless, when they were out of sight of the old farmer, who bore such a singular resemblance to Mr. Toil. The two travellers had gone but little farther, when they came to a spot where some carpenters were erecting a house. Daffydowndilly begged his companion to stop a moment; for it was a very pretty sight to see how neatly the carpenters did their work, with their broad-axes, and saws, and planes, and hammers, shaping out the doors, and putting in the window-sashes, and nailing on the clapboards; and he could not help thinking that he should like to take a broad-axe, a saw, a plane, and a hammer, and build a little house for himself. And then, when he should have a house of his own, old Mr. Toil would never dare to molest him.

But, just while he was delighting himself with this

idea, little Daffydowndilly beheld something that made him catch hold of his companion's hand, all in a fright.

"Make haste. Quick, quick!" cried he. "There he is again!"

"Who?" asked the stranger, very quietly.

"Old Mr. Toil," said Daffydowndilly, trembling. "There! he that is overseeing the carpenters. 'T is my old schoolmaster, as sure as I 'm alive!"

The stranger cast his eyes where Daffydowndilly pointed his finger; and he saw an elderly man, with a carpenter's rule and compasses in his hand. This person went to and fro about the unfinished house, measuring pieces of timber, and marking out the work that was to be done, and continually exhorting the other carpenters to be diligent. And wherever he turned his hard and wrinkled visage, the men seemed to feel that they had a task-master over them, and sawed, and hammered, and planed, as if for dear life.

"O no! this is not Mr. Toil, the schoolmaster," said the stranger. "It is another brother of his, who follows the trade of carpenter."

"I am very glad to hear it," quoth Daffydowndilly; "but if you please, sir, I should like to get out of his way as soon as possible."

Then they went on a little farther, and soon heard the sound of a drum and fife. Daffydowndilly pricked up his ears at this, and besought his companion to hurry forward, that they might not miss seeing the soldiers. Accordingly, they made what haste they could, and soon met a company of soldiers, gayly dressed, with beautiful feathers in their caps, and bright muskets on their shoulders. In front marched two drummers and two fifers, beating on their drums and playing on their fifes with might and main, and making such lively music that little

Daffydowndilly would gladly have followed them to the
end of the world. And if he was only a soldier, then,
he said to himself, old Mr. Toil would never venture to
look him in the face.

"Quick step! Forward march!" shouted a gruff
voice.

Little Daffydowndilly started, in great dismay; for
this voice which had spoken to the soldiers sounded
precisely the same as that which he had heard every
day in Mr. Toil's school-room, out of Mr. Toil's own
mouth. And, turning his eyes to the captain of the
company, what should he see but the very image of old
Mr. Toil himself, with a smart cap and feather on his
head, a pair of gold epaulets on his shoulders, a laced
coat on his back, a purple sash round his waist, and
a long sword, instead of a birch rod, in his hand. And
though he held his head so high, and strutted like a
turkey-cock, still he looked quite as ugly and disagreeable as when he was hearing lessons in the school-
room.

"This is certainly old Mr. Toil," said Daffydowndilly,
in a trembling voice. "Let us run away, for fear he
should make us enlist in his company!"

"You are mistaken again, my little friend," replied
the stranger, very composedly. "This is not Mr. Toil,
the schoolmaster, but a brother of his, who has served
in the army all his life. People say he's a terribly
severe fellow; but you and I need not be afraid of
him."

"Well, well," said little Daffydowndilly, "but, if you
please, sir, I don't went to see the soldiers any more."

So the child and the stranger resumed their journey;
and, by and by, they came to a house by the roadside,
where a number of people were making merry. Young

men and rosy-cheeked girls, with smiles on their faces, were dancing to the sound of a fiddle. It was the pleas-antest sight that Daffydowndilly had yet met with; and it comforted him for all his disappointments.

"O, let us stop here," cried he to his companion; "for Mr. Toil will never dare to show his face where there is a fiddler, and where people are dancing and making merry. We shall be quite safe here!"

But these last words died away upon Daffydowndilly's tongue; for, happening to cast his eyes on the fiddler, whom should he behold again, but the likeness of Mr. Toil, holding a fiddle-bow instead of a birch rod, and flourishing it with as much ease and dexterity as if he had been a fiddler all his life! He had somewhat the air of a Frenchman, but still looked exactly like the old schoolmaster; and Daffydowndilly even fancied that he nodded and winked at him, and made signs for him to join in the dance.

"O dear me!" whispered he, turning pale. "It seems as if there was nobody but Mr. Toil in the world. Who could have thought of his playing on a fiddle!"

"This is not your old schoolmaster," observed the stranger, "but another brother of his, who was bred in France, where he learned the profession of a fiddler. He is ashamed of his family, and generally calls himself Monsieur le Plaisir; but his real name is Toil, and those who have known him best think him still more disagree-able than his brothers."

"Pray let us go a little farther," said Daffydowndilly. "I don't like the looks of this fiddler at all."

"Well, thus the stranger and little Daffydowndilly went wandering along the highway, and in shady lanes, and through pleasant villages; and whithersoever they

went, behold! there was the image of old Mr. Toil. He
stood like a scarecrow in the cornfields. If they entered
a house, he sat in the parlor; if they peeped into the
kitchen, he was there. He made himself at home in
every cottage, and stole, under one disguise or another,
into the most splendid mansions. Everywhere there
was sure to be somebody wearing the likeness of Mr.
Toil, and who, as the stranger affirmed, was one of the
old schoolmaster's innumerable brethren.

Little Daffydowndilly was almost tired to death, when
he perceived some people reclining lazily in a shady
place, by the side of the road. The poor child entreated
his companion that they might sit down there, and take
some repose.

"Old Mr. Toil will never come here," said he; "for
he hates to see people taking their ease."

But, even while he spoke, Daffydowndilly's eyes fell
upon a person who seemed the laziest, and heaviest, and
most torpid of all those lazy and heavy and torpid
people who had lain down to sleep in the shade. Who
should it be, again, but the very image of Mr. Toil!

"There is a large family of these Toils," remarked
the stranger. "This is another of the old schoolmaster's
brothers, who was bred in Italy, where he acquired very
idle habits, and goes by the name of Signor Far Niente.
He pretends to lead an easy life, but is really the most
miserable fellow in the family."

"O, take me back! — take me back!" cried poor
little Daffydowndilly, bursting into tears. "If there is
nothing but Toil all the world over, I may just as well go
back to the school-house!"

"Yonder it is, — there is the school-house!" said the
stranger; for though he and little Daffydowndilly had
taken a great many steps, they had travelled in a circle,

instead of a straight line. "Come; we will go back to school together."

There was something in his companion's voice that little Daffydowndilly now remembered; and it is strange that he had not remembered it sooner. Looking up into his face, behold! there again was the likeness of old Mr. Toil; so that the poor child had been in company with Toil all day, even while he was doing his best to run away from him. Some people, to whom I have told little Daffydowndilly's story, are of opinion that old Mr. Toil was a magician, and possessed the power of multiplying himself into as many shapes as he saw fit.

Be this as it may, little Daffydowndilly had learned a good lesson, and from that time forward was diligent at his task, because he knew that diligence is not a whit more toilsome than sport or idleness. And when he became better acquainted with Mr. Toil, he began to think that his ways were not so very disagreeable, and that the old schoolmaster's smile of approbation made his face almost as pleasant as even that of Daffydowndilly's mother.

MY KINSMAN, MAJOR MOLINEUX.

AFTER the kings of Great Britain had assumed the right of appointing the colonial governors, the measures of the latter seldom met with the ready and general approbation which had been paid to those of their predecessors, under the original charters. The people looked with most jealous scrutiny to the exercise of power which did not emanate from themselves, and they usually rewarded their rulers with slender gratitude for the compliances by which, in softening their instructions from beyond the sea, they had incurred the reprehension of those who gave them. The annals of Massachusetts Bay will inform us, that of six governors in the space of about forty years from the surrender of the old charter, under James II., two were imprisoned by a popular insurrection; a third, as Hutchinson inclines to believe, was driven from the province by the whizzing of a musket-ball; a fourth, in the opinion of the same historian, was hastened to his grave by continual bickerings with the House of Representatives; and the remaining two, as well as their successors, till the Revolution, were favored with few and brief intervals of peaceful sway. The inferior members of the court party, in times of high political excitement, led scarcely a more desirable life. These remarks may serve as a preface to the following adventures, which chanced upon a summer night, not far from a hundred years ago. The reader, in order to avoid a long and dry detail of colonial affairs, is requested to dispense with an account of the train of circumstances that had caused much temporary inflammation of the popular mind.

It was near nine o'clock of a moonlight evening, when a boat crossed the ferry with a single passenger, who had obtained his conveyance at that unusual hour by the promise of an extra fare. While he stood on the landing-place, searching in either pocket for the means of fulfilling his agreement, the ferryman lifted a lantern, by the aid of which, and the newly risen moon, he took a very accurate survey of the stranger's figure. He was a youth of barely eighteen years, evidently country-bred, and now, as it should seem, upon his first visit to town. He was clad in a coarse gray coat, well worn, but in excellent repair; his under garments were durably constructed of leather, and fitted tight to a pair of serviceable and well-shaped limbs; his stockings of blue yarn were the incontrovertible work of a mother or a sister; and on his head was a three-cornered hat, which in its better days had perhaps sheltered the graver brow of the lad's father. Under his left arm was a heavy cudgel, formed of an oak sapling, and retaining a part of the hardened root; and his equipment was completed by a wallet, not so abundantly stocked as to incommode the vigorous shoulders on which it hung. Brown, curly hair, well-shaped features, and bright, cheerful eyes were nature's gifts, and worth all that art could have done for his adornment.

The youth, one of whose names was Robin, finally drew from his pocket the half of a little province bill of five shillings, which, in the depreciation of that sort of currency, did but satisfy the ferryman's demand, with

the surplus of a sexangular piece of parchment, valued at
three pence.   He then walked forward into the town,
with as light a step as if his day's journey had not already exceeded thirty miles, and with as eager an eye as
if he were entering London city, instead of the little
metropolis of a New England colony.   Before Robin had
proceeded far, however, it occurred to him that he knew
not whither to direct his steps ; so he paused, and looked
up and down the narrow street, scrutinizing the small
and mean wooden buildings that were scattered on either
side.

"This low hovel cannot be my kinsman's dwelling,"
thought he, "nor yonder old house, where the moonlight
enters at the broken casement; and truly I see none
hereabouts that might be worthy of him.   It would have
been wise to inquire my way of the ferryman, and doubtless he would have gone with me, and earned a shilling
from the Major for his pains.   But the next man I meet
will do as well."

He resumed his walk, and was glad to perceive that the
street now became wider, and the houses more respectable in their appearance.   He soon discerned a figure
moving on moderately in advance, and hastened his steps
to overtake it.   As Robin drew nigh, he saw that the
passenger was a man in years, with a full periwig of gray
hair, a wide-skirted coat of dark cloth, and silk stockings
rolled above his knees.   He carried a long and polished
cane, which he struck down perpendicularly before him,
at every step ; and at regular intervals he uttered two
successive hems, of a peculiarly solemn and sepulchral
intonation.   Having made these observations, Robin laid
hold of the skirt of the old man's coat, just when the
light from the open door and windows of a barber's shop
fell upon both their figures.

"Good evening to you, honored sir, said he, making a low bow, and still retaining his hold of the skirt. "I pray you tell me whereabouts is the dwelling of my kinsman, Major Molineux."

The youth's question was uttered very loudly; and one of the barbers, whose razor was descending on a well-soaped chin, and another who was dressing a Ramillies wig, left their occupations, and came to the door. The citizen, in the mean time, turned a long-favored countenance upon Robin, and answered him in a tone of excessive anger and annoyance. His two sepulchral hems, however, broke into the very centre of his rebuke, with most singular effect, like a thought of the cold grave obtruding among wrathful passions.

"Let go my garment, fellow! I tell you, I know not the man you speak of. What! I have authority, I have — hem, hem — authority; and if this be the respect you show for your betters, your feet shall be brought acquainted with the stocks by daylight, to-morrow morning!"

Robin released the old man's skirt, and hastened away, pursued by an ill-mannered roar of laughter from the barber's shop. He was at first considerably surprised by the result of his question, but, being a shrewd youth, soon thought himself able to account for the mystery.

"This is some country representative," was his conclusion, "who has never seen the inside of my kinsman's door, and lacks the breeding to answer a stranger civilly. The man is old, or verily — I might be tempted to turn back and smite him on the nose. Ah, Robin, Robin! even the barber's boys laugh at you for choosing such a guide! You will be wiser in time, friend Robin."

He now became entangled in a succession of crooked

and narrow streets, which crossed each other, and mean-
dered at no great distance from the water-side. The
smell of tar was obvious to his nostrils, the masts of
vessels pierced the moonlight above the tops of the
buildings, and the numerous signs, which Robin paused
to read, informed him that he was near the centre of
business. But the streets were empty, the shops were
closed, and lights were visible only in the second stories
of a few dwelling-houses. At length, on the corner of a
narrow lane, through which he was passing, he beheld
the broad countenance of a British hero swinging before
the door of an inn, whence proceeded the voices of many
guests. The casement of one of the lower windows was
thrown back, and a very thin curtain permitted Robin
to distinguish a party at supper, round a well-furnished
table. The fragrance of the good cheer steamed forth
into the outer air, and the youth could not fail to recollect that the last remnant of his travelling stock of pro-
vision had yielded to his morning appetite, and that noon
had found and left him dinnerless.

"O, that a parchment three-penny might give me a
right to sit down at yonder table!" said Robin, with a
sigh. "But the Major will make me welcome to the
best of his victuals; so I will even step boldly in, and
inquire my way to his dwelling."

He entered the tavern, and was guided by the murmur
of voices and the fumes of tobacco to the public-room.
It was a long and low apartment, with oaken walls, grown
dark in the continual smoke, and a floor which was
thickly sanded, but of no immaculate purity. A number
of persons — the larger part of whom appeared to be
mariners, or in some way connected with the sea — occupied the wooden benches, or leather-bottomed chairs,
conversing on various matters, and occasionally lending

their attention to some topic of general interest. Three or four little groups were draining as many bowls of punch, which the West India trade had long since made a familiar drink in the colony. Others, who had the appearance of men who lived by regular and laborious handicraft, preferred the insulated bliss of an unshared potation, and became more taciturn under its influence. Nearly all, in short, evinced a predilection for the Good Creature in some of its various shapes, for this is a vice to which, as Fast-day sermons of a hundred years ago will testify, we have a long hereditary claim. The only guests to whom Robin's sympathies inclined him were two or three sheepish countrymen, who were using the inn somewhat after the fashion of a Turkish caravansary; they had gotten themselves into the darkest corner of the room, and, heedless of the Nicotian atmosphere, were supping on the bread of their own ovens, and the bacon cured in their own chimney-smoke. But though Robin felt a sort of brotherhood with these strangers, his eyes were attracted from them to a person who stood near the door, holding whispered conversation with a group of ill-dressed associates. His features were separately striking almost to grotesqueness, and the whole face left a deep impression on the memory. The forehead bulged out into a double prominence, with a vale between; the nose came boldly forth in an irregular curve, and its bridge was of more than a finger's breadth; the eyebrows were deep and shaggy, and the eyes glowed beneath them like fire in a cave.

While Robin deliberated of whom to inquire respecting his kinsman's dwelling, he was accosted by the innkeeper, a little man in a stained white apron, who had come to pay his professional welcome to the stranger. Being in the second generation from a French Protestant, he seemed to have inherited the courtesy of his parent nation; but no variety of circumstances was ever known to change his voice from the one shrill note in which he now addressed Robin.

"From the country, I presume, sir?" said he, with a profound bow. "Beg leave to congratulate you on your arrival, and trust you intend a long stay with us. Fine town here, sir, beautiful buildings, and much that may interest a stranger. May I hope for the honor of your commands in respect to supper?"

"The man sees a family likeness! the rogue has guessed that I am related to the Major!" thought Robin, who had hitherto experienced little superfluous civility.

All eyes were now turned on the country lad, standing at the door, in his worn three-cornered hat, gray coat, leather breeches, and blue yarn stockings, leaning on an oaken cudgel, and bearing a wallet on his back.

Robin replied to the courteous innkeeper, with such an assumption of confidence as befitted the Major's relative. "My honest friend," he said, "I shall make it a point to patronize your house on some occasion, when" — here he could not help lowering his voice — "when I may have more than a parchment three-pence in my pocket. My present business," continued he, speaking with lofty confidence, "is merely to inquire my way to the dwelling of my kinsman, Major Molineux."

There was a sudden and general movement in the room, which Robin interpreted as expressing the eagerness of each individual to become his guide. But the innkeeper turned his eyes to a written paper on the wall, which he read, or seemed to read, with occasional recurrences to the young man's figure.

"What have we here?" said he, breaking his speech

into little dry fragments. "'Left the house of the sub-
scriber, bounden servant, Hezekiah Mudge, — had on,
when he went away, gray coat, leather breeches, master's
third-best hat. One pound currency reward to whoso-
ever shall lodge him in any jail of the province.' Better
trudge, boy, better trudge!'"

Robin had begun to draw his hand towards the lighter
end of the oak cudgel, but a strange hostility in every
countenance induced him to relinquish his purpose of
breaking the courteous innkeeper's head. As he turned
to leave the room, he encountered a sneering glance from
the bold-featured personage whom he had before noticed;
and no sooner was he beyond the door, than he heard
a general laugh, in which the innkeeper's voice might be
distinguished, like the dropping of small stones into a
kettle.

"Now, is it not strange," thought Robin, with his
usual shrewdness, — "is it not strange that the confession
of an empty pocket should outweigh the name of my
kinsman, Major Molineux? O, if I had one of those
grinning rascals in the woods, where I and my oak sapling grew up together, I would teach him that my arm
is heavy, though my purse be light!"

On turning the corner of the narrow lane, Robin found
himself in a spacious street, with an unbroken line of
lofty houses on each side, and a steepled building at the
upper end, whence the ringing of a bell announced the
hour of nine. The light of the moon, and the lamps from
the numerous shop-windows, discovered people prome-
nading on the pavement, and amongst them Robin hoped
to recognize his hitherto inscrutable relative. The result
of his former inquiries made him unwilling to hazard
another, in a scene of such publicity, and he determined
to walk slowly and silently up the street, thrusting his

face close to that of every elderly gentleman, in search
of the Major's lineaments. In his progress, Robin encountered many gay and gallant figures. Embroidered
garments of showy colors, enormous periwigs, gold-laced
hats, and silver-hilted swords glided past him and dazzled
his optics. Travelled youths, imitators of the European
fine gentlemen of the period, trod jauntily along, half
dancing to the fashionable tunes which they hummed, and
making poor Robin ashamed of his quiet and natural
gait. At length, after many pauses to examine the gorgeous display of goods in the shop-windows, and after
suffering some rebukes for the impertinence of his scrutiny into people's faces, the Major's kinsman found himself near the steepled building, still unsuccessful in his
search. As yet, however, he had seen only one side of
the thronged street; so Robin crossed, and continued the
same sort of inquisition down the opposite pavement, with
stronger hopes than the philosopher seeking an honest
man, but with no better fortune. He had arrived about
midway towards the lower end, from which his course
began, when he overheard the approach of some one who
struck down a cane on the flag-stones at every step,
uttering, at regular intervals, two sepulchral hems.

"Mercy on us!" quoth Robin, recognizing the sound.

Turning a corner, which chanced to be close at his
right hand, he hastened to pursue his researches in some
other part of the town. His patience now was wearing
low, and he seemed to feel more fatigue from his rambles
since he crossed the ferry, than from his journey of
several days on the other side. Hunger also pleaded
loudly within him, and Robin began to balance the propriety of demanding, violently, and with lifted cudgel,
the necessary guidance from the first solitary passenger
whom he should meet. While a resolution to this effect

was gaining strength, he entered a street of mean appearance, on either side of which a row of ill-built houses was straggling towards the harbor. The moonlight fell upon no passenger along the whole extent, but in the third domicile which Robin passed there was a half-opened door, and his keen glance detected a woman's garment within.

"My luck may be better here," said he to himself.

Accordingly, he approached the door, and beheld it shut closer as he did so; yet an open space remained, sufficing for the fair occupant to observe the stranger, without a corresponding display on her part. All that Robin could discern was a strip of scarlet petticoat, and the occasional sparkle of an eye, as if the moonbeams were trembling on some bright thing.

"Pretty mistress," for I may call her so with a good conscience, thought the shrewd youth, since I know nothing to the contrary, — "my sweet pretty mistress, will you be kind enough to tell me whereabouts I must seek the dwelling of my kinsman, Major Molineux?"

Robin's voice was plaintive and winning, and the female, seeing nothing to be shunned in the handsome country youth, thrust open the door, and came forth into the moonlight. She was a dainty little figure, with a white neck, round arms, and a slender waist, at the extremity of which her scarlet petticoat jutted out over a hoop, as if she were standing in a balloon. Moreover, her face was oval and pretty, her hair dark beneath the little cap, and her bright eyes possessed a sly freedom, which triumphed over those of Robin.

"Major Molineux dwells here," said this fair woman.

Now, her voice was the sweetest Robin had heard that night, the airy counterpart of a stream of melted silver; yet he could not help doubting whether that sweet voice

11   P

spoke Gospel truth. He looked up and down the mean
street, and then surveyed the house before which they
stood. It was a small, dark edifice of two stories, the
second of which projected over the lower floor; and the
front apartment had the aspect of a shop for petty commodities.

"Now, truly, I am in luck," replied Robin, cunningly,
"and so indeed is my kinsman, the Major, in having so
pretty a housekeeper. But I prithee trouble him to step
to the door; I will deliver him a message from his friends
in the country, and then go back to my lodgings at the
inn."

"Nay, the Major has been abed this hour or more,"
said the lady of the scarlet petticoat; "and it would be
to little purpose to disturb him to-night, seeing his evening draught was of the strongest. But he is a kind-
hearted man, and it would be as much as my life's
worth to let a kinsman of his turn away from the door.
You are the good old gentleman's very picture, and I
could swear that was his rainy-weather hat. Also he
has garments very much resembling those leather small-
clothes. But come in, I pray, for I bid you hearty welcome in his name."

So saying, the fair and hospitable dame took our hero
by the hand; and the touch was light, and the force was
gentleness, and though Robin read in her eyes what he
did not hear in her words, yet the slender-waisted woman in the scarlet petticoat proved stronger than the
athletic country youth. She had drawn his half-willing
footsteps nearly to the threshold, when the opening of
a door in the neighborhood startled the Major's housekeeper, and, leaving the Major's kinsman, she vanished
speedily into her own domicile. A heavy yawn preceded
the appearance of a man, who, like the Moonshine of

Pyramus and Thisbe, carried a lantern, needlessly aiding his sister luminary in the heavens. As he walked sleepily up the street, he turned his broad, dull face on Robin, and displayed a long staff, spiked at the end.

"Home, vagabond, home!" said the watchman, in accents that seemed to fall asleep as soon as they were uttered. "Home, or we'll set you in the stocks, by peep of day!"

"This is the second hint of the kind," thought Robin. "I wish they would end my difficulties, by setting me there to-night."

Nevertheless, the youth felt an instinctive antipathy towards the guardian of midnight order, which at first prevented him from asking his usual question. But just when the man was about to vanish behind the corner, Robin resolved not to lose the opportunity, and shouted lustily after him, —

"I say, friend! will you guide me to the house of my kinsman, Major Molineux?"

The watchman made no reply, but turned the corner and was gone; yet Robin seemed to hear the sound of drowsy laughter stealing along the solitary street. At that moment, also, a pleasant titter saluted him from the open window above his head; he looked up, and caught the sparkle of a saucy eye; a round arm beckoned to him, and next he heard light footsteps descending the staircase within. But Robin, being of the household of a New England clergyman, was a good youth, as well as a shrewd one; so he resisted temptation, and fled away.

He now roamed desperately, and at random, through the town, almost ready to believe that a spell was on him, like that by which a wizard of his country had once kept three pursuers wandering, a whole winter night, within twenty paces of the cottage which they sought.

The streets lay before him, strange and desolate, and the lights were extinguished in almost every house. Twice, however, little parties of men, among whom Robin distinguished individuals in outlandish attire, came hurrying along; but though on both occasions they paused to address him, such intercourse did not at all enlighten his perplexity. They did but utter a few words in some language of which Robin knew nothing, and perceiving his inability to answer, bestowed a curse upon him in plain English, and hastened away. Finally, the lad determined to knock at the door of every mansion that might appear worthy to be occupied by his kinsman, trusting that perseverance would overcome the fatality that had hitherto thwarted him. Firm in this resolve, he was passing beneath the walls of a church, which formed the corner of two streets, when, as he turned into the shade of its steeple, he encountered a bulky stranger, muffled in a cloak. The man was proceeding with the speed of earnest business, but Robin planted himself full before him, holding the oak cudgel with both hands across his body as a bar to further passage.

"Halt, honest man, and answer me a question," said he, very resolutely. "Tell me, this instant, whereabouts is the dwelling of my kinsman, Major Molineux!"

"Keep your tongue between your teeth, fool, and let me pass!" said a deep, gruff voice, which Robin partly remembered. "Let me pass, I say, or I'll strike you to the earth!"

"No, no, neighbor!" cried Robin, flourishing his cudgel, and then thrusting its larger end close to the man's muffled face. "No, no, I'm not the fool you take me for, nor do you pass till I have an answer to my question. Whereabouts is the dwelling of my kinsman, Major Molineux?"

The stranger, instead of attempting to force his passage, stepped back into the moonlight, unmuffled his face, and stared full into that of Robin.

"Watch here an hour, and Major Molineux will pass by," said he.

Robin gazed with dismay and astonishment on the unprecedented physiognomy of the speaker. The forehead with its double prominence, the broad hooked nose, the shaggy eyebrows, and fiery eyes were those which he had noticed at the inn, but the man's complexion had undergone a singular, or, more properly, a twofold change. One side of the face blazed an intense red, while the other was black as midnight, the division line being in the broad bridge of the nose; and a mouth which seemed to extend from ear to ear was black or red, in contrast to the color of the cheek. The effect was as if two individual devils, a fiend of fire and a fiend of darkness, had united themselves to form this infernal visage. The stranger grinned in Robin's face, muffled his party-colored features, and was out of sight in a moment.

"Strange things we travellers see!" ejaculated Robin.

He seated himself, however, upon the steps of the church-door, resolving to wait the appointed time for his kinsman. A few moments were consumed in philosophical speculations upon the species of man who had just left him; but having settled this point shrewdly, rationally, and satisfactorily, he was compelled to look elsewhere for his amusement. And first he threw his eyes along the street. It was of more respectable appearance than most of those into which he had wandered, and the moon, creating, like the imaginative power, a beautiful strangeness in familiar objects, gave something of romance to a scene that might not have possessed it in

the light of day. The irregular and often quaint architecture of the houses, some of whose roofs were broken
into numerous little peaks, while others ascended, steep
and narrow, into a single point, and others again were
square; the pure snow-white of some of their complexions, the aged darkness of others, and the thousand spark-
lings, reflected from bright substances in the walls of
many; these matters engaged Robin's attention for a
while, and then began to grow wearisome. Next he
endeavored to define the forms of distant objects, starting
away, with almost ghostly indistinctness, just as his eye
appeared to grasp them; and finally he took a minute
survey of an edifice which stood on the opposite side of
the street, directly in front of the church-door, where he
was stationed. It was a large, square mansion, distinguished from its neighbors by a balcony, which rested on
tall pillars, and by an elaborate Gothic window, commu-
nicating therewith.

"Perhaps this is the very house I have been seeking,"
thought Robin.

Then he strove to speed away the time, by listening
to a murmur which swept continually along the street,
yet was scarcely audible, except to an unaccustomed ear
like his; it was a low, dull, dreamy sound, compounded
of many noises, each of which was at too great a distance to be separately heard. Robin marvelled at this
snore of a sleeping town, and marvelled more whenever
its continuity was broken by now and then a distant
shout, apparently loud where it originated. But altogether it was a sleep-inspiring sound, and, to shake off
its drowsy influence, Robin arose, and climbed a window-
frame, that he might view the interior of the church.
There the moonbeams came trembling in, and fell down
upon the deserted pews, and extended along the quiet

aisles. A fainter yet more awful radiance was hovering around the pulpit, and one solitary ray had dared
to rest upon the open page of the great Bible. Had
nature, in that deep hour, become a worshipper in the
house which man had builded? Or was that heavenly
light the visible sanctity of the place, — visible because
no earthly and impure feet were within the walls? The
scene made Robin's heart shiver with a sensation of loneliness stronger than he had ever felt in the remotest
depths of his native woods ; so he turned away, and sat
down again before the door. There were graves around
the church, and now an uneasy thought obtruded into
Robin's breast. What if the object of his search, which
had been so often and so strangely thwarted, were all
the time mouldering in his shroud? What if his kinsman should glide through yonder gate, and nod and
smile to him in dimly passing by?

"O that any breathing thing were here with me!"
said Robin.

Recalling his thoughts from this uncomfortable track,
he sent them over forest, hill, and stream, and attempted
to imagine how that evening of ambiguity and weariness
had been spent by his father's household. He pictured
them assembled at the door, beneath the tree, the great
old tree, which had been spared for its huge twisted
trunk, and venerable shade, when a thousand leafy brethren fell. There, at the going down of the summer sun,
it was his father's custom to perform domestic worship,
that the neighbors might come and join with him like
brothers of the family, and that the wayfaring man might
pause to drink at that fountain, and keep his heart pure
by freshening the memory of home. Robin distinguished
the seat of every individual of the little audience ; he saw
the good man in the midst, holding the Scriptures in the

golden light that fell from the western clouds; he beheld
him close the book and all rise up to pray. He heard
the old thanksgivings for daily mercies, the old supplications for their continuance, to which he had so often
listened in weariness, but which were now among his
dear remembrances. He perceived the slight inequality
of his father's voice when he came to speak of the absent
one; he noted how his mother turned her face to the
broad and knotted trunk; how his elder brother scorned,
because the beard was rough upon his upper lip, to permit his features to be moved; how the younger sister
drew down a low hanging branch before her eyes; and
how the little one of all, whose sports had hitherto
broken the decorum of the scene, understood the prayer
for her playmate, and burst into clamorous grief. Then
he saw them go in at the door; and when Robin would
have entered also, the latch tinkled into its place, and he
was excluded from his home.

"Am I here, or there?" cried Robin, starting; for all
at once, when his thoughts had become visible and audible in a dream, the long, wide, solitary street shone out
before him.

He aroused himself, and endeavored to fix his attention
steadily upon the large edifice which he had surveyed
before. But still his mind kept vibrating between fancy
and reality; by turns, the pillars of the balcony length-
ened into the tall, bare stems of pines, dwindled down to
human figures, settled again into their true shape and
size, and then commenced a new succession of changes.
For a single moment, when he deemed himself awake,
he could have sworn that a visage — one which he seemed
to remember, yet could not absolutely name as his kinsman's — was looking towards him from the Gothic window. A deeper sleep wrestled with and nearly overcame

him, but fled at the sound of footsteps along the opposite pavement. Robin rubbed his eyes, discerned a man passing at the foot of the balcony, and addressed him in a loud, peevish, and lamentable cry.

"Hallo, friend! must I wait here all night for my kinsman, Major Molineux?"

The sleeping echoes awoke, and answered the voice; and the passenger, barely able to discern a figure sitting in the oblique shade of the steeple, traversed the street to obtain a nearer view. He was himself a gentleman in his prime, of open, intelligent, cheerful, and altogether prepossessing countenance. Perceiving a country youth, apparently homeless and without friends, he accosted him in a tone of real kindness, which had become strange to Robin's ears.

"Well, my good lad, why are you sitting here?" inquired he. "Can I be of service to you in any way?"

"I am afraid not, sir," replied Robin, despondingly; "yet I shall take it kindly, if you'll answer me a single question. I've been searching, half the night, for one Major Molineux; now, sir, is there really such a person in these parts, or am I dreaming?"

"Major Molineux! The name is not altogether strange to me," said the gentleman, smiling. "Have you any objection to telling me the nature of your business with him?"

Then Robin briefly related that his father was a clergyman, settled on a small salary, at a long distance back in the country, and that he and Major Molineux were brothers' children. The Major, having inherited riches, and acquired civil and military rank, had visited his cousin, in great pomp, a year or two before; had manifested much interest in Robin and an elder brother, and, being childless himself, had thrown out hints respecting

11 *

the future establishment of one of them in life. The
elder brother was destined to succeed to the farm which
his father cultivated in the interval of sacred duties; it
was therefore determined that Robin should profit by his
kinsman's generous intentions, especially as he seemed
to be rather the favorite, and was thought to possess
other necessary endowments.

"For I have the name of being a shrewd youth," observed Robin, in this part of his story.

"I doubt not you deserve it," replied his new friend,
good-naturedly; "but pray proceed."

"Well, sir, being nearly eighteen years old, and well
grown, as you see," continued Robin, drawing himself
up to his full height, "I thought it high time to begin
the world. So my mother and sister put me in handsome trim, and my father gave me half the remnant of
his last year's salary, and five days ago I started for this
place, to pay the Major a visit. But, would you believe
it, sir! I crossed the ferry a little after dark, and have
yet found nobody that would show me the way to his
dwelling; only, an hour or two since, I was told to wait
here, and Major Molineux would pass by."

"Can you describe the man who told you this?" inquired the gentleman.

"O, he was a very ill-favored fellow, sir," replied
Robin, "with two great bumps on his forehead, a hook
nose, fiery eyes; and, what struck me as the strangest,
his face was of two different colors. Do you happen to
know such a man, sir?"

"Not intimately," answered the stranger, "but I
chanced to meet him a little time previous to your
stopping me. I believe you may trust his word, and
that the Major will very shortly pass through this street.
In the mean time, as I have a singular curiosity to wit-

ness your meeting, I will sit down here upon the steps, and bear you company."

He seated himself accordingly, and soon engaged his companion in animated discourse. It was but of brief continuance, however, for a noise of shouting, which had long been remotely audible, drew so much nearer that Robin inquired its cause.

"What may be the meaning of this uproar?" asked he. "Truly, if your town be always as noisy, I shall find little sleep, while I am an inhabitant."

"Why, indeed, friend Robin, there do appear to be three or four riotous fellows abroad to-night," replied the gentleman. "You must not expect all the stillness of your native woods, here in our streets. But the watch will shortly be at the heels of these lads, and —"

"Ay, and set them in the stocks by peep of day," interrupted Robin, recollecting his own encounter with the drowsy lantern-bearer. "But, dear sir, if I may trust my ears, an army of watchmen would never make head against such a multitude of rioters. There were at least a thousand voices went up to make that one shout."

"May not a man have several voices, Robin, as well as two complexions?" said his friend.

"Perhaps a man may; but Heaven forbid that a woman should!" responded the shrewd youth, thinking of the seductive tones of the Major's housekeeper.

The sounds of a trumpet in some neighboring street now became so evident and continual, that Robin's curiosity was strongly excited. In addition to the shouts, he heard frequent bursts from many instruments of discord, and a wild and confused laughter filled up the intervals. Robin rose from the steps, and looked wistfully towards a point whither several people seemed to be hastening.

"Surely some prodigious merry-making is going on," exclaimed he. "I have laughed very little since I left home, sir, and should be sorry to lose an opportunity. Shall we step round the corner by that darkish house, and take our share of the fun?"

"Sit down again, sit down, good Robin," replied the gentleman, laying his hand on the skirt of the gray coat. "You forget that we must wait here for your kinsman; and there is reason to believe that he will pass by, in the course of a very few moments."

The near approach of the uproar had now disturbed the neighborhood; windows flew open on all sides; and many heads, in the attire of the pillow, and confused by sleep suddenly broken, were protruded to the gaze of whoever had leisure to observe them. Eager voices hailed each other from house to house, all demanding the explanation, which not a soul could give. Half-dressed men hurried towards the unknown commotion, stumbling as they went over the stone steps that thrust themselves into the narrow foot-walk. The shouts, the laughter, and the tuneless bray, the antipodes of music, came onwards with increasing din, till scattered individuals, and then denser bodies, began to appear round a corner at the distance of a hundred yards.

"Will you recognize your kinsman, if he passes in this crowd?" inquired the gentleman.

"Indeed, I can't warrant it, sir; but I'll take my stand here, and keep a bright lookout," answered Robin, descending to the outer edge of the pavement.

A mighty stream of people now emptied into the street, and came rolling slowly towards the church. A single horseman wheeled the corner in the midst of them, and close behind him came a band of fearful wind-instruments, sending forth a fresher discord, now

that no intervening buildings kept it from the ear. Then
a redder light disturbed the moonbeams, and a dense
multitude of torches shone along the street, concealing,
by their glare, whatever object they illuminated. The
single horseman, clad in a military dress, and bearing a
drawn sword, rode onward as the leader, and, by his
fierce and variegated countenance, appeared like war
personified ; the red of one cheek was an emblem of fire
and sword; the blackness of the other betokened the
mourning that attends them. In his train were wild
figures in the Indian dress, and many fantastic shapes
without a model, giving the whole march a visionary
air, as if a dream had broken forth from some feverish
brain, and were sweeping visibly through the midnight
streets. A mass of people, inactive, except as applaud-
ing spectators, hemmed the procession in ; and several
women ran along the sidewalk, piercing the confusion
of heavier sounds with their shrill voices of mirth or
terror.

"The double-faced fellow has his eye upon me," muttered Robin, with an indefinite but an uncomfortable
idea that he was himself to bear a part in the pageantry.

The leader turned himself in the saddle, and fixed his
glance full upon the country youth, as the steed went
slowly by. When Robin had freed his eyes from those
fiery ones, the musicians were passing before him, and
the torches were close at hand ; but the unsteady brightness of the latter formed a veil which he could not
penetrate. The rattling of wheels over the stones sometimes found its way to his ear, and confused traces of a
human form appeared at intervals, and then melted into
the vivid light. A moment more, and the leader thundered a command to halt : the trumpets vomited a
horrid breath, and then held their peace ; the shouts and

laughter of the people died away, and there remained only a universal hum, allied to silence. Right before Robin's eyes was an uncovered cart. There the torches blazed the brightest, there the moon shone out like day, and there, in tar-and-feathery dignity, sat his kinsman, Major Molineux!

He was an elderly man, of large and majestic person, and strong, square features, betokening a steady soul; but steady as it was, his enemies had found means to shake it. His face was pale as death, and far more ghastly; the broad forehead was contracted in his agony, so that his eyebrows formed one grizzled line; his eyes were red and wild, and the foam hung white upon his quivering lip. His whole frame was agitated by a quick and continual tremor, which his pride strove to quell, even in those circumstances of overwhelming humiliation. But perhaps the bitterest pang of all was when his eyes met those of Robin; for he evidently knew him on the instant, as the youth stood witnessing the foul disgrace of a head grown gray in honor. They stared at each other in silence, and Robin's knees shook, and his hair bristled, with a mixture of pity and terror. Soon, however, a bewildering excitement began to seize upon his mind; the preceding adventures of the night, the unexpected appearance of the crowd, the torches, the confused din and the hush that followed, the spectre of his kinsman reviled by that great multitude,—all this, and, more than all, a perception of tremendous ridicule in the whole scene, affected him with a sort of mental inebriety. At that moment a voice of sluggish merriment saluted Robin's ears; he turned instinctively, and just behind the corner of the church stood the lantern-bearer, rubbing his eyes, and drowsily enjoying the lad's amazement. Then he heard a peal of laughter like the ringing of sil-

very bells; a woman twitched his arm, a saucy eye met
his, and he saw the lady of the scarlet petticoat. A
sharp, dry cachinnation appealed to his memory, and,
standing on tiptoe in the crowd, with his white apron
over his head, he beheld the courteous little innkeeper.
And lastly, there sailed over the heads of the multitude a
great, broad laugh, broken in the midst by two sepulchral
hems; thus, " Haw, haw, haw, — hem, hem, — haw, haw,
haw, haw ! "

The sound proceeded from the balcony of the opposite
edifice, and thither Robin turned his eyes. In front of
the Gothic window stood the old citizen, wrapped in a
wide gown, his gray periwig exchanged for a nightcap,
which was thrust back from his forehead, and his silk
stockings hanging about his legs. He supported himself on his polished cane in a fit of convulsive merriment, which manifested itself on his solemn old features
like a funny inscription on a tombstone. Then Robin
seemed to hear the voices of the barbers, of the guests
of the inn, and of all who had made sport of him that
night. The contagion was spreading among the multitude, when, all at once, it seized upon Robin, and he
sent forth a shout of laughter that echoed through the
street; — every man shook his sides, every man emptied
his lungs, but Robin's shout was the loudest there. The
cloud-spirits peeped from their silvery islands, as the
congregated mirth went roaring up the sky ! The Man
in the Moon heard the far bellow. " Oho," quoth he,
" the old earth is frolicsome to-night ! "

When there was a momentary calm in that tempestuous sea of sound, the leader gave the sign, the procession resumed its march. On they went, like fiends that
throng in mockery around some dead potentate, mighty
no more, but majestic still in his agony. On they went,

in counterfeited pomp, in senseless uproar, in frenzied merriment, trampling all on an old man's heart. On swept the tumult, and left a silent street behind.

*   *   *   *   *

"Well, Robin, are you dreaming?" inquired the gentleman, laying his hand on the youth's shoulder.

Robin started, and withdrew his arm from the stone post to which he had instinctively clung, as the living stream rolled by him. His cheek was somewhat pale, and his eye not quite as lively as in the earlier part of the evening.

"Will you be kind enough to show me the way to the ferry?" said he, after a moment's pause.

"You have, then, adopted a new subject of inquiry?" observed his companion, with a smile.

"Why, yes, sir," replied Robin, rather dryly. "Thanks to you, and to my other friends, I have at last met my kinsman, and he will scarce desire to see my face again. I begin to grow weary of a town life, sir. Will you show me the way to the ferry?"

"No, my good friend Robin, — not to-night, at least," said the gentleman. "Some few days hence, if you wish it, I will speed you on your journey. Or, if you prefer to remain with us, perhaps, as you are a shrewd youth, you may rise in the world without the help of your kinsman, Major Molineux."

Cambridge: Electrotyped and Printed by Welch, Bigelow, & Co.

www.ingramcontent.com/pod-product-compliance
Lightning Source LLC
Chambersburg PA
CBHW030801020726
47499CB00006B/1717